NEW YORK TIMES BESTSELLING AUTHOR

KAYLEE RYAN

CHAPTER
Marshall
ONE

"DONE," I SAY to myself as I hit Send on the email and push back from my desk. I've been here at the office since early this morning. It's usually my two oldest brothers, Royce or Owen, who arrive first, but now that they both have wives and babies at home, they don't live to work like they used to.

Riggins Enterprises launched a new marketing campaign last month. It was my brainchild that I worked tirelessly on for months, and I'm happy to report that our reach is better than ever. Our accounts are growing in all regions, and it's not just me boasting. The proof is in the numbers. Just ask my brother Owen. He's the numbers guy, and he's thrilled with the increase we've seen. Royce, my oldest brother, is the CEO, and he's made sure to tell me several times in the last month what a marketing genius I am. Yes, I made him say it while I recorded it. I gotta take my praise where I can get it.

"You two are my favorites." Layla's voice carries down the hall. "Don't tell Sawyer."

"Don't tell Sawyer what?" my sister-in-law Sawyer asks.

My sisters, well, my brothers' wives, are here, and that's the perfect excuse to take a break. Standing from my chair, I make my way to Layla's desk at the reception area. "What's that?" I immediately ask when I spot a container of something sitting on the corner of Layla's desk.

"We were bored," Aspen tells me. The shiny new engagement ring that my brother gave her last month sparkles as she moves her hand to point at the container.

"How bored are we talking?" I ask. "Bored, as in, let's make some box brownies, or bored as in I whipped up a batch of homemade peanut butter bars. There's a difference," I tell them.

"Bored as in, we whipped up a batch of homemade magic bars," my almost sister-in-law Aspen tells me with a grin.

"A bunch of hocus pocus," I say, reaching for the container. Pulling off the lid, I'm assaulted with the smell of fresh baked goods, and this is my sister's baking we're talking about. You can't have just one, so of course, I grab two.

"Careful, Marsh," my middle brother Grant says as he approaches his wife, Aurora. "You might catch the magic bug," he teases.

"I call bullshit. You just want the bars to yourself," I say as I shove a bite of the magic bar into my mouth.

"My wife made the recipe," he fires back. "I can have them anytime that I want them. Right, babe?"

"That's right." Aurora smiles at him.

"How are you two feeling?" Sawyer asks Aurora and Aspen.

If you're confused, let me catch you up. My oldest brother, Royce, is married to Sawyer. She works here at Riggins, and they have a hella cute baby boy named Roan. He's five months old, and I'm his favorite uncle. He can't tell you that yet, but I'm confident that he will.

Next in line in the Riggins family tree is Owen. The second oldest and married to Layla, who also works here at Riggins. Layla and Sawyer work closely together to keep the five of us in line. They, too, have a hella cute little boy. His name is Carter. He's a year-and-a-half old, and if I ask him who his favorite uncle is, he points to me. We're going to pretend that he doesn't do the same thing with my brothers. Let me have my moment.

Grant is my middle brother. He's married to Aurora, who is Aspen's sister. Aurora and Aspen own Warm Delights. However, it caught fire about five months ago, and they're still dealing with insurance, waiting to rebuild. That's okay because she's expecting their first baby in a couple of months.

Conrad is the second to the youngest brother. He's engaged to Aspen, Aurora's sister, and they, too, are expecting a baby in a couple of months. She and her sister are due only a week apart. Neither planned it that way. It just sort of happened. By the end of the year, there are going to be two more baby boys joining the Riggins clan, and we're all thrilled. Although, no one is more excited than my parents.

That leaves me—Marshall Riggins, the youngest of the Riggins brood and the last holdout. My dad and my brothers believe in what they call the magic of love. The five of them claim that when you find the one woman you're supposed to spend the rest of your life with, it's magical.

They claim that it changes you.

I've watched all four of my brothers fall in love. Each of them has found the woman they are meant to love forever, hence giving me four sisters, two nephews, and soon-to-be two more nephews. I don't know if the "magic of love" is just something they all say to keep the rest of us from giving them shit about tying themselves to one woman for the rest of their lives, or if it's real.

I don't believe in magic, but I do believe in love.

I watched my parents growing up, and yeah, it would be nice to have that one day, but for me, I don't know how to find it. How do you know if someone is with you for the right reasons? My family is well known, and yeah… I just don't know. My mom is constantly telling me that I'll never meet the woman I want to bring home to meet her at a club. However, I don't really hit the clubs much anymore. It was something I always did with my brothers, and well, they all have families now. It's just not the same without them.

Now, instead of a night out at the club, we gather together and build baby furniture or rearrange the furniture in their houses. Fun times. No, truthfully, it's always a good time when I get to hang out with my family. My brothers, all four of them, are my best friends, so any time I can snag time with them and their wives or fiancées is a win.

Just don't tell them that. I don't want that shit going to their heads.

My phone rings, pulling me out of my head and back to the present conversation. Tugging it out of my pants pocket, I see Mom's face. "Hey, Momma," I greet her.

"What has you so chipper?"

"Oh, you know, just hanging out with my siblings eating magic bars."

"Tell Aurora and Aspen to save one for me."

I move the phone from my face and place it on speaker. "You're on speaker. Tell them yourself," I tell Mom.

"Girls, save one of those for me."

"Don't worry, we made extra," Aurora tells her.

"Are we still on for dinner tonight for Dad's birthday?" I ask.

"Yes. You all are going to be here at six, right?" Mom checks.

"We'll be there earlier than that," Royce tells her. "How's my boy?" My mom watches Roan and Carter, she and my dad together, and you'd have thought she cured world hunger with how happy it makes her.

"He's napping. Carter has already had his nap, and he's outside with your dad playing in the sandbox."

"Mom, don't let him eat the sand," Owen speaks up.

"Owen Riggins, I raised you and your brothers, and I think I'm perfectly capable of watching my grandsons. Besides, a little sand never hurt anyone." Her tone is teasing.

"We're on our way," Owen fires back. There's a tilt to his lips.

We all know he's just playing with her. Our mother is a superwoman. She has to be to have raised all five of us.

"Oh, hush." Mom chuckles. "Anyway, Marshall, can you do me a favor?"

"Sure, what's up?"

"I didn't get a chance to go out today to pick up my arthritis medication. Do you mind stopping by the drugstore to pick it up for me?"

"Sure. Do you need anything else?"

"Not that I can think of."

"Same pharmacy as last time?" I ask.

"Yes. Thank you, Marsh. You know you're my favorite, right?" she asks.

My brothers make their displeasure with her statement known, while my sisters laugh, and I sneak another magic bar while making a mental note to run an extra mile on my treadmill tonight.

My mother's laughter flows through the speaker. "I love you all. I'll see you soon." The line goes silent. Locking the screen, I shove my phone back into my pocket.

"See, I told you I was the favorite." I point at my chest, a smirk playing on my lips.

"You're the baby, not the favorite. There's a difference," Grant counters.

"Well, you're the middle man."

"That's why she loves me best." He smiles, satisfied with his comeback.

"We should let you get back to work," Aspen says, looking over her shoulder at Conrad, who's standing behind her with his hands resting on their unborn son.

"We should. I think it's nap time before we head to your parents,'" Aurora agrees.

"Fine," Grant grumbles. He leans in and kisses her, then bends to place a kiss on her swollen belly.

"You're leaving these, right?" Layla asks, moving the container of what's left of the magic bars closer to her.

Aurora and Aspen both laugh. "Yes, those are yours."

"You have to share," I remind them like the spoiled youngest child that I am. Hell, it wouldn't matter if I was the oldest like Royce or the middle man like Grant. I'd fight for another taste of anything that my two baking sisters-in-law make. It's legit that good.

After a round of hugs, we all go back to work. Their surprise visit was just the afternoon pick-me-up we all needed. I know it was for me. Sitting back at my desk, I return a few calls and get lost in work for a few more hours.

A little after four, I leave the office. I want to run by the pharmacy for Mom, and then head to their place before everyone gets there. I need snuggle time with my nephews, and my damn brothers will steal them away. I might be the youngest of the family, but I'm also the smartest. I'll have a good hour of Uncle Marsh, Carter, and Roan time before the rest of my family descends.

After parking my car in front of the pharmacy, I grab the keys and head inside. I make my way to the back of the store to pick up Mom's prescription. There's a line, but that's nothing new. I don't know that I've ever been here to pick up a prescription when I didn't have to wait.

The woman in front of me appears to be my age, and she has a baby in an infant seat with her. She's swaying the seat back and forth, and I know from my nephews it's a trick parents use to soothe the baby. Royce and Owen even strap the kids in and take them for a drive. I remember Mom telling Owen when Carter was born that she and Dad did the same thing with each of us when we were babies.

She adjusts her stance and stumbles a little. On instinct, I reach out and brace my hands on her hips to steady her.

"I'm so sorry." She's quick to apologize.

"Don't be. You have your hands full." I motion to the baby, swaddled in lots of pink with wide eyes, as she takes in the new surroundings.

The woman blows out a puff of air. "You have no idea," she mumbles.

"How old is she?" I ask. It's partly to make casual conversation. The other part is that I can feel the stress coming off her in waves. If I've learned anything from my two oldest brothers being dads, it's that talking about their kids always brightens their days. Well, their kids and their wives. Besides, I'm getting good at this baby stuff. I'd say she's close to Roan's age at five or so months old.

Sure enough, the woman smiles down at the baby. "Five months today."

I lean over closer to the baby. "Happy five months, sweet girl," I coo at her. Don't judge. Babies are cute as hell. It's not until I stand back up to my full height and I see the mom's wide eyes, I realize I might come off as a creeper. Fuck.

"Sorry," I say sheepishly. "I have a five-month-old nephew and a one-and-a-half-year-old nephew. They're the best," I add, hoping it makes me seem less like a creeper.

"Next!" The line moves forward, and it's the woman's turn.

I tune her out as she talks to the pharmacy technician, and yes, that's what they're called. I hooked up with a woman who was a pharmacy tech and had to hear all about her job and how she wanted to be a pharmacist. I'm not a complete dick. I listen when they talk. That still doesn't mean that we're going to ride off into the sunset together.

The baby begins to cry, and I assume it's because her momma is no longer swaying back and forth with her. I'd offer to do it for her, but I've reached my limit for creeper today, so instead, I stand back and watch as the little girl's cries grow louder. It's not until I notice her mom's shoulders slump that I tune into the conversation.

"I'm sorry. Without insurance, that's the cost of the medication."

"It was only ten dollars the last time," the woman says, with desperation in her voice.

"I'm sorry, ma'am. That was because you had a coupon from the drug company."

Those same shoulders that slumped begin to shake. Here's something you might not know about me, I hate to see anyone cry. What's worse is a woman in tears. What's worse is a woman with a baby in tears. And even worse than that, a woman with a baby, they're both crying, and apparently, the mom can't afford the baby's medication. At least I assume it's for the fussy baby with the red-rimmed eyes.

I step forward and place my hand on the woman's shoulder. "Allow me," I say, pulling my wallet out of my pants pocket and pulling out some cash.

"No. I can't let you do that," she protests, tears pooling in her eyes, and from the looks of it, threatening to fall.

"Let me ask you something. Is this for her?" I point to the baby, who is now crying even louder.

She nods. "Ear infection."

"Let me help you. No strings. Just pay it forward one day when you are able." I can tell she's wavering by the way she bites down on her bottom lip. "Take it for her."

She nods. "Thank you. I'll pay you back... when I can."

I wave her off. My underwear that I'm currently wearing costs more than this prescription. If that doesn't put things into perspective, I don't know what does. "As I said, one day, you'll be able to pay it forward." I hand the cash to the tech, and she quickly rings up the prescription. She hands me my change, and I go to put it back in my wallet but instead, I pull out two more one-hundred-dollar bills. I grab the bag and pretend to be looking inside and drop the money before closing it tightly. "Diaper bag?" I ask her.

"Yes, please. I'm so embarrassed. I can't thank you enough for this. I will never forget your kindness, and I promise to pay it forward."

"You're more than welcome. That's all that I ask." Bending over, I offer my index finger to the little girl. She takes it, and her cries die down to a whimper. "Hey, sweetheart. Mommy has your medicine, and you'll start feeling better soon."

Her breath shudders, and I swear she can understand what I'm telling her because she's no longer crying.

Taking my finger back, I stand and face the mom. "Good luck. I hope she feels better soon."

"Thank you…" Her voice trails off.

"Marshall. Marshall Riggins." I wait for recognition to take hold, but I see nothing in her eyes that says she recognizes me or my last name.

"Thank you, Marshall. I'm Wren, and this is Madeline."

"It's nice to meet you."

"You too. Thank you again. I just… thank you, Marshall Riggins."

"You're welcome, Wren, and you too, Madeline. Feel better, sweetheart," I tell the baby. With a nod, she walks away, and I step up to the counter. "Hi, I have a prescription for Lena Riggins," I tell the tech.

"That was really nice of you."

I shrug. "It wasn't a hardship, and it looked like they needed it."

The older lady nods and turns to retrieve Mom's prescription. When she comes back, what she tells me has my gut twisting. "You know, her husband used to work here. He was in pharmacy school. Only had a year to go when it happened."

I shouldn't ask, but I have to know. "What happened?"

"Not my story to tell."

I want to yell at her and tell her she shouldn't have brought it up, but I keep my cool, pay for Mom's prescription and get the hell out of here.

In my car on the way to my parents,' I can't help but think of the woman. She wasn't wearing a wedding ring, but apparently has a husband, an infant, and is obviously struggling financially. It's not often that I think about life outside of my work and my family. I'm not a snob. You just live within the comfort you've always known. I've been very fortunate in life, and right now, that luck is sitting like lead in my stomach.

CHAPTER
Wren
TWO

BY THE TIME I reach our tiny apartment, just two blocks from the pharmacy, I'm exhausted. Madeline and this seat together are heavy. Add the diaper bag, my purse, and the fact that we got zero sleep last night, and I'm dead on my feet.

My sweet girl fell asleep on the walk. The movement, I'm sure, as her seat bounced against my hip did the trick. I hate to wake her up, but she needs this medicine. The sooner we get it started, the sooner she will start to feel better.

As carefully as possible, I place her seat on the floor next to our small couch. I hold my breath waiting to see if she's going to wake up. Thankfully, she stays sleeping. I just need a minute—just a quick moment in time to catch my breath. I had to sell our cars when Travis died. I also had to give up our apartment. It wasn't huge, but compared to the crackerjack box that we live in now, it was a mansion. It also didn't have paper-thin walls with neighbors that argue all hours of the night. However, it's a warm, safe roof over our heads. That's something.

Madeline whimpers, and my heart breaks for her. This is the second ear infection in two months. With a heavy sigh, I stand from the couch and grab the diaper bag, digging out the bag from the pharmacy. I hate that I couldn't even afford the medication she needs. I have exactly thirty dollars to my name until I get paid tomorrow. We're running low on diapers, and thankfully, I breastfeed. I never thought that was something that I would do. It just didn't feel like it was for me, and well, my husband died, and baby formula is expensive. At first, it made me uncomfortable, but now, it's our bonding time.

Taking the bag to the small galley kitchen, I reach inside for the medicine. Pulling out the bottle, I gasp when I see two one-hundred-dollar bills and a fifty-dollar bill. Hot tears prick my eyes.

Marshall Riggins.

The handsome stranger that helped me more today than he could ever imagine. Fifty dollars for medication isn't in the budget. Not when I have to pay for childcare and diapers. My stomach grumbles from hunger as if it senses that I have money that I wasn't expecting to have. It's an incredible gift, but I can't accept it. I know he meant well, but I just can't. Paying for Madeline's medication was more than enough.

Nashville is a big city, but surely someone knows who he is. Maybe I can hop on a computer at work and search for him. I sold Travis's and my laptops after he passed. I liquidated everything that I could to keep us on our feet.

A tear rolls down my cheek as I place the money back into the bag. Two hundred and fifty dollars feels like a million at this point, but I still can't keep it. His generosity will forever be with me and is greatly appreciated, but the medication was more than enough. I meant what I told him. As soon as I'm able, I'll be paying it forward. I can't pay forward three hundred dollars.

Madeline begins to cry. Wiping at my cheeks, I work to get her medication ready and take it with my back to the small living area. "Hey, sweetie," I coo to her. She doesn't seem to care as her cries grow louder. She's hungry and her ear hurts. Luckily the pediatrician had samples of Tylenol. The nurse was so sweet and gave me three bottles — more than enough to get us through this ear infection.

I had to give up my job at the local day care when I gave up the apartment. I needed to find something closer to our new place, work, and Madeline's day care. I have to be at my job for ninety days before I can get health insurance. That's Monday. I was able to maintain the bills and my old apartment until Madeline was born. After that, we had to move. I should have moved sooner and saved some of our cash. I just… couldn't. That was my home with Travis, and I was pregnant. I needed things for our daughter. She needed a bed. In hindsight, I wish I could have pulled myself out of my funk of missing him to see that saving that money was the better option. Grief does that to you. It keeps you from thinking clearly.

"Come here." I lift my daughter from her car seat, and she quiets down a little. "I know you don't like the icky medicine, but I promise it will make you feel so much better." I position her on my lap and place the syringe in her mouth. She takes it with a grimace as she chokes back a sob. "Shh," I coo as I rock her a little in my arms.

Placing the medicine dropper on the table, I settle back against the couch and pull up my shirt. My girl knows exactly what's happening as she roots to latch on. Her cries stop completely.

"All better," I say, soothing her. Resting my head back against the couch, I fight the exhaustion that weighs heavy on me. Doing this alone is hard. Travis was a foster kid, raised in a children's home from the time he was ten. Families didn't want to foster or adopt the older kids, so for eight years, he lived in the home as a ward of the state. I was his only family.

As for me, my mom passed when I was a little girl from a ruptured ovarian cyst. It was a freak thing. I was seven, so I don't remember much. Just that my dad had our neighbor pick me up from school, and when he came home, he told me my mom was gone. That she was with the angels. Later I learned what it meant, and my dad, well, he retreated into himself. He stopped socializing. He went to work and took care of me the best that he could. He passed three years ago at home alone in his sleep from a heart attack.

Travis was my family. We had each other, and together, we were building a life, making it work. I look down at our daughter, and my heart clenches in my chest. I never got the chance to tell him I was pregnant. We weren't trying, but he would have been thrilled regardless. I blink hard, fighting back the tears that once again threaten to fall.

"It's just you and me, Maddie. I promise you we're going to get through this. I don't know how," I whisper. "But I promise you that we will. Things will get better for us. They have to." Knowing if I don't get up and get moving that I'll fall asleep here, I stand and head to the bathroom. After giving Madeline a bath and packing the diaper bag for tomorrow, I make a mental note to go out in the morning for diapers. Unfortunately, I can't take Madeline back to day care until she's fever-free for twenty-four hours. I have to miss another day's work, which is going to cut us short next week, and I'm still in my ninety-day probation period. I missed two days already when I first started this job because she had an ear infection as well. My only hope is that my boss means it when she tells me that she understands that I'm a single mom. I made sure to express that many times in my interview and when I accepted the nurse aide position. The thought of losing this job when I'm so close to insurance causes my stomach to roll.

"Okay, sweet girl. It's time for bed." As if she knows what I'm saying, Madeline rubs at her eyes. "Mama's tired too," I tell her. I rock her for a few minutes until she's sound asleep. Carefully, I place her in her bed and tiptoe out of her room.

In the kitchen, I make myself two pieces of toast with peanut butter for dinner and drink two glasses of water before moving to the couch and settling in for the night. The apartment is one bedroom, so I gave it to Madeline. I sold my bed because we don't have room for it, but that's okay. The couch is comfortable. It's just me, and we don't have a whole lot of visitors.

The shrill sound of my daughter crying jolts me from sleep. It's just after midnight. I'm guessing the Tylenol from earlier has worn off. Time for another dose of that as well as her antibiotic, a diaper change, and a little boob. Hopefully, I'll be able to get her back to sleep.

"Hey," I coo when I enter her room. "It's all right," I tell her. "Mommy's here." She sniffs but her cries quiet when I pick her up—that lasts until I lay her down to change her. "I've got you," I say, picking her back up, and she shudders from her cries. "You have to take your medicine, and then you can eat," I tell her. Some might say I'm crazy for talking to my five-month-old like she can understand me, but what they don't understand is that she is my person, my heart, and my entire world.

She's all that I have.

It takes me two tries to get both of her medicines down her. She's screaming at this point. I'm just waiting for the neighbors to complain, not that they have a leg to stand on. They argue at all hours of the night. I've never said a word, even when they wake Madeline.

Twenty minutes later, my girl is asleep. Again, I lay her as carefully as I can into her crib and wait a few minutes making sure that she's going to stay asleep before going back to the living room and plopping back down on the couch.

I'm exhausted, but I can't fall back to sleep. Grabbing a paperback I've read more times than I can count, I try to get lost in the story, but it's no use. I know it by heart, and it's not holding my attention. Tossing the book aside, I close my eyes and will myself to fall asleep. I don't know how long I lie here, but eventually, I drift off. My daughter must be feeling better because it's not until 6:00 a.m. that her cries wake me up again. Six solid hours she slept. Too bad I can't say the same for myself.

A diaper change and breakfast, and my girl is ready for some medicine. Her fever is gone, and she seems to be more settled and doesn't appear to be in pain. I decide to pass on the Tylenol for now, but I'll be sure to put it in the diaper bag in case we need it while we're out. I'm in the middle of changing her outfit when my cell phone rings. It's old as hell, a flip phone, and it's prepaid, which means I don't have many minutes each month. However, with Madeline, I feel as though I need a phone in case of an emergency.

"Hello?" I greet my best friend, Carrie. She and I have been friends since middle school, and she's been a godsend since losing Travis.

"Hey. I'll be quick," she says, knowing I don't like to waste my minutes. I can only afford a small amount each month. "You're off today, right?"

"Yes, but just because Maddie is sick again."

"Shit. Well, I was going to suggest coffee. How about I bring it to you?"

"You don't have to do that."

"Of course, I do. I'm about fifteen minutes away. Let me hit the drive-thru, and I'll be there. Can I pick anything up for you?"

"No. Thank you, though."

She doesn't argue with me like I know that she wants to. "I'll see you in a little while," she says, ending the call.

"Well, it looks like Aunt Carrie is coming to visit," I tell Madeline. She coos up at me. With her belly full and the medicine working, she's back to my happy baby girl. Placing her in her swing, which she's almost too big for, I straighten up my blankets and pillows on the couch and wash the few dishes that are in the sink. I'm wiping off the counters when there's a knock at the door. Dropping the dish towel, I rush to let Carrie inside. "Hey," I greet her.

"Morning."

"Are you off today, I guess? I didn't ask."

"Yes. I worked a twelve-hour yesterday for a girl, and she took my shift today."

Carrie is a nurse. Something I decided after six months at my old job that would come in handy. When Dad passed, I had just finished college with an associate's degree in early childhood education. I loved my job but could see the benefits of also having a nursing degree. Travis and I discussed it, and I was going to go back to school when he finished.

When I realized I couldn't afford to stay in our apartment on my income alone, I began to look for a new place, and a new job within walking distance. I knew I would need to sell our cars to help make ends meet. When I wasn't having any luck, Carrie suggested becoming a certified nurse's aide. Being a nurse, she claimed they were in high demand. So, while I was pregnant and working, I took the twelve-week course and passed my certification.

Carrie is my biggest supporter of going back to school and becoming a nurse. However, I just don't know how I could make it work. Financially I could probably get some help, but then I'd spend even more time away from Madeline, and that's not something that sounds appealing at all.

"What's all that?" I ask as she starts unloading the small brown bag she is carrying.

"Breakfast."

"Carrie—" I start and stop knowing it's no use. My best friend is one in a million.

"None of that." She looks over her shoulder at me and winks.

"And the tote?" I ask.

"Oh, I had to bring some stuff for my niece." She starts to empty the tote and tears well in my eyes when I see a pack of diapers, wipes, and two outfits. I made the comment that Madeline was growing so fast a few days ago, and my guess is that those outfits are the size I told her Madeline was almost in.

"Carrie, you didn't have to," I tell her, choking up.

"I know I didn't. I wanted to. I'm happy to help. I know things are tight for you, and honestly, Wren, you've been through it. You've had a lot of shit roll downhill to you, and this isn't much in the grand scheme of things."

"You do this almost every time that you visit."

She shrugs. "I can afford to, and I want to. I know if I were in your shoes, you would do the same." She folds up the tote and shoves it into her purse. "Now, get your ass over here and eat with me. I miss my best friend. Tell me all the things," she says, grabbing her sandwich and coffee and settling on the couch. My apartment is too small for a dining room table, and the galley kitchen is too small for one as well.

My stomach grumbles from hunger, but my best friend, being the rock star that she is, ignores it when I take a seat next to her, sandwich and coffee in hand. I take a bite of my sandwich—bacon, egg, and cheese on a bagel—and it's the best thing I've eaten in weeks. In between bites, I tell her about Madeline being sick and the stranger yesterday at the pharmacy.

"Wren, you know I can float you—" she starts, but I stop her.

"I get paid today, and my health insurance kicks in on Monday. It was just a bad time and a tough spot."

"You should have called me."

"I would have. I didn't have time to. He just stepped up and said to pay it forward someday. Then I found he dropped cash into the bag when he handed it to me."

"Wow. Was he wearing a ring?" she jokes.

"I was too embarrassed to look," I tell her honestly. "Anyway, I'm going to look him up when I get to work on Monday and try to find him. I need to return the money."

"You need it."

"I know, but I'm not his responsibility."

"How are you going to find him? Did he give you a name?" She doesn't respond to my comment. She knows me well enough to know that my mind is made up.

"He said his name was Marshall Riggins." As soon as his name is out of my mouth, she chokes on the last bite of the sandwich she just shoved into her mouth. "You all right?" I ask her.

"Yes. Wren, do you not recognize that name?"

"No. Should I?"

She stands and goes to her purse she left on the kitchen counter and walks back to take her seat on the couch. The entire time her fingers are flying across the screen of her cell phone. "Marshall Riggins is one of the Riggins brothers. Riggins Enterprises?" she asks.

"Oh. Yeah, that's the big building downtown, right? What do they do anyway?" I ask her.

"They're in logistics. They coordinate trucks and deliveries all over the world."

"So Marshall? He owns the business?" I ask.

She nods, grinning wildly. "He does, with his four brothers. They're all hot as hell."

"Yeah, he was easy on the eyes."

"I thought you weren't looking?" she teases.

"I looked enough," I confess.

"Well, hold onto your panties because this is Marshall and his brothers." She turns her phone screen to show me, and sure enough, the handsome stranger from yesterday is in the photo with four other guys who all have similar features.

"Wow."

"Right? It says that Marshall is the youngest of the five and the only single one left."

"Don't start," I tell her.

"Hey, I'm just saying. You're young and you're beautiful. What happened to Travis was tragic, but you have to keep living. Live for him, and for her." She points to the swing. "Speaking of my niece, can I get some snuggles?"

"Have at it."

She stands and lifts Madeline from her swing and snuggles her close. "Hey, sweetie," she says softly. Madeline babbles at her, and my heart swells. I'm so glad she's feeling better, and I thank God every single day that he brought my best friend into my life. She's been my rock. She was there when I lost my dad, and she was with me when I lost Travis. I know that I wouldn't have made it this far without her and her kind heart.

CHAPTER THREE
Marshall

"THE NUMBERS ARE good," Owen says. "The new marketing campaign has definitely increased our client list. All locations are above where they were last year," he explains.

"That's because our little brother is a marketing genius." Royce nods toward me.

"Keep 'em coming," I tease, motioning him to keep the compliments rolling in. All four of my brothers laugh.

"I'm surprised you're not recording him saying that," Conrad muses.

"That's because I already did." Reaching for my phone that's sitting on the table, I pull up the video of Royce in his office a couple of weeks ago telling me that same thing.

"I should have known." Conrad shakes his head at my antics.

Before I can reply, there's a knock at the conference room door. We all turn to look to see Layla standing just inside the doorway. "Sorry to interrupt. Marsh, you have a visitor."

"I'm not expecting anyone. Is there a meeting I forgot about?" I ask her as I pull out my phone to check my calendar.

"N-No. No meeting." She shakes her head. "I normally wouldn't interrupt, but well, I think you need to come with me."

"Babe?" Owen stands.

"It's fine," Layla assures her husband. "I just don't think that Marshall wants to keep this one waiting." She gives me a look I can't decipher as I stand from the conference table.

"We're done here anyway. If you stay any longer, your head's not going to make it out the door," Royce teases.

"It's not my fault I got all the brains," I quip as I follow Layla out of the conference room and down the hall to her desk, which is also the reception area. As soon as I turn the corner, I freeze when I see the woman from the pharmacy last night.

"Hi." She waves.

I take her in, and she seems to be more rested than yesterday, and the baby she's swinging back and forth in her seat isn't crying. Stepping forward, I crouch down so I'm eye level with the baby. "Hey, sweet girl, are you feeling better?" I ask her.

"She is. Thank you for that. Now that I know where you work, I can repay you."

I stand back to my full height. "I told you that's not necessary. Pay it forward one day when you see someone in need."

She nods and places the baby and the seat on the floor, then digs in the diaper bag and thrusts her hand out toward me. "I believe this is yours."

I don't have to look into that white envelope to know that it's the extra cash I snuck into the bag. The baby begins to fuss, so instead of taking the money, I lift the seat into my arms and begin to rock her. "That's yours," I tell her.

"It's not." She shakes her head adamantly. "I appreciate the gesture, but I can't accept this."

"It's a gift."

"The medication was enough." She tries again to hand me the envelope, but I ignore it.

"How did you find me?" I ask her.

"My best friend, Carrie. When I told her about your generosity, she recognized your name."

"Not you?"

"Not me what?"

"You didn't recognize my name?" I watch her closely to see if she's lying, but when she tells me no, I believe her.

"So what are you girls doing today?" I ask the baby girl. "Madeline, right?" I ask the mom. "And you're Wren?"

She nods. "We came to give this back to you."

"Other than that."

"Nothing. I couldn't work today because Madeline can't go to day care until she's fever-free for twenty-four hours."

Heavy footsteps and the voices of my brothers carry, and I know they're about to round the corner to see who my visitor is.

"Oh, who's this?" my sister-in-law Sawyer asks. She stops next to me and peers down at the angel in the car seat.

"This is Madeline and her momma, Wren." She gives me a questioning look, and I shake my head as subtly as I can. She thinks they're mine, or at least the baby. They're not. I would have remembered Wren. Her short blonde hair rests just above her shoulders, and her blue eyes are piercing, almost like looking up at the sky on a cloudless day. I'm guessing she's about five foot four or so comparing her to my six-foot-one frame. She's sexy as hell, and if I hadn't seen her with her daughter, I never would have guessed she was a mom. Or a widow if the woman at the pharmacy's story checks out.

"She's what? Five months?" Sawyer asks.

"Yes," Wren replies.

"I have a five-month-old little boy at home," Sawyer explains.

"Aren't you the cutest?" Layla chimes in. I didn't even realize she'd joined us from behind her desk. "I have a one-and-a-half-year-old. Boy."

"We have lots of boys. Two more on the way," I tell Wren. "These are my sisters-in-law, Sawyer and Layla. I have two more who are both expecting boys a week apart," I explain. Doing so helps me seem like less of a creeper from our interaction yesterday.

"What? You can introduce our wives but not us?" Royce asks.

"What are we, chopped liver?" Owen jokes. It's so good to see him coming out of his shell. We have Layla and their son, Carter, to thank for that.

I chuckle. "These knuckleheads are my brothers. Royce, Owen, Grant, and Conrad," I point as I say their names.

"That one's mine," Royce says, pointing to Sawyer.

"And this one's mine," Owen says, placing his hand on Layla's shoulder.

"Ours aren't here," Grant speaks up.

"We should open a bakery in the building," Conrad muses.

"That's not a bad idea." I point at him. "It would make our morning stops so much easier."

"It's nice to meet you all. I just—" Wren starts. When I look at her, I see a flush to her cheeks.

"Come with me." With Madeline in her seat in one hand, I place the other on the small of Wren's back and lead her away from my loud, nosey family and to my office. Once we're inside, I shut the door. "Sorry about that. There's a lot of us, and we sometimes forget how overwhelming it can be for all of us to be in the same place at once. Especially for someone new."

"Here." She thrusts the envelope at me.

"I'm not taking that back," I tell her as I place the infant seat on my desk. "What do you think, Madeline? Can you help me out here? Can you tell your momma to keep the money?" The cutie grins at me and sticks her hand in her mouth.

"Marshall," Wren sighs.

I turn to face her. "Look, what I'm going to say is going to make me sound like an as—butthole." I quickly catch myself before cursing. Not that Madeline is old enough to understand, but regardless. "I'm just going to say it, but know that it's coming from a good place, and I'm not trying to be rude or degrading." I wait for her to nod as she crosses her arms over her chest. "I don't need the money." She opens her mouth to argue, but I raise my hands to stop her. "My family has worked hard to grow this company to what it is today. I'm proud of that. I'm proud to be a part of it. My brothers and I were handed our family legacy, and we've expanded and grown. The business is thriving. The shoes I'm wearing cost four times what I gave you. I can afford to help you, Wren, and I want to help you."

"I'm not your responsibility."

I nod. "You're right. You're not. You're a complete stranger to me, but that's okay. What is the point of my having all of this money and not being able to use it for good? How do you expect me to sleep at night knowing you and your daughter are struggling, and I have the means to help?"

"What? Are you going to try and save the world?"

"No. Not the world. I just want to help." I shrug.

"Why?" Her tone is softer. "I'm not sleeping with you." There's a tic in her jaw, and she shuffles her stance from one foot to the other. She's nervous.

I can't hold in my laughter, and it's so loud it startles the baby, making her cry. "I'm sorry," I tell the baby as I rock her seat back and forth on my desk. "Look, this isn't some scheme to get into your pants. I was there at the right time to offer assistance. That's all this is. I can help, so let me help."

"I-I don't know what to say," Wren says, her voice cracking.

"You say thank you, and when you get back on your feet, and you see someone in need, you help them out. It's that simple."

"Thank you for paying for her medication. I can't tell you what that means to me. And this—" She holds up the white envelope. "This is a gesture too kind and one I will never forget, but I'm sorry, Marshall, I can't keep it." She places the envelope on the edge of my desk and lifts her daughter still in her seat from my desk. "Thank you for your generosity. I'll never forget it." With that, she walks out of my office.

I stand rooted to my spot. I should run after her, insist that she take the money, but I saw the look in her eyes. Determination and pride both prevent her from taking the gift. I thought I could convince her, but I guess I was wrong.

What's even more shocking is that she truly didn't seem to know who we were. Not one ounce of recognition flashed in those big blue eyes when she met my family.

I wish that she would have taken the money. It wasn't much, but I'm sure it would have given her a little bit of relief. I release a heavy sigh as I sit back at my desk. There is nothing I can do. I gave it my best shot.

It's barely been ten minutes since she left when a shadow falls over my desk. Glancing up, I see my brother Royce standing in front of my desk.

"What's up?"

"Wren seems nice."

"I don't know. I guess so."

"How did you meet?" he asks.

I see shadows outside my office door, and I know the rest of my family is out there listening in. "You can all come in," I call out. One by one, my brothers shuffle into the room. "I don't know her. I was at the pharmacy last night picking up Mom's prescription, and she was in front of me in line. She doesn't have insurance and didn't have enough money to pay for the baby's medicine. I stepped up and paid for it for her."

"Aww." I hear from the hallway.

"Come on in," I tell my sisters.

"Marsh." Layla comes to me and gives me a hug, followed immediately by a hug from Sawyer too.

"You're one of the good ones," Sawyer tells me.

"Hey!" Royce snakes an arm around her waist and pulls her into his lap.

"I'm just saying."

"Anyway," I start again. "I insisted on paying and told her to pay it forward. It was only fifty dollars." I shake my head. "My underwear costs more than her baby's prescription. When the lady handed me back my change, I slipped the fifty and two more hundreds into the bag before handing it to her." I point to the white envelope that's still lying on the corner of my desk. "She brought it back to me. Said she can't accept it."

"How did she know where to find you?" Owen asks.

"I gave her my name. Apparently, when she told her best friend, she's heard of our family, much like everyone else in this town, and that led her here today."

"So the baby?" Grant asks.

I knew this was coming, which is why I throw my head back in laughter. "She's not mine," I tell them once my laughter is under control. "Cute as hell, but not mine."

"She seems nice," Layla comments.

"Yeah, she's on hard times. After she left the pharmacy, the woman checking me out said that her husband used to work there. She's not wearing a wedding ring, so I'm assuming they split. Said it wasn't her story to tell, so that's all the intel she was willing to give me."

"That's so sad," Sawyer whispers.

"It is. And I hate it because I can help, you know?" All six of them nod their agreement. "Anyway, she insisted on not taking the money." Again, I point to the envelope on my desk. "So, that's it. I did what I could. At least I know I tried to help her."

"You did help her," Layla speaks up. "Trust me. That money for the medication was just as hard for her to accept. If it had not been for her daughter, she wouldn't have accepted that either."

Layla knows tough times. She had a rough childhood, and into adulthood wasn't much better. My brother fell in love with her hard and fast, and now she's one of us. That doesn't mean that any of us forgets her struggles in life before she came into our lives.

"Yeah," I agree. "She's stubborn."

"Not stubborn," Layla corrects me. "She's proud. She's... I'm sure, busting her ass to work and be a mom, and handouts are hard to take. No matter how desperately you need them."

"Like shoes," Owen whispers, kissing her temple.

"Anyway, that's it. The baby's not mine, and I'll probably never see them again."

"Well, damn," Conrad speaks up. "I was hoping for something juicier than that. Not to mention, Mom would have flipped to have a granddaughter with all the boys." He grins.

"It's the Riggins' genes," Grant chimes in. "We're studly like that." The words are barely out of his mouth before he's laughing at his own remark. That's okay, though, because the rest of us are laughing too. Four Riggins grandchildren, all boys. Mom and Dad had the five of us, all boys, so he's not wrong. Mom would flip. She's over the moon to have four new daughters-in-law. Well, three and one soon-to-be daughter-in-law, if we are getting technical. The Riggins ladies are still outnumbered.

"Well, that was anti-climatic. I guess we should get back to work." Royce taps Sawyer on the leg so that they can both stand. I watch as the six of them leave my office. We're one big nosey family, but I wouldn't have it any other way.

CHAPTER
Wren
FOUR

"**T**WO MORE BLOCKS, Maddie. Can you hold on for Mommy?" I ask my daughter as I quicken my pace. I had some errands to run today and Maddie has been an angel, but she's at her wit's end. I thought she would make it until we got home to eat, but my daughter isn't a happy camper.

I have two choices. I can stop somewhere and feed her, or I can let her scream until we get home. My heart can't handle the screaming, so stopping it is.

The only issue with stopping is that I can't really go to a café or restaurant and not buy anything, so I need to find a place outside. Up ahead, I see what looks like a bakery that is closed. There's a park bench with flowers out front and an awning to provide us with a little shade. "This will have to do," I tell Madeline. Not that she's listening. She's pissed and hungry, and her cries are growing louder by the second.

Luckily, I pumped, so I'm not whipping my breast out in public. Don't get me wrong, I would, but luckily, I don't have to.

Madeline isn't picky. She takes a bottle with ease, which is a good thing since she's in day care. A very expensive day care, but I only want what's best for her. It takes the majority of our money each month, but it's worth it for my peace of mind while I'm at work.

"Warm Delights," I say the name of the bakery out loud. "Closed due to fire." I hate that for the owners. I couldn't imagine putting all of your hard work and money into a business only to have it brought down by a fire. I'm sure they had insurance. At least I hope they did. Just the thought of the loss causes a ping of sadness to grip my heart. Loss is loss any way you look at it.

"I'm working on it," I tell my daughter as she wails even louder. I quickly pull a bottle from the diaper bag and set it on the bench next to me before unstrapping her from her seat. I think it's time I start using the stroller. It's a pain because my apartment is on the third floor, and we don't have an elevator, so just taking the seat is easier. However, as she gets older, she's getting too heavy for me to pack both all over the city.

"There you go," I say, placing the bottle in her mouth. Like I knew she would, she latches on easily and drinks greedily.

"How old is she?" a female voice asks, startling me. "Sorry." She smiles kindly. "I didn't mean to scare you."

"Five months," I tell her, my pulse slowing when I take in the woman's friendly smile.

"I have a nephew who just turned five months," she says.

"She's becoming more interactive, getting to that fun age. At least that's what I'm told." I laugh. "That's what the books I've read say."

"I have a nephew who's one-and-a-half, and he's a ball of fun, so I can see that," she says.

Her nephews are the same ages as Marshall's. Yes, a week later, I'm still thinking about the man. His kindness is not something you see much of these days. It helps that he's easy on the eyes. I might be a widowed mother to an infant, but I'm still a woman. There isn't a woman, hell, maybe not even a man who would disagree that Marshall Riggins and his brothers are definite eye candy.

"I'm Aspen," the woman introduces herself.

"I'm Wren, and this is Madeline." Something flashes in her eyes, but she quickly masks it.

"This is my store, well, mine and my sister's."

"I'm sorry about the fire." I nod toward the sign on the door.

"Thank you. I was inside," she says, taking a seat next to me on the bench. "It was pretty scary, but we're okay," she says, placing her hands on her swollen belly.

"Thank goodness."

"Yeah, I didn't know I was pregnant until the hospital ran bloodwork on me that night. I was taken to the Emergency Room. I'd passed out from smoke inhalation."

"Wow. I'm glad you're both okay."

"Thank you."

"Are you going to rebuild?" It's none of my business, but she's so easy to talk to.

"Yeah, my sister, Aurora, this was always her dream. To own her own bakery. We're in the process of fighting with the insurance company. Faulty wiring caused the fire. This is an old building." She shrugs. "These things just happen, but yeah, the plan is to rebuild, or maybe we'll move locations. I'm not sure. We've been bouncing ideas around. What about you? What do you do?" she asks. She seems completely content to sit here on this bench and talk to me, a complete stranger.

"Is it okay that I'm here?" I nod down at the bench. "I just needed a place to stop and feed her. We live a few blocks away, and the alternative was to let her scream the rest of the way."

"Of course it is. This little cutie needed to fill her belly." She smiles at Madeline.

"Thank you." I return her kind smile. "I'm a nurse's aide." I answer her earlier question.

"I don't think I could do needles and stuff." She shivers.

"I don't have to. As an aide, I do things like help with baths and life tasks. I'm currently working at an assisted living facility for the elderly. It's my job to help with tasks they can no longer do on their own. As far as needles, I wanted to be a nurse. I was working in a day care and could see the benefits of having a nurse on staff. I decided that I wanted to further my education to do just that."

"I commend everyone in the healthcare industry. That's just not for me." She shakes her head. "What stopped you?"

"My late husband; he was going through pharmacy school. I was working full-time at a day care facility. When I told him my idea about nursing to help my current role, he was supportive. We made the decision I would start school again when he finished. It wasn't about more money for me, I wanted to do it to be able to help the kids." I swallow hard at this next part. "He passed away. Unexpectedly, and then I found out I was pregnant, and life just… happened, I guess."

"Is that still a dream of yours?" she asks.

"Yeah, maybe someday. Honestly, I wish I could just be her momma." I laugh. "She is by far the greatest blessing in my life." I clear my throat. "Besides, right now I'm not even using my associate's degree in early childhood education. I couldn't find a job, so I'm using my CNA training instead. Whatever it takes to pay the bills."

Aspen places her hands over her swollen belly. "I'm sorry for your loss. I can't imagine how hard that was for you and to be raising her alone."

"Thank you." This is part of why I don't like to talk about Travis's death. It gets awkward. People never know what to say.

"Any sage parenting advice?" Aspen chuckles.

I could give her the biggest hug right now for the conversation change. "Take lots of pictures, and don't blink. I can't believe she's already five months old."

"Got it. Lots of pictures and no blinking." She laughs.

"I have so many pictures on my camera that I need to get developed." My camera is old, but it still takes decent photos. Thankfully SD memory cards are inexpensive, and I choose carefully which images to save. Sometimes I find new cards lying around the house, and I know that it's Carrie who's bringing them over. I don't know what I would do without my best friend.

"I'm sure I'll be the same way. Although, I have a feeling my fiancé is going to give me a run for my money."

"Sounds like you've found one of the good ones."

"Definitely. My sister is married to his brother. She and I are both incredibly lucky to marry into, well, I'm going to be soon-ish, their family."

"No wedding date?" I ask.

"No. I don't want to be pregnant for the wedding."

"What does he think? Your fiancé?"

"He'd marry me now, right here in my leggings and an oversized T-shirt." She smiles. It's one of those genuine smiles, the ones you can't stop from tilting your lips.

"That's true love," I tell her. "I know we just met, but can I give you a piece of advice?"

"Definitely."

"Life is short, Aspen. Too damn short. I never thought I'd be where I am right now. Raising my daughter all on my own. A widow at the age of twenty-four." I pause to collect my thoughts. "It all happened so fast. I say if you love him, and he loves you, who cares if you're pregnant in your wedding photos? All that matters is that the two of you are so in love that you can't wait to start your lives together."

She nods and wipes a tear from the corner of her eye. "I don't know what happened to your husband, and I'm not going to ask. Maybe one day you will tell me. However, that piece of advice is probably some of the best I've ever been given." She smiles down at Madeline with watery eyes before looking back up at me. "You and I are going to be good friends. And my fiancé, well, let's just say when I tell him I'm ready to set a date now, he's going to track you down and try to buy you a new car or something crazy like that." She huffs out a laugh.

"Seriously?" I ask, my mouth dropping open.

"I wouldn't put it past him. Hey, what are you doing right now?"

"Heading home now that this one has her belly full. Why?"

"My sister and I are getting together with her sisters-in-law at my place, and well, I guess they're going to be mine too. Sooner now rather than later." She winks. "Why don't you join us?" she offers.

"I don't have a sitter."

"No sitter needed. They'll have their kids with them. The husbands will be there too, but they'll stay in the basement doing whatever it is they do when they all get together."

"I don't know." It's on the tip of my tongue to turn her down, but at the same time, meeting new friends is a good thing. I really like Aspen. My gut tells me she's good people just from sitting here talking to her.

"Please? You'll fit right in with all of us, I promise. Besides, when I tell my fiancé it was you who convinced me we need to do this wedding thing sooner rather than later, he's going to at least want to meet you."

"I don't have a car," I confess, dropping my head in embarrassment.

"That's fine. I'll drive you."

"I can't ask you to do that."

"You didn't. I offered. Come on. I want you to meet my sister and my future sisters-in-law. Please?" She folds her hands as if she were praying and juts out her bottom lip.

"Does that work with your fiancé?" I ask her.

"Oddly enough, I never have to beg or ask now that I think about it. He likes to take care of me." She shrugs.

"Sounds like you're a lucky woman." Travis and I were good together, but he was never overly affectionate. I think it was because he didn't have that growing up. He was good to me, and we loved one another, but the kind of love that Aspen is talking about? I've never had that. Travis was my best friend. I loved him and he loved me. We made a beautiful baby girl together, and I'll forever have a piece of him.

"Come on, Wren, please?" she begs.

"Are you sure that I won't be intruding?"

"Positive. It's at my house, so I have the final say. Please. It's only about fifteen minutes from here. I'll drive you and drive you home. It's not like you have to worry about me drinking." She chuckles and points to her watermelon-sized belly.

"I don't have the car seat base."

"I have one, and I think our seats are similar."

"It's in your car already?"

"Yep. My fiancé is just a little excited about being a dad. My bag is already packed and ready to go. He gets it honest," she says with a shrug.

I really want to go. I want to keep talking to her, and it would be good for Madeline to be around other kids other than just at day care. "If you're sure you don't mind."

"Yes!" She claps her hands. "This is going to be so much fun. I can't wait to introduce you to everyone."

"Wait, did you need to do something? Did I talk your head off and keep you from it?"

"No." She waves me off. "I just went for a drive and found myself driving past the shop." She points behind us. "I saw you and this little cutie sitting here, and I don't know, something just told me to stop and say hello."

"Well, I'm glad you did."

"Me too. Now, come on. My husband-to-be is grilling burgers. And before you ask, yes, there's plenty. We always have plenty."

"I'm crashing your Saturday night," I tell her.

"Nonsense. You're just adding to it." She stands and grabs the diaper bag. "Come with me." She leads me to a fancy white SUV. She opens the back door and steps back. Sure, enough, Madeline's car seat fits into the base perfectly. "See, it's meant to be."

With a smile and a nod, I climb into the passenger seat, headed for the unknown with a woman I just met but already feels like a close friend.

The drive is short, just about fifteen minutes, just like she said. The driveway is lined with cars, trucks, and SUVs. "Um, Aspen, how big of a get-together are you having?"

"Just a small one. My sister, her husband, my fiancé, and his three other brothers."

"I think maybe this was a bad idea," I tell her as I eye the long line of vehicles.

"Come on. You're going to fit right in. I promise. I'll grab the bags. You get the baby." Her grin is infectious.

Climbing out of the car, I grab Madeline, who is surprisingly still awake, and walk behind Aspen as she enters the house. "Honey, I'm home!" she calls out.

"In the kitchen!" a deep voice answers.

I follow along behind her, and when we reach the open floorplan kitchen, my mouth falls open. Standing around an island bigger than any I've ever seen in my life is none other than Marshall Riggins and his brothers, and the two women I met who I know are his sisters-in-law when I stopped to give him back his money.

"Aspen?" I murmur.

She turns to look at me. "You good?" she asks.

"Who is your fiancé?"

A slow smile pulls at her lips. "Conrad Riggins." She sees it on my face, and now I understand the look I caught from her earlier. She recognized my name.

"I should go."

"Wren?" Marshall is on his feet and walking toward us. "Hey, fancy seeing you here." He reaches for Madeline's car seat, and my hands are shaking, so I let him.

"I—" I don't know what to say.

"Come on in, and I'll introduce you to my sister." Aspen tugs on my arm, but I stop and look at Marshall.

"We're right behind you, Momma." He smiles at me, and I don't know how but it puts me at ease.

CHAPTER FIVE
Marshall

I T SEEMS AS though the blonde pixie and her daughter are showing up everywhere I am these days. I don't know why she's with Aspen or how they know each other. What I do know is the shock written all over her face. She had no idea what she was walking into. I could see the tremble in her hands, so I took the baby from her.

"Hey, sweetheart," I coo down at the adorable little girl.

"Who do we have here?" Aurora asks.

"This is Madeline," I tell her. I don't need to give her further explanation. I know that my brothers have already filled her in. What I don't know is how Aspen ended up with Wren and why she brought her here.

Setting the car seat on the kitchen island, I work to unbuckle the five-point harness and lift Madeline from her seat. "You're a tiny thing," I tell her, resting her against my shoulder. She cuddles up to me, her little fists clutching at my shirt. My heart squeezes as she snuggles into my chest.

"That baby looks good on you, Marsh," Conrad says, placing his arm over Aspen's shoulders.

"She likes me," I fire back. My eyes find Wren's, and she's got her head tilted to the side, watching me hold her daughter. I guess I should have asked for permission, but she was too damn cute to just leave her in there.

"Hand her over, baby hog," Grant says, stopping next to me.

"I saw her first," I argue.

"We don't get little girls in this house, and the next two won't be girls either, so we all get a turn." He holds out his arms, waiting for me to hand Madeline over to him.

"Fine," I grumble and carefully move her to his arms. She juts out her bottom lip like she's going to cry. "She likes me better," I say, crossing my arms over my chest.

"Tell Marsh he's wrong," he coos to Madeline. "You like Uncle Grant, don't you, Madeline?"

Wren and her daughter have been a constant topic of conversation in my family since she showed up at the office to give me back the money I tried to slip her. They're all big fans of Wren. Our money and our name mean nothing to her. That's big... no, that's *huge,* and my brothers, my sisters-in-law, and even my parents have made that known.

They act like there's some love connection there when all I was trying to do was be a nice guy. Thankfully they haven't spouted anything about the damn magic they're all the time talking about. The women in my life have mentioned the word fate a few times, but I ignore them. I was simply in the right place at the right time. It's not a crime to be a good person. And well, Wren proved she is as well, but I still wish she would have kept that money.

Madeline begins to cry regardless of Grant's efforts to console her. I see Wren headed this way from where she stands on the other side of the island, but I beat her to it. "Come here, sweetheart." I take her from Grant, and she immediately stops crying.

"Who would have thought Marshall would be the damn baby whisperer," Grant complains.

"I'd be afraid of you too," Conrad says. "Let me try." He takes Madeline from my arms, and she's okay for about a minute before she starts to cry. He hands her back to me, and she stops.

"You jokers are doing it wrong. You have to soothe her." Royce steps in front of me. "Hand her over, little brother. I'll show these knuckleheads how it's done."

"I'm sorry, sweet girl. We can humor them, right?" I ask Madeline before handing her over to Royce. He coos softly to her. I have no idea what he's saying, but he lasts about two minutes, longer than Grant and Con, before she begins to fuss, and he immediately hands her back.

"He does the same thing with Roan." Sawyer laughs. "Daddy hates to hear him cry."

"It's the worst," Royce confesses. "I never know what he wants. I'm failing at this dad gig."

"You're not failing," Layla tells him. "It takes time to learn, and my guess is that Roan can sense that his crying makes you nervous, which makes him nervous."

"That's what I keep telling him," Sawyer agrees.

"Clearly, as the more seasoned father, I've got this." Owen walks around the island and holds out his arms like he's already cradling the baby. "Baby me," he says.

It's still sometimes hard to see my brother so laidback with kids and us even. Layla has opened him up, and it's the best thing. "Here you go." I gently place Madeline into his arms. She immediately grabs for his beard, and a slow smile tilts his lips. He thinks that he has this in the bag.

"You're a cute little thing, aren't you?" he asks Madeline.

"She and Roan are the same age," I tell him.

At the sound of my voice, Madeline turns to look at me, and again that little lip of hers pokes out, and she begins to cry. Royce isn't the only one who can't handle a baby crying, so I reach for her. She snuggles into my chest and immediately quiets down. "I've got you," I tell her softly, rubbing my hand up and down her back.

"I think it's safe to say she likes you." Aurora smiles at me.

"She's not used to being around a lot of people. She's in day care, but they have an all-female staff. She's never really been around men," Wren confesses.

That makes me wonder what happened to her husband. Did he leave them? How is it possible that he was married to a woman like Wren and had this adorable little girl, and he was able to walk away? I don't know Wren, but from what I do know, she's a good person and cute as hell. He's an idiot.

"We're best buds, right, Maddie?" I ask the baby.

"I can take her," Wren tells me.

"It's fine. Go ahead and eat. I'll watch her while you do."

"It's okay. I'm used to eating and holding her."

"Which is why you should take a break," I reply.

"She's content," Aspen chimes in. "Let's get a plate. We'll be right here if she starts to get fussy."

"Are you sure you don't mind?" Wren asks me.

"Positive." I move to one of the barstools and take a seat. Madeline has her little fist wrapped around my shirt, with her head resting on my shoulder. She's perfectly content, and I admit that her wanting me over my brothers has me wanting to puff out my chest in victory. It's stupid and childish, but it's still facts. As the youngest Riggins brother, I'm constantly behind all of them, and well, Madeline just moved me to the top spot.

Conversation flows all around us. Royce has Roan in a similar position as I do Madeline, and Carter is in his high chair, the one Con bought just for him for get-togethers like this. I have one at my place too, and so do Royce and Grant. Our family is growing and changing, and we're all here for it.

"Have the two of you set a date yet?" Layla asks Aspen.

"No, but I've been thinking about it." Aspen smiles at Wren, who returns her smile in earnest. "I'm thinking sooner rather than later."

"What?" Conrad drops his fork to his plate and turns to look at his fiancée, giving her his full attention.

Aspen smiles. "Life's short, and at the end of the day, I want to be your wife. Even if I look like a whale in my wedding dress."

"You're a fucking goddess," Conrad is quick to reply.

No one bothers to tell him to watch his language around the kids. He is laser-focused on Aspen, and we all know that he's lost in her and their conversation.

"And that's why I love you." Aspen places her hand on his cheek and smiles softly at him.

"What changed your mind?"

"Wren."

Every head in the room turns to look at Wren, even Conrad. I watch as she visibly swallows and squares her shoulders. "I lost my husband," she murmurs. "A week later, I found out I was pregnant. Life is short. You have to take what it gives you while you can." She looks away, averting her gaze.

I feel like a dick. I called her late husband an idiot without knowing the story. I'm glad I didn't say that shit out loud. I'm ready to stand and go to her, but I'm surprised when Conrad beats me to it. He kisses Aspen on the temple and moves to stand next to Wren. I watch as he talks softly to her. So soft that the conversation is just for them. Then, he hugs her. He wraps his arms around her and pulls her into his chest. I might not be able to hear their conversation, but I can see the way her body visibly shakes with her tears.

I want to tell him to stop. Whatever he said, or maybe it's his embrace that's causing her tears, but he needs to stop. I can't take it. I watch as he releases her, and she wipes at her eyes. That's my cue, but Aspen, Aurora, Layla, and Sawyer all crowd around her and guide her out of the kitchen.

"Damn," Grant mutters.

"Did you know?" Royce asks.

I have to clear my throat before I can answer. "No. The lady at the pharmacy said her husband used to work there but didn't give me specifics."

"I can't imagine doing this on my own," Owen says, handing Carter a cracker.

"Yeah," I say, snuggling Madeline a little closer. She begins sucking on her hand. "I think she's getting hungry."

"We've got this," Conrad says. "I think we should give her time with the ladies," he says. He grabs the diaper bag, pulling it toward him. He roots inside and finds a bottle and pulls off the cap, handing it to me.

"Wait, you need a bib," Royce tells him.

"And a burp cloth," Owen adds.

"Let me look." Grant pulls the bag to him and shoves his hand into the side pocket, pulling out both items with a look of victory on his face. "Got 'em."

He helps me get the bib on Madeline without much fuss and tosses the burp cloth over my shoulder. I place the bottle in her mouth, and she drinks greedily. "What if she's off schedule?" I ask them. "Your wives always talk about keeping the babies on a schedule," I tell them.

"She's hungry," Conrad points out.

"Yes, but if it's too early, Wren might get pissed."

"Meh." Owen waves me off. "One time isn't going to hurt anything. She's not going to be pissed."

"What do you think, Maddie? Is Mommy going to be mad at us?" The cutie smiles around her bottle, flaps her arms and begins to drink again. "Okay, you're right. I'm on your side. You have to stand up for me," I tell her. "We're in this together."

Fifteen minutes later, Madeline has sucked her bottle dry and is snoozing away in my arms. That's how the women find us when they enter the kitchen. "She was hungry," I tell Wren as soon as she lays eyes on us.

"She ate before we got here."

"Well, she ate again." I hold up the empty bottle with my free hand.

"Thank you for taking such good care of her."

I look down at the baby in my arms. "She was an angel."

"I should get her home," she says, stepping next to me.

"I'll put her in her seat." I move to the other side of the counter and place the sleeping baby into her seat. She sighs but doesn't wake up. I quickly strap her in, something I've done a million times with my nephews.

"I'll be right back," Aspen tells Conrad.

"I can take them," I offer. I wasn't going to head out this early, but something inside me is telling me that I need to take them home. I need to know where she lives, and I just... need to make sure she's okay.

"Wren?" Aspen asks.

"I live in town. I'm sure it's on the way."

"Are you sure you don't mind?" Wren asks.

"Positive."

"Wait. I need a car seat base."

"I have one."

Surprise crosses her face. "You do?"

"Of course I do." I point at my chest. "Favorite uncle."

"Here we go." Owen laughs.

"Wren, put us out of our misery so we don't have to listen to this nonsense," Conrad tells her. "Everyone knows I'm the favorite uncle."

"That would be me." Grant raises his hand.

"Clearly, it's me," Royce chimes in.

"I've got you all beat," Owen says, crossing his arms over his chest.

"Fine." Wren laughs. It's a musical sound, and after seeing her tears, a welcome sight. "We better go before a fight breaks out."

"Nah, they're all bark and no bite," Aspen tells her. "Before you leave, we need to exchange numbers." She hands Wren her phone, and she quickly types in her number and hands it back. "Great. I'll give it to the others," Aspen tells her.

"Um... okay. Thank you." I can tell by her reply she thinks Aspen is just being nice. She has no idea what she's up against. They like Wren, and that means she's in the circle. Hell, she was in the circle before Aspen brought her here. Which reminds me I still need to find out how they ended up here together.

"Ready?" I ask Wren.

"Yes. Thank you, Marshall. It seems you've been bailing me out a lot lately."

"It's no problem. I'll see you all later." I wave to my family as they shout out their goodbyes.

I load Madeline into the back of my car. I double-check to make sure her seat is secure, then step back, allowing Wren to do the same thing. I don't take it personally as she's her momma, and it's her job above all else to keep her safe. In fact, I admire that about her.

Once we're in the car, I ask for her address, and I don't need a GPS to get me there. I know the building. "So, how did you end up with Aspen?" I ask.

"I stopped to feed Madeline. We were walking home, and she was fussing, and I knew she couldn't make it a few more blocks. I just so happened to stop in front of her bakery. She was driving by and said that something told her to stop and talk to me. We talked, and she invited me over. I had no idea she was your family. I'm not stalking you or anything."

A deep chuckle escapes my throat. "I didn't even consider it. It was good to see you again. I'm glad you came." I'm not just blowing smoke up her ass. Wren seems cool, and after learning all that she's been through, a little Riggins Family interaction is exactly what she needed.

"Your family is great."

"Thanks. How about yours? Do they drive you as crazy as mine do?"

"You know you love them, and no. I don't have any family. My parents passed, and my late husband, Travis, that was his name. He grew up in foster care and had no immediate family that he was aware of. My best friend, Carrie, she's my family."

Did you hear that crack? That's my heart. It's cracked right down the middle for this woman and her daughter. "Well, you can borrow mine anytime that you want. I promise you'll want to give them back," I tease her.

"Stop." She laughs. "They're amazing. You're lucky to have them."

"I am," I agree. "I'll still loan them to you."

"Deal."

A few minutes later, I'm pulling into the parking lot of her apartment complex. "I'll grab Madeline and carry her up for you. You grab the diaper bag."

"I can manage. You've done too much already."

"Nope. I'm walking you up." Climbing out of the car, I'm in the back and releasing the car seat before she can stop me.

"There's not an elevator, so it's a long walk for you to only turn around and do it all over again."

"What? You think I'm out of shape?" I have half a mind to lift my shirt and show her just how in shape I am but refrain. I've already came off as a creeper when we first met. I don't need her to rethink that stance because I'm flashing her my abs.

"No. It's just a lot."

"Well, my momma raised me to be a gentleman. Besides, I promised Madeline I would."

"Oh, you did, did you?" she asks, amusement in her voice.

"Yep. And I never break a promise." So, it's a little white lie. I don't care because it makes her smile.

"If you have a hankering to get your cardio in, who am I to stop you." She shrugs, grabs the diaper bag, and leads us into the building.

My eyes scan the place. It's an older building but seems to be well kept. When we finally reach her door, she turns to face me. "It's not much, but it's home to us."

"I'm not here to judge you, Wren." She nods and opens the door, motioning me inside.

"You can just set her seat down by the couch. I'll get her out and change her for bed."

I do as she asks, all while taking in the small apartment, hoping she doesn't see my eyes roaming. "Here you go, little lady," I whisper to Madeline. "Sleep tight." I don't know why I do it, but I kiss the tips of my fingers and place them softly on her forehead.

"Thank you," Wren whispers.

"Here." I hand her my phone. "Add your number. I'll text you with mine. If you ever need anything, call me."

"You've already done so much."

"That's what friends are for. Besides, I can always get it from Aspen." Just then, my phone pings with a message. "Never mind," I say when I pull the phone back to look at the screen. "Aspen just sent your number in a group text." I quickly add her to my contacts and send her a message. The diaper bag vibrates, and I grin. "Now you have mine. I'll see you later, Wren. Use that number if you need it." I walk to the door. "Lock up after me."

"I always do."

I give her a nod and step out of her apartment, closing the door behind me. The lock clicks into place, and I smile before turning and walking away.

CHAPTER
Wren
SIX

I T'S BEEN TWO weeks since I've seen a member of the Riggins family. However, every day I'm talking to one of the women in the family. It's been surreal the way they're all in my life, as if they've always been there. Sawyer and I have talked on the phone a few times about the kids, the same with Layla. Aspen and I have talked every day since I met her, and Aurora has called me a few times as well to ask baby-specific questions.

I went from having one best friend and a very small circle surrounding me to four additional women, who are strong, confident, and so full of kindness their hearts have to be ready to burst out of their chests. I don't know what I did in a former life to have them so suddenly thrust into mine, but I'm grateful.

I didn't know how nice it would be to have friends who are moms. Someone to talk to about what's going on with Madeline and with me. I love Carrie. She has been with me through thick and thin, but she's not a mom. And sometimes, it's hard for her to relate to me and the questions I have about motherhood.

My phone rings from its place on the kitchen counter, and I rush to answer it before it wakes my sleeping daughter. "Hello."

"Hey, Wren, it's Aspen. You need to get a bag packed for you and for Maddie. We're going to the lake."

"Um... the lake?" I ask.

She chuckles. "Sorry, I wanted to get that out before you had a chance to shoot the offer down. Yes, the lake. My future in-laws have one on their property. We hang out there a lot."

"I don't know. I don't want to intrude." This is what I say every single time she's asked me to meet up. First, it was her house, which led to dinner with her family. The second was coffee with her and Aurora when she insisted on picking me up for. The third was lunch with her, Aurora, Layla, Sawyer, and the little boys. She picked me up then as well.

"Come on. You know you're not intruding. I'll come pick you up." I knew she was going to say that.

"Why can I not say no to you?" I laugh.

"Because I'm awesome," she replies. "Now, get to packing."

"Maddie is napping."

"Okay, well, it will be about an hour or so before I get there. I have to pack for myself too. I'm not taking much. A swimsuit, my cover-up, and a hoodie and sweats in case it gets cold tonight."

"It's the middle of the summer."

"Yeah, but you never know, and I swear since the moment I found out that I was pregnant, my thermostat has been broken."

"Okay. I guess we can do that. I don't have a suit, but I don't plan on swimming. Come to think of it, Maddie doesn't have one either."

"She won't need it. Just bring a onesie she can get dirty and a change for after."

"Are you sure it's okay if I join you? This sounds like a family thing."

"I promise you are not intruding. The girls and I will sit with the kids, and Aurora and I won't be skiing or doing any of the other water sports since we're pregnant. We'd love the company."

"I hate that you're always chauffeuring me around."

"It's not an issue, Wren. I promise. I'll be there in an hour."

"Okay. Thank you for the invite."

"Yay! I'm so glad you're coming with us. I'll see you soon." She ends the call before I can ask her if I should bring anything. I mentally calculate the funds in my checking account. I don't have time to make anything. I can just offer to pay for what I eat, or maybe I'll just bask in their company and pass on the food. I feel as though I'm a sponge. Every time I've met up with them, someone has picked up the tab. I try to only ever order a drink, but they always insist on more. One of these days, I'm going to need to take a turn, and that's going to take a hit to my account. Maybe I can try to pick up an extra shift soon? I'll see if Carrie can watch Maddie for me while I do. I hate to leave her another day, but it's only fair I take my turn to pay.

Tiptoeing into Madeline's room, I pull a small insulated backpack from her closet to pack extra bottles and food. I grab her a few extra outfits and diapers. I toss in some toys as well as a few extra blankets. Checking in on her, she's still sleeping, so I make my way back to the living area and go through the diaper bag, adding the additional items. It's fully stocked with diapers, wipes, more toys, bibs, and a couple of outfits. I'm certain I'm going overboard, but I want to make sure that I have anything that we might need.

I grab a couple of bags of breast milk from the freezer that will also serve as ice packs and toss in a few jars of baby food. It's overkill, but that's just me. That's who I am. I toss in several clean bottles so that all I have to do is pour the milk inside. I have four bottles in the fridge, so I take those as well, just to be safe. After adding a few ice packs and double-checking I have everything, I zip up the bag and set it on the floor next to the diaper bag.

As for me, I make sure I have my wallet, my phone, and my sunglasses, and I'm good to go. I won't be swimming, and it's summertime so I seriously doubt I'm going to need any additional clothes as night falls. I should probably put a little more effort into my appearance, but I don't have the energy. Lucky my hair is short and layered, so it always lays well. I've been blessed in the hair department. I always seem to have this beachy wave thing going on, and I don't hate it.

I'm wearing a tank top and cutoff jean shorts, and I'll slip my feet into some flip-flops. This is me. This is who I am, and not once have any of the girls ever made me feel bad about it. Hell, they're all usually dressed very similar to me. Amazingly, I just fit with them.

Madeline begins to stir, which tells me that naptime is over. I'm grateful because I need to run, well, walk to the pharmacy and grab some sunscreen for her. The thought of packing her down all those stairs, only to pack her back up and then down again right after, doesn't sound appealing to me at all. Maybe Aspen won't mind stopping.

Grabbing my phone, I call her.

"Hey. I just left my place."

"We're ready. I have a favor to ask."

"Sure. What's up?"

"Do you mind stopping after you pick us up so I can buy some sunscreen for Maddie? I have some, but the bottle is almost empty."

"Sure, but you won't need to. Lena, that's the boys' mom, my future mother-in-law, she keeps stocked on all of that for everyone, but especially the grandkids. And there are plenty of places to keep the littles out of the sun. Lena and Stanley took care of that as soon as they found out Owen and Layla were expecting Carter. There's a pavilion, I guess you would call it, as well as the gazebo."

"Wow. Okay, well, if you're sure."

"I'm positive. Look, I know you don't know much about the Riggins family, but they're well-off. They take family seriously, and I promise you that you and Maddie are welcome. I wouldn't put you in a position where you wouldn't be."

"Thank you." I don't know what else to say to that. I've been going at life all alone except for Carrie, who works her tail off, so

I don't get to see her as often as we like. This is all new to me, having people in my corner.

"You bet. I'll come up and help you carry everything down."

"Absolutely not. I'm packed. We're going to head down now so you don't have to wait on us."

"I can help carry a diaper bag."

"But you don't need the trek up and down the flights of stairs."

"The exercise will do me some good."

"Save it."

"You did it."

"What do you mean?"

"I mean, you did it while you were pregnant."

"I didn't, actually. I moved into this place when Maddie was about two months old."

"Oh, I didn't realize."

"It's a long story, but I'll fill you in some time."

"I'd like that. I'll see you soon."

"Bye."

"All right, missy, are you ready for a day at the lake?" My daughter coos at me like she's excited. "Well, Mommy's not sure what I'm getting us into. I apologize if this is a boring day for you." She just smiles and blows bubbles, and my heart trips over in my chest. I love this little girl with everything inside me. Travis left me with the most amazing gift. When I miss him, I think about Madeline; I will always have a part of him with me.

After getting Madeline strapped into her seat, I put the backpack on my back, shove my purse into the diaper bag, and sling it over my shoulder. "Let's do this," I tell my daughter, tickling her belly. She rewards me with a grin.

By the time I reach the main level of my building, I feel like I've ran a damn marathon. When I step outside, the heat of the day hits me, and I debate my sanity for agreeing to spend the day at the lake with my almost-six-months-old daughter. I have no idea what I was thinking agreeing to this. It's going to be hot, and she and I are both going to be miserable. I'm thinking about calling Aspen to cancel when she pulls in front of my building in her SUV.

"Hi." She waves, rolling down the window. "The car seat base is on your side," she tells me.

"Thank you for this," I say, placing the seat into the base and unloading my bags to the floorboard. I check to make sure the seat is secure before closing the back door and climbing into the passenger seat.

"No problem. I'm glad you're joining us."

"Where's Conrad?" I ask her.

"He's already there. He and his brothers took the boat out early this morning to do some fishing before it got too hot. I expect them to have the grill fired up by the time we get there."

"Oh, I should stop and pick something up to bring with us," I offer, despite knowing I can't afford much.

"That would be a negative. You're a guest. Besides, the guys would be pissed if I let you. This is what they do, and they always have enough food to feed an army."

"If I don't get a chance to, please thank him, well, all of them for me."

"Not necessary, but you'll get the chance. We have a day of fun in the sun. They're all going to be there. I think Jase and Sam are coming as well. They'll have their little girl, Aria, with them. She's older than Carter, but I don't know exactly how old she is. What I do know is that she's a cutie."

"Jase and Sam? Have I met them?" I'm trying to work through all the names they've mentioned, and Jase and Sam are not one of them.

"No. Jase is Royce's best friend. Sam used to work for him until she got pregnant. That's when Royce hired Sawyer, and well, you know how that turned out." She chuckles.

"Layla and Sawyer both work for the family business, right?" I ask just to make sure I have it straight.

"Yes. Aurora and I have the bakery. Well, we did have the

bakery. We will again soon. We're just not sure what that will look like or even if it's going to be in the same location. Sam is a stay-at-home mom now, and she's loving every minute of it from what I hear from Sawyer. They became close when Sam was training Sawyer remotely."

"So much to learn."

"Oh, well, there will be two more. My future in-laws, Stanley and Lena, will probably show up at some point today as well. We told them all about you and how Maddie took to Marshall. I wonder if that was a fluke thing or if it will happen again?" she muses.

Every time I think about how easily Madeline took to Marshall, I get a warm feeling in my chest. "I'm not sure. She's not spent a lot of time around men, so it was just as big a shock to me as it was to all of you."

"That's right." She reaches over the console and places her hand on my arm. "I'm sorry for your loss. I can't imagine doing this on my own."

"No one ever does, not until you have to."

"Well, I think you're a badass."

"Thanks. I think," I say, and we both burst out laughing.

"Hey, should we call your friend Carrie and invite her?" she offers.

"Thank you, but she's working a double today at the ER." Just like that, this family has taken me in as one of their own, offering to invite who they now know is my only family to join us. It's overwhelming and wonderful all at the same time.

"Damn, it's such a nice day out too."

"That's the life of healthcare."

"We'll definitely have to invite her next time," she tells me as she pulls up to a large building. "This is it."

"Where's the lake?"

"Oh, it's back away on the property. One of the guys is supposed to be here to drive us. If not, we'll call them, and someone will come and pick us up."

Together we climb out of the car just as a UTV stops beside us. Conrad grins when he sees his wife. "You ladies need a ride?"

"Good timing." Aspen smiles.

"Brought the one with the base." He motions to the second row of the UTV, and sure enough, there's a car seat and a base, which I'm assuming is for Carter and Roan.

"Thank you."

"We're always prepared when it comes to the baby in the family," he tells me. "Let me help you," he offers, but I wave him off.

"I've got it." I quickly snap the car seat into the base and place my bags at my feet. "All set."

"Babe? You got everything you need?" Conrad asks Aspen.

"Yep."

Conrad takes off, and within a few minutes, we're stopping at a lake. Not a pond, but a lake. I thought maybe they just called it the lake, but no, it's an actual lake. There are two boats, some jet skis, and a whole lot of Riggins.

What did I get myself into?

CHAPTER
Marshall
SEVEN

I HEAR THE UTV pull up, and I turn to wave, and I'm taken aback when I see Wren and baby Madeline in the back seat. Setting my water bottle down on the table, I head toward them to see if they need any help.

"Fancy meeting you here." I smile at Wren and hold my hand out for the car seat. "I can take her."

"You don't have to," she counters.

"I know I don't have to. I want to. Besides, it's been a couple of weeks since I've seen my friend Maddie." I give her what my momma calls my charming smile.

"You might as well hand her over. He's just going to pout until you do," Conrad jokes.

"You heard the man. Hand me the baby." I hold out my hands again, and this time she hands me the infant car seat, baby Madeline and all. "Hey, cutie pie." I smile down at her. "You ready for a day in the sun?" She gurgles up at me, blowing bubbles, and that's as close to a yes as I'm going to get and the only reply I need.

"We need to see if she'll let me hold her," Conrad says with the diaper bag slung over his shoulder, with me trailing behind him.

"What just happened?" I hear Wren ask Aspen.

"They stole your daughter. I wouldn't plan on getting her back anytime soon." She laughs.

"I'm her favorite," I inform Conrad. It's not like I'm making it up. We all saw it.

"That was luck," Conrad counters. "I get first dibs this time."

"Is this normal?" Wren asks. Her voice is close so I'm assuming she and Aspen followed us.

She laughs. "Afraid so. All five of them are competitive."

I glance over my shoulder at Wren. "Tell him she likes me better."

A hint of a smile graces her lips as she shakes her head at our antics. "It might have been a fluke." She shrugs.

"See," Conrad jests.

"Fine, but I'm telling you that she likes me best." I sway Madeline in her car seat from side to side. It's a way to rub it in that I'm the one that has her now. She likes me best, they just won't admit it.

"You hope that when your children reach adulthood that they will act their age, but somehow when all five of my adult children get together, this never happens," Mom says with humor lacing her voice.

"I'm Lena," she introduces herself to Wren.

"Wren, and my daughter, Madeline. Thank you for having us. Your place is beautiful."

"We're happy to have you. And from the looks of it, my boys are happy to see your daughter."

"She's a cutie," Aspen chimes in.

"There are not enough babies to go around, and Maddie likes me better," I tell my mom.

"So I've heard," she reminds me.

"They told you?" I ask Mom.

"They did. The older four were pouting and swore it had to be because you held her first. Hence the reason Conrad is on a mission to prove their point."

"He's wrong," I tell them. "You'll see," I say with confidence when really, I have no idea. Madeline seemed to like me well enough the first time so that's what I'm banking on.

"Come here, cutie," Conrad says softly, lifting Madeline from her seat. He rests her on his shoulder, and she seems to be doing okay. "Told you so," he says.

"Are you cheating on me, Maddie?" I lean around to look at the baby, and her lip puckers up when she sees me. "I know he's scary-looking, but he's a good guy," I tell her. Instead of soothing her, she starts to cry.

Out of the corner of my eye, I see Wren step closer, ready to rescue her daughter, but I beat her to it. "Come to Marsh, Maddie," I coo. Conrad accepts defeat and hands her over to me. "I've got you," I whisper to her, and she stops crying. Something happens when she smiles up at me. Her gummy smile with her eyes wet from tears grips my heart as it bounces wildly in my chest.

"Well, I wouldn't have believed it had I not witnessed it," Mom says.

"I told you she likes me better," I boast. "Isn't that right, Maddie?"

"I don't understand it," Wren speaks up. "She's never taken to someone like that, and definitely not a man."

"What can I say? I have a way with the ladies. I've been telling my family this for years, and they refuse to believe it. The proof is with the baby."

"Perfect. Now we're going to have to hear him gloat," Conrad grumbles.

"Hey, Wren, glad you could make it," Grant greets her. "I see you're being a baby hog again," he says to me.

"Hey, Con got the first try, and she wanted me."

"Bullshit," Grant says.

"Grant Riggins, you watch your mouth around these babies. And he's telling you the truth. Conrad held her first. When she saw your brother, she began to cry."

"Marsh is scary." Grant laughs.

"No. She wanted me. We're buds." I rub my hand up her little back, and she snuggles into my neck. It's as if she's tied a string around my heart and attached it to her little fist.

"I can take her," Wren interrupts us.

"Nope. I've got her. You go grab something to eat."

"I can take her. I'm used to multitasking," Wren offers.

"Well, today, you don't have to. Go grab something to eat. You too, sis," I tell Aspen.

"Come on, ladies. Let's get you a plate. Marshall, you stay close." Mom points her finger at me.

I'm a grown man with my momma pointing a finger at me while holding a baby, like I'm going to leave her on the table all alone or something. I get it. She's trying to reassure Wren. "I'll stay close. Go make a plate. Maddie and I are going to make our rounds and say hello." I capture Wren's gaze. "I'll keep her safe. I promise."

She hesitates, but when Aspen links her arm through Wren's, she lets Aspen and my mother lead her away. "All right, cutie pie, it's time to say hi to my other brothers, and then there are a few new people for you to meet." My first stop is Dad.

"Who do we have here?" he asks.

"This is Madeline."

"Ah." He nods. "This is the little one who likes you the best."

"It's been confirmed a second time. Con held her first this time, and she, of course, wanted me."

"Where's Wren?" Royce asks.

"She went with Mom and Aspen to grab something to eat."

"And she left Madeline with you?" he asks.

"She did. You know I'm her favorite," I remind him.

"I think we need to test your theory," Royce suggests.

"We already did. She cried for me when Con had her." I stand a little taller. I don't know why this pleases me as much as it does. It's not like she's my niece. Usually, it's because I have one-up on my brothers. It's that, but it's something else too. Maybe it's because I know her momma is struggling to give her the best life that she can. Maybe it's because I know her daddy is no longer here. Then again, maybe it's just the little girl in my arms and that string she's apparently attached to my heart.

"That's because I haven't held her," my dad boasts. "Let me try."

"She's comfy," I reply.

"Come on, Marsh. Let Dad hold her."

"Fine," I grumble. "Maddie, this is my dad. His name is Stanley. He's nice. I promise." I whisper the words before transferring her into my dad's arms. I watch as she stares up at him.

"Aren't you a cute little thing," Dad says softly. He only has eyes for Madeline. "I raised five boys, and now my boys have boys. I'm not used to holding little girls." He's rambling, and she seems fine, which takes the wind out of my sails.

"I guess it wasn't just you," Owen says, joining us.

"Well, I'm the favorite brother, so there." At the sound of my voice, Madeline turns to look at me and juts out her little lip. When it starts to quiver, I don't give Dad the chance to refuse, I take her from him, and she settles against my chest, just like she did earlier. As if the spot is hers and hers alone.

"Huh," Dad says, shoving his hands in his pockets.

"I win." I grin at him.

"So it seems."

"They're just jealous," I whisper to Madeline. "Come on. There are still more people for you to meet." I give my dad and brothers a nod as I turn.

"He doesn't even see it," my dad says as I walk away.

I have no idea what he's rambling on about. It's easy to see that I'm her favorite.

"Hey, Mommy, I think we're hungry," I say after about thirty minutes of walking around and letting Madeline meet everyone and say hi to those who have already met her.

"I can take her." Wren starts to stand.

"I can do it. Just point me in the right direction."

"She breastfeeds." Aurora smirks.

"I do, but she takes a bottle." Wren is quick to reply. Her cheeks are rosy from embarrassment.

I can't help it. My eyes stray to Wren's tits, and yeah, I've noticed them before, but I'm looking again. You can't tell me she breastfeeds and expect me not to look at her chest. It's just not possible.

"Marshall." Her voice pulls my attention back to the moment. "My daughter." She holds her hands out for me to hand over the baby.

"Did you eat?"

She looks down at her plate that is still half full. "I'm working on it."

"I'll feed her." I don't give her time to argue. I walk over to where we left the car seat and find the diaper bag.

"You don't have to do this," she says from behind me.

"I know, but I've already eaten, and I'm not doing anything else. Look." I point to where Royce is sitting on a lounge chair feeding Roan. "I'll go sit with Royce. It will be fine."

"We're not your responsibility, Marshall." Her voice is a little defensive and dare I say sad? It's almost as if she wants to be my responsibility but is afraid of what that might mean.

"I didn't say that you were. I'm just helping out. We're all just hanging. You never get a chance to get a break. Enjoy yourself."

"How do you know?"

"Wren, you're a single mom. I'm guessing that your time isn't even in your vocabulary unless you're working. Go. I'll be right over there." I point again to Royce and Roan. "Any special instructions?"

"No."

"Come on, Maddie. Let's fill that belly."

"Take these," Wren calls out.

Turning back, I take the thin blanket and bib from her hands, then head toward Royce. "Look, Maddie, it's Roan. You two are the same age," I tell her.

"You look good with a baby," Royce says.

I'd smart off, but I know my older brother and he's being completely serious. "One day, brother," I tell him.

"You volunteer to feed her?"

"Yeah. Wren was still eating, and all the women are chatting up a storm." I shrug. "I wasn't doing anything else. I assume she doesn't have many days to just sit and gossip and relax, so I'm helping out."

"Gossip? You think the woman are gossiping?"

"Probably about me." I laugh. "They're all scheming for who to hook me up with, I'm sure. Heaven forbid I'm the last Riggins holdout to start a family."

"It's more than that, Marsh. It's the magic of finding love and knowing that person will be with you by your side through all of life's up and downs."

"Well, when I find her, I'll be sure to let you know." There's no point in arguing with him about this. I've been round and round with my dad and all four of my brothers about their "magic," and no matter how many times I dispute their concept, it doesn't do me a bit of good.

"I don't think you'll have to tell us. I think we'll just know. Look at me. Everyone knew Sawyer was good for me and that we should be together, but I fought it."

"That's you. I'm not fighting anything. I'm not dating. There is no woman in my life who's going to suddenly make me believe in this magic sh—stuff y'all are always rambling on about."

He grins. "Just do me a favor, Marshall, when it hits you, when you realize you've found your magic, don't run from it like I did. Embrace it. Embrace her. Trust me, little brother, your life will be a hell of a lot easier because of it."

"How so?" I take the bait.

"I wasted time with Sawyer. I could have had this"—he nods down to his son, who is sleeping in his arms—"a hell of a lot sooner if I hadn't been so stubborn."

"It all worked out in the end."

He nods. "It did. The same way it's going to work out for you as well."

"When I have to admit you to the nursing home for losing your mind, I'll be sure to tell them it's been going on for years," I tease.

His grin grows wide. "You know, as the oldest, I'm always right."

"Okay. Let's go with that." I move my attention to Madeline, who is now snoozing in my arms. She sucked down her bottle like a champ and then dozed off.

"Thank you," Wren says, appearing next to me. "I can take her now."

"She's comfortable."

"You need to be enjoying your day. Not babysitting." She places her hands on her narrow hips.

"I am enjoying my day. I'm thinking about taking a nap with Maddie."

"Marshall," she sighs.

"Go take a ride on the boat." I point to where my dad and Owen are getting ready to take the boat for a spin.

"I can't just leave her here with you."

"Yes, you can. I'll look after her. I'm the only one she likes anyway besides you."

"You don't know that. You've not let anyone else try," Royce chimes in.

"I did. Dad and Con both tried."

Royce just smirks. "He's responsible even though he sometimes doesn't act like it," he tells Wren.

"Thank you. I knew you were my favorite," I reply.

"Hey, Wren," Sawyer calls out. "Let's go. Let the guys handle the littles for a while."

I glance over to see Owen now has Carter as Layla, Aurora, Aspen, and Mom are already on the boat. "Go. We're fine. You aren't going far, and I have the number of every single person on that boat. If I need you, I'll call you."

"Are you sure?" she asks, chewing on her bottom lip.

"I'm sure. Now go. Have fun."

She leans down and kisses Madeline on the forehand, and her scent wraps around me. Something vanilla and uniquely Wren. "Mommy loves you. Be good for Marshall." She stands and looks over her shoulder at Sawyer, who is waiting patiently before turning her gaze back to me. "Thank you, Marshall."

"You're welcome." She turns to leave, and I watch every single step she takes. I can't seem to peel my eyes away from her. Unfortunately, Royce notices.

"She's cute."

"She is," I agree. Thankfully he doesn't comment further. I don't need my big brother to join my sisters, one of who is his wife, and is part of the "let's set Marshall up on a date to find his magic" campaign. No, thank you.

If the magic is real like they say it is, I'll find it on my own.

CHAPTER
Wren
EIGHT

W HEN I APPROACH the boat, Lena, Marshall's mom, must see the worry written all over my face. She offers me her hand to help me board. "He's the youngest, and he plays that card well." She smiles kindly. "However, I can assure you, that baby girl of yours couldn't be in better hands. Marshall will take good care of her."

I nod. "Thank you. I feel guilty. He should be out having fun, not babysitting."

She shrugs. "He offered. If I know anything about my five sons and their father? They don't do anything that they don't want to do."

"Take advantage of the break," Aspen says, stepping onto the boat with the help of Marshall's dad, Stanley.

"Good luck getting her away from him. That boy, hell, all of my boys are baby hogs," Stanley grumbles good-naturedly. "This is for you." Stanley hands me a life jacket. "I don't plan on driving crazy with such precious cargo on board." He looks at his wife with so much love in his eyes I feel my cheeks flush. He then turns his gaze to his daughters-in-law, two of which are expecting, and then he lands on me. "Suit up, ladies." He grins before turning and heading to the steering wheel.

"What are you waiting on, old man?" Lena calls out once we're all suited up. Stanley winks at her, and we're off.

The wind whips through my hair as the spray of the warm water from the lake splashes against my skin. We're all laughing and hanging on as Stanley increases his speed, propelling us across the lake. When we reach the opposite side, where we can no longer see the shoreline, Stanley kills the engine and turns to face us.

"I thought we could float here for a little while," he tells us.

"This is perfect," Aurora says from her seat on the side of the boat. She tilts her head back, and even though she has sunglasses on, I know her eyes are closed as she lets the warmth from the sun wash over her.

"Kick back and relax," Aspen tells me.

"I'm not sure I even know what that word means anymore," I confess.

"Anytime you need a break, you bring that sweet girl to me," Lena speaks up.

"Oh, I couldn't do that."

"Of course you can. I know you don't know us well, but today is a good start at changing that." Her wink is accompanied by a kind smile.

Hot tears prick my eyes. I've been doing everything on my own. Sure I have Carrie, and she's a huge help, but this… these people, they understand motherhood. They don't know me, but they're offering to help me, to give me a break. The offer alone is more than I ever could have hoped for.

I swallow hard, forcing the emotions down as I nod and give her a watery smile. It's all I can manage right now. Lena seems to understand as she changes the subject asking Aspen about the wedding.

"Soon," Aspen tells her. There's something in her tone of voice, almost as if she might be hiding something. Of course, I don't know her well enough, but it sure seems like she might have something up her sleeve.

I don't know how long we float on the water, soaking up the sun and enjoying each other's company. They make me feel included, and it's as if I've known all of them for years. I've never had a lot of friends, I had Carrie, who I have been friends with since we were little, and then there was Travis. Other than that, it was work and a night class here or there when we could afford it.

"We better head back," Sawyer says. "Royce is probably giving Roan sugar, and he'll be up all night." She laughs.

"Did he learn nothing from Owen feeding Carter cake icing?" Layla laughs.

"Please tell me that Marshall isn't giving any of that to Madeline," I groan.

"I'd say you're safe. Owen is there, and he remembers all too well the sleepless cranky night we had with Carter."

"This was a bad idea," I mutter, making them all laugh.

"It will be fine. If he did, you could leave that sweet angel with us overnight," Stanley tells me. "Momma can get a good night's rest." He smiles. He doesn't give me time to reply before he's starting up the engine and pointing the boat back to the shore where everyone else is waiting for us.

When we reach the boat dock, I'm eager to get to my daughter. Stanley tells us all to hold tight while he ties off the boat and then steps off. One by one, he helps each of us off the boat.

"Come on, let's go see your girl." Aspen links her arm through mine, and I'm surprised when Aurora does the same on the other arm. The three of us walk toward the pavilion, and what I see has my heart stuttering in my chest.

Owen, Royce, Jase, and Marshall are all on loungers. Eyes closed sleeping, as all four kids slumber on their chests. My eyes lock on Marshall, and something inside me shifts. His big strong hand is resting on Madeline's back, holding her close. My daughter is slumbering away as if she's slept on his chest a thousand times.

"It's a good thing I'm already pregnant," Aurora whispers.

"Right? Ovary explosion," Aspen agrees.

"Where are the others?" I ask, forcing myself to look away from the scene before me. Aurora points, and I see Conrad and Grant both napping on a lounge chair as well. They don't have babies in their arms, but that doesn't take away from their hotness factor. Really, the genes in this family are insane.

"Should we wake them?" Aspen asks.

"Nah, let's let them sleep," Aurora tells her.

"I should take Madeline," I comment.

"She's fine. Let's go grab something to drink and talk wedding plans," Sawyer says, pulling lightly on Aspen's arm and leading the way to the cooler.

I glance back at Marshall and Madeline, and I'm torn. I feel bad that he's had her all day.

"She's okay, Wren. I promise. The Riggins men don't do anything they don't want to. Marshall snatched her right up and volunteered to watch her. They're all sleeping. When she wakes up, you can take her back. For now, enjoy the break we know that you never get." Aurora places her arm over my shoulders, and we follow after Aspen and Sawyer.

I know it sounds crazy that I'm just leaving my daughter with him, but something deep inside me knows that I can trust him with her. That I can trust all of them with both of us. My gut has never steered my wrong, so I'm going to do exactly as Aurora suggested, and try to relax. She's right. I never get a break, and I'm okay with that, but since it's being offered, and it's obvious that Marshall isn't giving my daughter back anytime soon, I might as well try and enjoy myself.

Sawyer hands me a glass of lemonade. "Lena made it. It's the best you'll ever have," she says as she continues to pass out Solo cups of lemonade.

"So good," Aurora sighs, taking a huge drink.

"So, Aspen, wedding planning," Sawyer prompts.

"I don't really want anything big. Just all of us, and at the end of the day, I want to be Conrad's wife." She shrugs.

I'm listening to the conversation, but my eyes keep straying to Marshall. Why do I find it so damn sexy the way he's holding my daughter as if he's protecting her?

"Earth to Wren." Aspen waves her hand in front of my face. "We lost you." She smirks.

"I just… I can't seem to look away," I admit. What I don't say is that for the first time since losing Travis, I notice a man as more than just an acquaintance. Marshall Riggins is sexy on a normal day, but with my sleeping daughter on his chest, Aspen was right. Ovary explosion.

"So, is it the man or the man and the baby?" Layla asks.

"Both," I confess. With my free hand, I cover my face to try and ward off my embarrassment.

"No need to hide. Not from us. You're forgetting that we're all married or soon-to-be married to a Riggins."

"Hey!" Sam interjects.

Sawyer waves her off. "Jase might as well be a Riggins. Besides, he's just as sexy."

"Did you just call my husband sexy?" Sam asks, amusement in her voice.

"Yep." Sawyer grins. She has zero shame in admitting it. "I'm married, but I'm not dead. All six of them are sexy. You know I'm right."

"Agreed." Layla chuckles. "And, Wren, we know how it is when you first meet them, and the tension. We get it."

"Oh, there's no tension. At least not before today." I glance back over at Marshall and Madeline.

"He's good with her," Aurora comments.

"He's a good guy." This from Layla.

"He acts like a big goofball, and he is," Aspen adds.

"But he has a heart of gold. They all do," Sawyer chimes in.

"I have a feeling that Marshall is going to fall harder than the rest of them," Sawyer says.

That grabs my attention. "What do you mean?"

"All of them"—she points to the guys—"have fallen in love differently. We each"—she motions to our small group—"have our own love stories. However, the common denominator is that when our men finally accepted that they had fallen head over ass in love, they didn't stop fighting until we were so wrapped up in them, until our hearts were entwined that there was no going back for any of us," Sawyer explains.

"Sounds like a fairy tale."

"What about you? Your husband?" Layla asks. Her tone is soft, as if she's afraid her asking might upset me.

"Travis and I were different. We were friends first, and one day we were more. I can't even tell you when it happened. Then, my father died, and the next thing I know, we're getting married." I pause, collecting my thoughts. "I loved him. He gave me the greatest gift I'll ever receive." I glance over at Madeline, where she's still sleeping on Marshall's chest. "It wasn't a grand tale of love. It just kind of happened, and we just were." It's the best way that I can explain it. I loved him. Of course, I did. However, our love was uniquely ours.

"You're young," Sam speaks up. "Please don't take this the wrong way, but you're young, and there's still time for you to find your fairy-tale love."

"I agree," Layla adds. "I'm not dismissing your husband and the love that you shared. I believe that everything happens for a reason. While losing him was tragic, maybe Madeline was his purpose?"

"You deserve a love that consumes you, Wren," Aspen adds.

I swallow hard, pushing back the tears. "Maybe one day." I'm not opposed to finding love again. I miss Travis every single day. He left me the best part of him, and that love that we shared will live on through our daughter, as for me. I'm open to finding love again. I am young, and surely being a widow isn't how my story ends. Maybe when Madeline is older, and we're more financially stable, I can think about getting back into the dating pool.

A whimper comes from where the guys are sitting, and we all turn our heads. Madeline is stirring. "That's my cue," I tell the girls. Placing my Solo cup of lemonade on the ground, I stand and head toward my daughter. As I get closer, I can see that Marshall's eyes are still closed, but his hand is gently rubbing Madeline's back.

"Shh," he whispers. "I've got you, baby girl," he murmurs to her. "It's all right."

I watch in fascination as she quiets down. Her little body shudders as she sinks into him. With each step that carries me closer to them, I fight back the tears. My little girl will never know her daddy, and that hurts worse than losing him. Her losing him will always be the greater tragedy. I know from first-hand experience, losing your parents never fades.

I stop next to the lounge chair, and Marshall's eyes slowly slide open and lock with mine. Neither of us says a word. I can't seem to think as his blue eyes bore into my soul. There's a connection that is flowing between us, one like I've never experienced before. My blood whooshes in my ears, and I know he has to be able to hear my heart as it threatens to beat right out of my chest.

"Hey, Momma," his deep raspy voice greets me.

"Hey." I swallow thickly. "I can take her."

"We're napping."

I know. I'm suddenly jealous of my daughter. She doesn't realize how lucky she is to be lying on his toned muscular chest. "She'll be waking up soon."

"Why don't you lie here with us?" He pats the side of the lounge chair. There's plenty of room for me to snuggle up to them, but I won't.

"Thanks for watching her," I tell him, ignoring his offer. Instead, I bend down and lift my daughter from his chest. She stretches, and her eyes blink open. Me? Well, I'm trying to ignore the fact that my fingers feel as though they've been lit on fire, just from the soft brush of my skin against his chest when I picked her up.

"I need to change her."

"I'll grab the bag," he says. He's standing and tossing the diaper bag that I didn't realize he moved beside his lounge chair over his shoulder.

"I can get it," I tell him.

"This is momma's day off, right, Maddie?" She gives him a gummy smile, and he seems to melt from that simple act. "There's my girl," he says, running his index finger over her cheek.

"Where can I change her?" I ask him, working hard to disguise the swell of emotion in my throat.

"Let's use the back of my truck." He places his hand on the small of my back and leads me to a large deck box. "There are blankets in here. Mom thinks of everything," he says, reaching into the box and pulling out a weathered quilt. "We can lay this down on the bed so it's softer for her."

I nod because what else can I do? This gorgeous man and his family have been so great to me, and my run-in with Marshall led me to Aspen, and the girls, my new friends. It's because of him I feel a lot less alone in this big world. He leads us to a large black pickup truck. "This is me," he says, lowering the tailgate and spreading the quilt. "All set," he says, placing the diaper bag beside the quilt.

"Th-Thank you, Marshall. For everything."

He takes me by surprise when he reaches out and tucks my hair behind my ear. "You're welcome," he says, his voice once again husky, but this time it's not from sleep. His eyes capture mine, and he leans in. I think he's going to kiss me. Do I want him to kiss me?

Madeline grunts and nuzzles my chest, pulling our attention. "She's hungry. At least she thinks she is." I laugh nervously.

"She drank all of her bottles, but that was a couple of hours ago."

"I have more."

"You can," he nods to my chest, "you know, feed her here. We can sit here so you're out of eyeshot if you're nervous about it."

"I'm not." I shake my head. "I mean, it's natural, right?"

"Right." He swallows hard. "But we should stay here."

"Why?" My hackles rise.

His hand slides behind my neck, and he leans in close. "Because I don't want my brothers to see you."

"I'll be covered."

"It's the thought."

"Will they be offended?" I didn't get that impression from any of them.

"No." He shakes his head. "I just—Never mind. It will be fine. You can feed her here or under the pavilion out of the sun."

I don't know what he was going to say, but his facial expression looked angry or pained even. I decide to let it go. I have more important matters to handle, like feeding my daughter. "Thank you." I make quick work of changing her diaper and dressing her. "All better?" I ask Madeline, lifting her from the quilt. "Can you tell Marshall thank you for watching you and letting us use his truck?" I know she can't actually do it, but it's my roundabout way of thanking him. I turn to face him. "Thank you, Marshall."

"You're welcome. Come on, let's go feed her." He grabs the quilt and shuts the tailgate. Once again, he places his hand on the small of my back and leads me to the pavilion.

The heat of his palm sears through the thin fabric of my shirt, and it makes me feel things I shouldn't be feeling when it comes to Marshall. It's been a long time since I've been privy to the warm touch of a man, and my body is reacting to that. It's not him. At least that's what I'm telling myself.

CHAPTER *Marshall* NINE

I CAN'T STOP touching her. I don't know what's wrong with me, but I can't seem to keep my hands to myself. I almost kissed her. I was so close to closing the distance between us and pressing my lips to hers. She smells so damn good, and her skin is the softest I've ever felt on a woman.

With my hand on the small of her back, I lead her back to the pavilion. I ignore my family as they watch us. "Here," I say, pointing to the lounge chair that Madeline and I napped on earlier. Wren takes a seat and settles in. My pulse is racing as I wait for her to feed her daughter. I've seen a woman breastfeed their baby. Sawyer does it all the time with Roan. It's never bothered me before.

It doesn't bother me now. It's the fact that everyone will see her. I have this unfounded sense of protectiveness that's bubbling up inside me when it comes to Wren and Madeline. I don't understand it, and I know that it's irrational, but I can't seem to stop my reacting. Instead, I'm hovering over them like they're mine.

They're not.

Taking a seat next to her on the lounge chair, I ignore Royce as his eyes bug out. He's going to silently ask me what the hell I'm doing, and I don't have an answer. Silent or spoken, I don't know what's come over me.

I almost kissed her.

It warrants repeating.

She's a single mom, not some random woman at a club. I know better, yet I was close to doing it anyway. Shaking out of my thoughts, I watch as Wren reaches for the diaper bag, and I find that I'm holding my breath. I should have offered her the cool air conditioning of my truck to feed Madeline. Why is this bothering me? My eyes are glued to her, and when she pulls a bottle from the diaper bag, I expel a heavy breath.

She notices and smiles at me. "I came prepared."

I nod because I can't seem to form words at the moment. She could have told me this ten minutes ago, but then again, why would she? How she chooses to feed her daughter isn't up to me. And let's talk about her smile? Does she know how potent it is? And even more so, why does it affect me the way that it does? Why does it have my heart racing and my lips tingling to taste hers?

"She was hungry," I say when Madeline latches onto the bottle and drinks greedily. I need to try and focus my attention elsewhere. Anywhere but on the adorable little girl's mother.

"She's a good eater," she says, her eyes locked on her daughter.

"She did the same thing for me earlier," I tell her. At the sound of my voice, Madeline turns to look at me. She grins around her bottle. It's brief, her hunger winning out, but the effect that smile has on me is the same. That little fist of hers may as well reach into my chest and squeeze my heart. She's so tiny and looks so much like her momma. Wren is going to have to beat the boys off with a stick when she gets older.

Reaching out, I offer Madeline my finger, and she clamps her tiny hand around it, not missing a beat as she sucks down her bottle. Bracing myself on the lounger, I lean over Wren's legs and watch the two of them, all while Madeline keeps a tight grip on my finger. I wish I could understand why these two ladies fascinate me so much, but I've got nothing. Just this overwhelming urge to spend time with them.

Protect them.

Maybe I've had too much sun.

The first time I saw Wren, I thought she was gorgeous, but nothing more. Suddenly today, I'm all up in her space, and every protective instinct that usually only comes to the surface for my family is coming to the surface for these two.

"Marsh, you ready?" I hear Royce ask me.

No. I'm not ready for whatever it is you want me to do. I want to sit right here and watch Wren and Madeline. I turn to look at him. "Ready for what?"

"Guys turn on the boat," he says, clamping a hand down on my shoulder.

"Come to Mommy," Sawyer coos as she takes Roan from Royce.

It's on the tip of my tongue to tell him I'm fine where I am, but maybe a little distance is necessary. The last thirty minutes has my head all jumbled. Time with my brothers sounds like exactly what I need to shake out of this... funk? I'm not sure what to call it. "Yeah, I'll be right there." I turn back to Wren. "You'll be here when I get back?" I ask her.

"Aspen is my ride so I'm here until she's ready to go."

"Good." I give her leg a gentle squeeze, and on instinct, I lean down and kiss the back of Madeline's hand that's gripping mine. "I'll be back soon, Maddie." Carefully, I remove my finger from her grip and stand. I have to force myself to turn away from them and follow Royce to the boat. Dad, Grant, Owen, and Conrad are already on board.

"Come on, slowpokes," Dad calls out.

Royce and I are quiet as we board the boat. I take a seat in the back, hoping to get a few minutes to myself. Unfortunately, my oldest brother isn't having that as he takes a seat next to me. "Marshall."

That's it. All he says is my name, and there is so much said with just one word. He wants to know what's going on with me. He wants to know if I'm okay, and he's telling me that he's here for me. Yeah, I got all that with just the way he said my name.

"I'm good," I assure him.

"Is there something between you and Wren?"

Isn't that the million-dollar question? "No." It's an honest answer. This is all on me. Wren is completely innocent in the fact that I almost kissed her. Sure, she didn't look like she was going to stop me, but I initiated the move out of nowhere. She didn't even see it coming. The funny thing is, I didn't see it coming either. It just sort of happened.

"You sure about that?"

No. "Yep." I don't know what I expected, but it's not his raucous laughter. I don't bother to acknowledge him. Instead, I leave him sitting on the back of the boat, his head thrown back in laughter.

"What's up with him?" Dad asks when I approach him where he's driving the boat.

"Too much sun," I murmur.

"Wren seems nice," he says casually.

"Yep." I'm stellar at conversation today it seems.

"And Madeline, she sure is cute."

"She is." I nod. He's not wrong on either count, but I got on this boat and left them to get some distance, not to talk about them.

"You want to drive?" he offers.

"Yes." He moves from behind the wheel, and I take over. I laser my focus on the water ahead and controlling the boat. Picking up speed, we crash through the water, and although I'd like to say that Wren and her daughter are no longer in my mind, that would be a lie. Instead of clearing my head from thinking of them, I imagine Madeline a little older, laughing as the boat bounces over the water, and Wren's smile as she watches her.

What the hell? What's happening to me?

I don't know how long we're out on the water. I stay at the helm, driving around the lake. I hear my brothers and my dad laughing and having a good time, and normally, I'm right there with them. It's not that I'm having a bad time. I'm just... out of sorts, I guess. I didn't sleep the greatest last night. That has to be it. Even as I think of the excuse, I dismiss it.

"Hey, Aurora just texted me. They've got the grill fired back up. Let's head back so we can help," Grant tells me.

"On it." We're already headed back to shore so I keep the boat pointed in that direction. My head is still a mess, but I'm hoping that when we get back, I'll be thinking more clearly.

Docking the boat, we all climb off and head toward the pavilion area that Dad built when Carter was born. It's a nice addition and a nice reprieve from the sun on these hot summer days. We used to use the gazebo for that, but our family is growing by leaps and bounds, and it's just not big enough for all of us comfortably anymore. Besides, Dad had fans installed under the pavilion, and the flow of air is like a tall glass of ice-cold water on hot days.

I take my time trailing behind my brothers and my dad, approaching the pavilion. My eyes scan the area. Mom and Layla are at the grill. Sam and Aria are playing in the small sandbox area. Mom insisted we build it for the kids. Sawyer, with Roan in her arms, is already headed toward Royce. Aurora is already in Grant's arms as he kisses her. Aspen is sitting at the picnic table holding Madeline, with Wren sitting next to them. They're laughing and talking about who knows what, but I'm glad she fits in so well with them.

Conrad approaches and kisses Aspen, then holds out his arms for Madeline. I stop walking and watch the four of them. Conrad bounces Madeline, and from where I'm standing, she seems to be doing okay with him holding her. I know that's a good thing, but there is a part of me that's... what is this feeling? Jealousy? It makes no sense, but I can't call it anything but that. I'm jealous that that sweet baby girl is letting my brother hold her. I was supposed to be the only one.

On their own accord, my feet carry me to them. I don't stop until I'm on the same side of the picnic table as Wren and drop down next to her. "Maddie." I shake my head. "My girl is cheating on me." I keep the cool, calm, collected pretense that I'm known for present when I feel anything but on the inside.

"I knew she would come to her senses," Conrad jokes.

"Maddie, girl, you're killing me." I chuckle. At the sound of my voice, she turns her little head to look at me. Unable to help myself, I reach across the picnic table and offer her my hand. She juts out her little lip, and I pull my hand back. I don't want to make her cry. However, that's exactly what happens. She begins to fuss, and in no time, she's full-on crying.

Without giving it a second thought, I stand and walk around the table. Conrad hands her to me. "Hey, what's wrong, baby girl?" I ask her. Instantly she stops crying. I stop walking and look up to find three sets of eyes on me.

"Marsh," Aspen breathes.

"Dissed again." Conrad laughs. He's trying to make light of the situation, but from the look on his face, he's just as affected by the moment as I am.

This little girl, she wants me.

When I finally look at Wren, she has tears in her eyes. "Hey." I rush around the table to soothe her. "What's wrong? I'm sorry. I didn't think. She was crying, and I wanted to help," I explain in a rush. "Here." I go to hand her the baby, but she shakes her head.

"I'm not mad at you," she says, giving me a watery smile.

"You hear that, Maddie? Mommy's not mad at me, yet she still has tears in her eyes."

"It's hard to explain," Wren whispers.

"Try me."

Her eyes flash around us. I'm sure taking in my family. "It's nothing."

"Wren?" I wait for her eyes to find mine. "Take a walk with me?"

She hesitates for a couple of heartbeats before eventually nodding. "Okay."

I don't look back at my family. I wait for Wren to stand and together we walk away. I don't really know where we're going, but I do know that I want to know... no, I need to know what caused her tears.

"Have you seen the gazebo?" I ask her.

"No. I've heard about it. This place is beautiful. I can't believe you grew up here."

"It is pretty great," I agree. "Dad bought this land, built the house, and then the lake. Our family name comes with attention, and he wanted a place he could just spend time with his family without the fanfare of who we are. He dug the lake, and it seems as if he's constantly adding something. It's our own little oasis."

"You spend a lot of time here." It's not really a question, more of an observation on her part.

"We do. My brothers and I have so many good memories growing up here. Now their kids will have the same. It's pretty cool to watch."

"What about you? Do you want kids?"

"Someday." I pause before saying more and decide to just roll with what feels right. "My family gives me a hard time because I'm the last holdout. They have this magic theory when it comes to love."

"This sounds like something I need to hear," she says, her tone lighter than just moments before.

"That's a story for another day. What about you? Did you ever go camping out and boating when you were growing up?"

"No." She shakes her head. "My mom died when I was seven, and my dad, I lost him a few years before I lost Travis. Heart attack."

Fuck.

I swallow hard at the emotions threatening to consume me, hearing all that she's lost. "I'm sorry." I know those two words will do nothing to bring back her parents or her husband, but that's the best I've got at the moment.

"Thank you. Dad worked a lot after Mom passed. He was heartbroken. He was never quite the same after she died. He loved me and made sure I had everything I needed. He never missed a soccer game growing up, but the light in his eyes, the happy... it was dulled when we lost her."

"I can't imagine losing my parents. I know it's the circle of life, and that's how it's supposed to work, but damn, I hope it's a long damn time before I have to go through that."

"For your sake, I hope so too."

"Here it is." I point to the gazebo.

"Wow. That's beautiful. The backdrop of the lake and the trees... it looks like a postcard."

"I guess you're right. I've never really thought of it that way."

We continue to walk toward the gazebo and my shoulders relax now that it's just the three of us. "Let's sit." I nod toward the gazebo.

"Do you want me to take her?"

I look down at the baby resting against my chest and smile. "Nah, she's good." Madeline is just along for the ride, her eyes taking it all in. I hope we can use this time to get to know one another better. I need this time with her to figure out what the hell is going on with me. Why today, of all days, all of these emotions are waging a war inside me when it comes to Wren and Madeline?

CHAPTER
Wren
TEN

"TELL ME WHAT I said to upset you."

Marshall is looking at me with so much worry and concern in his eyes, I'm once again battling tears. I don't want to talk about this, but I don't see a way out. "I mentioned that Madeline hasn't been around many men. In fact, maybe a handful. All of her day care workers are women, so it's supermarkets, or pharmacies, things like that. To see her so taken with you, it's a little hard to see."

"Being a single mom is hard." He says the words matter-of-factly, as if he knows the struggle.

"What do you know about being a single mom?" My voice is calm, but I feel a bit of annoyance festering inside me. He can't possibly know what it's like to travel a day in my shoes.

"I don't. However, I do know what my brothers and I put my parents through. I would imagine that doing it on your own is a heavy burden to carry."

"My daughter is not a burden," I snap.

"No." He's quick to answer. "Madeline is not a burden, but the burdens of life, and raising her on your own, that's what I was referring to."

I nod because I can't find my voice. I should apologize for snapping at him, but my emotions are all over the place. I'm so out of my comfort zone with this gorgeous man, and then there's the incident earlier. I'm pretty sure he was going to kiss me.

I would have let him.

Then there was his response to me breastfeeding Madeline. At first, I thought he was just being prudish and judgmental, but that wasn't it at all. He was jealous. I may not be in the dating game these days, but I know jealousy when I see it. I can't wrap my head around why.

More than that, why was I going to let him kiss me? And why was I disappointed when he didn't? These are all questions I don't have answers to.

When I lost Travis and then found out about Madeline a week later, I resolved myself to the life of a single mother. I accepted I would be doing this on my own.

Now, sitting here with Marshall, it makes me wonder about the possibilities the future might hold. I can finally see past my grief and realize that maybe somewhere out there, there's a man who will love both of us. We are a package deal, after all.

"Sure, it's not easy," I finally answer. "But nothing in life worth having comes easy."

"Now you sound like my dad." He smiles. The corner of his mouth quirks up just a bit, and there's a dimple there I've never noticed before. "Tell me about him. About your husband."

I should have known this question was coming. "Travis and I met in high school. We had freshman English together and were seated next to each other. We were paired up on a project, and we became fast friends."

"Nice." He nods. "High school sweethearts."

"Not exactly. We were friends all through high school. I didn't have a lot of friends. My social circle was pretty much nonexistent. I always felt guilty for Dad having to work so hard to cover bills, and things I needed, so as soon as I could get someone to hire me, which happened to be my freshman year, I started working."

"I can see that from you," he comments. "You were the girl who tried to hide in the shadows. Did anyone not tell you that you're too beautiful to go unnoticed?"

I smile and shake my head. He's charming and he knows it. "Anyway, it was a local pizza joint. I picked up as many shifts as I could so there wasn't much time for a social life. Travis was a foster kid, but he was never placed. He lived in the children's home, and they weren't allowed to be out unless it was with a mentor who was approved by the home or a school function. Sometimes the home would take them on trips or to get ice cream and pizza."

"I see where this is going." He nods.

"Is this your story or mine?" I tease. It feels good to be so comfortable with him.

"I'm just saying." He chuckles.

"Anyway, yes, he came to where I worked about once a month or so, and when I took my breaks, we would sit and talk. He had big dreams of a better life than the one he grew up in. He was treated well in the home, but he wanted more. He wanted a good job and a family of his own."

"Damn," Marshall mutters.

"He studied hard and got into college. He wanted to be a pharmacist. He was extremely smart and dedicated to school. We talked when we could and met up for pizza."

"That was your thing. I like it." He nods.

"Anyway, when my dad died, he was there for me. I had to sell the house to pay off debts, and Travis offered for me to stay with him. One thing led to another, and we started to date. Six months later, we were married. I was working with the dream of adding the title of RN to my name. The plan was for Travis to graduate, and then I would go back to school."

This time he doesn't comment. Instead, he holds my stare. "When he asked me to marry him, I said yes. He was my best friend, and it seemed like the right choice."

"Wren."

"He was a year from being done. Then he could take his licensure, and then it was my turn." A lump of emotion forms in my throat when I think about the day I got the call.

"What happened?"

"There was a guy who came into the pharmacy, coincidently, the one where I met you." I try to smile, but it's no use. "The guy wanted pain medication. It was two weeks too early, and he argued with Travis. He was screaming and raging mad. At least that's what they tell me. Finally, the pharmacist on duty intervened and told the guy they were going to call the cops if he didn't leave. He knocked over an endcap display and stormed out."

My heart is in my throat when I think about Rodney sitting me down in his office to tell me the events of that day. "Rodney was Travis's mentor and the managing pharmacist. He's the one who told me what happened." I pause and swallow hard.

"You don't have to." Marshall is quick to tell me. He places his hand on my thigh while the other holds my now-sleeping daughter close to his chest. "If it's too painful, you don't have to keep going."

"I'm okay," I assure him. He doesn't move his hand, and it gives me the comfort and the strength I need to keep going. "When they closed that night, Rodney and Travis were the last two to leave. They had a shipment come in they didn't get to during the day and the pharmacist has to sign off on all of them. Travis offered to stay and help get everything signed in and put away so they weren't behind the next day. It was something they did often.

"Anyway, Rodney said that it happened so fast that neither of them had time to react. As soon as they stepped out the back door, the gun went off." I suck in a deep breath as the emotions of that day come roaring back. The phone call that changed my life.

"I'm right here," Marshall says as he slides his arm around my shoulder and pulls me into his chest. It's not lost on me that my daughter and I are now finding comfort in his arms. "You don't have to go on. It's fine," he assures me.

I've made it this far. I want to keep going. I want to get this conversation out of the way and hopefully not have to retell it for a long damn time. "The guy was waiting for them. He shot Travis in the chest and took off. By the time the paramedics got there, it was too late."

"Oh, Wren," he murmurs, holding me a little tighter.

"They found him, about six blocks over in an alley tweaking with a needle stuck in his arm. They hauled him off to jail."

"Is he still there?"

"Yes. They're supposed to notify me, since it was murder, if he's ever released."

"I don't have words for you. My heart breaks for you and for Maddie," he says softly.

"I found out a week later that I was pregnant. It was the day we buried him. I was able to write him a letter, and I placed one of the many home tests that I took in an envelope and buried it with him."

"I'm so sorry for your loss," he murmurs. "Those words don't seem adequate."

"He always wanted a family." I reach over and place my hand over his that's resting on Madeline's back. "He would have loved her."

"He does love her," Marshall says with conviction in his voice. "He's up there smiling down on both of you."

"You really believe that?"

"I do."

"So, the tears." I lift my head so that we are looking eye to eye. "To see her so taken with you is hard because her daddy isn't here. A man I know would have loved her and worked his ass off to give her everything he never had. She's missing out on the love of a father in her life, and it just kind of got me choked up."

"What about you? He was your husband."

"I loved him. He was my best friend. My other best friend, Carrie, we met in middle school and have stayed close over the years. She claims I loved him but wasn't in love with him."

"And what do you think?"

"I think it doesn't matter. I think that my husband left this earth way too soon. I think that he wanted a family more than anything, and it's my job to raise her and try to give her the world. Just like he would have."

"Those are tall orders to fill on your own."

I shrug. "Maybe, but that won't stop me from trying. I'll make sure she knows how much he wanted her and loved her. Even without him ever knowing while he was here, I know that to be the truth." Taking a deep breath, I slowly exhale. "Maybe one day Madeline and I will find a man who can love us both as he did. Because if I know anything, I know he loved me. Not just as his best friend, but as the love of his life."

"And you feel guilty for that?"

I shrug. "A little. I assume that too will pass with time."

He pulls me back into his chest. He doesn't speak, and neither do I as we watch the sun slowly set over the horizon. I feel raw and exposed, but I also feel light. As if a burden has been lifted from my shoulders. I didn't want to have this conversation with Marshall, but I'm glad that I did. It was therapeutic in a way.

I don't know how long we've been sitting here, with both me and Madeline in his arms, but the sun has long since set over the horizon, and I know Madeline will be waking up soon. I'm ready to suggest we head back when he speaks first, stopping me.

"I almost kissed you today."

"I know."

"Would you have let me?"

"Yes." The honest reply is out of my mouth before I can stop it. I want to ask him why he was going to kiss me. Why me when he could have anyone he wants, but I keep the question locked deep inside.

I feel him nod. "You ready to head back?"

"Yeah, she's going to need to eat."

He stands and offers me his hand to help me stand as well. Lacing his fingers with mine, we walk hand in hand back to where his family is waiting. I'm sure they're wondering what happened to us.

As we come into view, he drops my hand, and I can't help but feel disappointed. I shouldn't. I'm a single mom who just released a ton of baggage at his feet tonight. He might have almost kissed me, but he didn't follow through. Marshall doesn't need a ready-made family. Not when he can have his own.

"We were about to send the search party," Conrad calls out when he sees us.

"I told them you'd get hungry and head back." Grant laughs.

"Does that mean you're firing up the grill?" Marshall asks his brother.

"The ladies are already on it," Owen tells him.

Marshall takes a seat at the picnic table and I sit next to him. His brothers and their wives and his parents eventually join us at the long table that I'm sure is custom made. We all eat, laugh, and they treat me as if I'm one of them. Marshall passes Madeline to his mom, who coos over her as if she were her own flesh and blood. I can't help but wonder what it would be like to truly be a member of this wonderful family.

CHAPTER ELEVEN
Marshall

AFTER OPENING THE passenger door, I place the five large pizzas in the seat and close the door. When Grant called to tell me that my sisters-in-law were having a girls' night, I volunteered to pick up the pizzas since I live in town. He and my brothers are going to get together with my nephews and hang out.

I'm excited to get some nephew time. I haven't seen them since last weekend at the lake. Even then, I spent most of my time with Wren and Madeline. I've expended a lot of time thinking about her this week—more than I should. I even found myself driving past her place on my way home. I told myself it was to avoid traffic, which was a lie. I was hoping to, I don't know, see her? Give her a ride to her place? Carry Madeline upstairs for her? Just do something to take a little bit of burden off her shoulders. I know it's not my place, but after hearing her story last weekend, it's all I've been able to think about.

Life is so unfair. She's been through so much loss and heartache. And Madeline, the thought of that sweet baby girl never knowing her daddy, it gets me all up in my feels.

Then there was the almost kiss. The one that I pulled out of, only to find out that she would have let me. What the fuck do I do with that information? I'll tell you what I've done. I've replayed that entire day over and over in my mind. I know she's a single mom, and hooking up with her would be a dick move, but I still wanted to kiss her. If I'm being honest, I can see myself doing a whole hell of a lot more with her, but I kept myself in check. Here I am a week later and I have regrets. I shouldn't, but I do.

Pulling into Grant's driveway, I see that Owen, Royce, and Conrad are already here. That brings a smile to my face. My brothers are lost without their wives. Hopefully, I can distract my two oldest brothers long enough to steal some Uncle Marshall hugs from Roan and Carter.

Once I'm parked behind Owen, I grab what I need before rushing around to the passenger side to gather the pizzas. I don't bother knocking when I get to the front door. That's now how we roll. We're all family and welcome at each other's homes any time, night or day. Some might think that's weird or rude, but that's who we are. Pushing open the door, it's on the tip of my tongue to call out that the favorite uncle has arrived, but I walk into utter chaos.

My brothers are talking over one another. Royce is holding Roan, who has his little lip jutted out like he's about to lose his shit. Carter is gripping Owen's shirt like he's afraid he might disappear. Jase is walking the floor with Aria, holding his hand over her ear while the other is pressed to his chest.

My eyes dart to Conrad and Grant, and that's when I see her and where the crying is coming from.

"Maddie," I say her name out loud. Grant is trying to soothe her, but nothing seems to be helping. "What in the hell is going on?" As fast as my feet will carry me, I rush toward them. I place the pizzas on the table and take Madeline from Grant. "Shh, it's okay," I say soothingly. "What's wrong, baby girl?" Madeline shudders in my arms as her cries begin to quiet at the sound of my voice.

I glance at my brothers. "What's going on? Why was she crying and where's Wren?"

"Wren went out with the girls. We told her we would watch Madeline."

"I've got you," I tell her when she whines. Placing her on my shoulder, I rub up and down her back. "Why was she crying?"

"We don't know. We were debating on who to call, Mom or Wren," Conrad confesses, running his hands through his hair. "I don't know if I can do this."

"Of course you can," I tell him. My voice is calm, careful not to set Madeline off on another meltdown. "I didn't know she was here or that Wren was going."

Grant shrugs. "Aurora was upset that Wren wasn't going to make it because she didn't have a sitter. I knew Owen and Royce were coming, and they've got this dad thing down, so I thought we would be fine. It was Con and me against one tiny little girl. I thought we had it covered."

"You should have called me." I give all four of my brothers a pointed look. Jase, too, for good measure.

"I did," Grant reminds me.

"I mean to tell me Madeline was going to be here."

"Why?"

"I would have come sooner."

"I called you thirty minutes ago."

"Exactly. I could have had pizza delivered or had one of you pick it up."

"She literally just started to cry maybe five minutes before you walked in," Conrad defends.

"When was the last time she ate?" I ask as I go through my mental checklist of what I know about babies. Sure, my only experience is my nephews, but I'm rolling with it.

"About an hour ago."

"Does she need changing?" I lift her from my chest and smell her diaper.

"Uh, Marsh, did you just smell her ass?" Conrad asks.

"It's a thing," Owen tells him.

"He's right," Royce agrees. "It's a hell of a lot easier than undressing all the wiggly arms and legs to check. The smell test is a must."

"You should probably be taking notes." Owen points at Grant and then Conrad.

They both have looks of sheer panic on their faces.

"How you feeling, Maddie?" I place her back against my chest. She snuggles in close and exhales loudly. I know she can't answer me, but my voice seems to calm her so I'm going with it.

"Damn," Grant mutters. "She really does like you better," he grumbles.

"We're never going to hear the end of this," Conrad adds.

"Wait until you have to tell Wren that you made her daughter cry and needed your baby brother to help you calm her down."

"He's cast some kind of baby voodoo on her. Look at her, all calm and shit." Grant begins pacing, his hands locked behind his head.

"Language," I chastise him.

"Pizza!" Carter cheers when he finally spies the five large boxes on the table.

"That's right, little man. Uncle Marsh brought you pizza," I tell him. "Who's your favorite uncle?" I ask. Naturally, he points at me, which has all four of my brothers and even Jase protesting.

"No pizza for you, Maddie. You're still too little," I tell the baby. I take a seat on the couch and seek out Royce. "Bring me Roan," I tell him.

"You've got your hands full, bro." He chuckles.

"Nope. I've got this. Carter and Aria can eat pizza, and it's going to take all five of you to make that happen. Bring me my nephew." I'm feeling smug as hell that Madeline stopped crying as soon as I had her in my arms. Add Carter's declaration of me being his favorite uncle, and I'm on cloud nine.

Reluctantly, Royce brings Roan over to where I'm sitting and places him in my arms. Madeline grips my shirt as Roan reaches over to grab her hand. She releases her hold, and they settle, staring at one another.

"Hey, Royce," I call out. "Grab your camera and take a picture of this." He does as I ask and then taps out what I assume is a message to Sawyer. "Send it to me too," I tell him. He nods, and my phone vibrates in my back pocket.

I know what you're thinking. I'm a single guy, unattached. Do I really want to be hanging out on my brother's couch snuggling two adorable babies? The answer is a resounding yes. I love my family, and the new generation of little Riggins is no exception. As for Madeline, this little girl has me tied around her little finger already. She's cute as hell, just like her momma. I don't know if it's because I know their story or if maybe it's my heart breaking for her and that need for a father's love. Whatever it is, she's got me hooked. I'll take Madeline snuggles any day.

Once Royce is done eating, he takes Roan, and Conrad offers to take Madeline. "Nah, I'm good," I tell him. I make my plate with one hand and eat the same way. Instantly my mind goes to Wren. This is her life. She's a single mom, and I can imagine that she eats every meal when she's with her daughter this way. If she even eats. She's a tiny thing, so my guess is that she's often too exhausted to do so.

Then I remember how we met, and she didn't have money for Madeline's medication. Does she have money for food? There's an ache in my chest at the thought of her going hungry. Damn, that's a hard subject to tackle, and I don't know how to bring it up without offending her. Maybe I'll just have to randomly stop by sometimes with dinner. Or better yet, I can have it delivered from a secret admirer so she won't know it's me.

"Earth to Marshall." Grant waves his hand in front of my face. "Where did you go?" He cocks his head to the side.

"Just thinking. What's up?"

"Wren said to feed Madeline now so that she stays on her schedule for tonight."

"Got it." I stand, tossing my plate in the trash. "Where's her diaper bag?" Grant points to the floor, and I see four diaper bags lined up. Two very girly and two that I recognize as Roan and Carter's. Lucky for me, I know which one is Madeline's. I don't know what that says about me and how much Madeline and her momma have invaded my life. Not that I'm complaining. I grab a bottle, bib, and burp cloth and make myself comfortable on the couch.

My brothers and Jase join me, with their kids in tow. The rest of the night, we watch an MMA fight, snack, and eventually, all the kids crash, but none of us bother to put them down. Grant has Carter, and Conrad has Roan. Royce takes Aria, and she snuggles up to him like it's something she's always done.

I can't help the smile that tilts my lips. A few years ago, the five of us would have laughed our asses off if you told us this is how we would be spending our Saturday nights. I know I would have. However, now that I'm here, and I'm living it, I know this is the better option.

The main event is just about to start when the women come through the door. I keep my eyes on the screen and my hand resting on Madeline's back. Sam makes her way to Jase, Sawyer to Royce, Layla to Owen, Aurora to Grant, Aspen to Conrad, and that leaves me.

Me and Wren.

I can feel her stare, but I hold off on looking over at her. I don't know why but I need her to come to me. "Hey." Her hand rests on my shoulder. "I can take her."

"Nah, I'm good. Have a seat, the fight's about to start." As if my brothers and Jase needed me to announce it, they all start talking about who they think is going to win, all while their wives are content to just sit and listen. I've moved to the recliner so I tap the armrest. "Have a seat," I tell Wren.

"No. I'm okay."

"Come on, sit down." Reaching out, I wrap my hand around her wrist and give a gentle pull. She relents and takes a seat on the arm of the recliner. The room is dark. We dimmed the lights to help the kids sleep, so no one can see us. Hell, they're not worried about what we're doing. They're wrapped up in each other and the fight. That's why I slide my arm around her waist and pull so her back is resting against the back of the chair.

"Marshall," she whispers.

"I've got you," I whisper back.

The fight goes all five of the five-minute rounds, and normally, I'd be looking for a knockout or submission, but not tonight. I'm all for the fight dragging on. I have Wren in one arm and Madeline in the other. They both feel… perfect. This moment feels important. I'm not going to analyze it or question it. I'm just going with what feels right.

Wren and Madeline. That's what feels true to me.

All too soon, the fight is over, and everyone begins to gather their kids and bags and head out. "You ready to go?" Aspen asks Wren.

"I can take them. I'm going that way." It's a valid excuse. All of my brothers have moved out of town. I'm still there in my condo. Something I've been thinking of selling and getting out of the city, but tonight I'm thankful that I'm still there.

"Are you sure?" Wren asks.

"Of course I am. It's on the way." Again, a valid excuse. However, I'd use it even if it wasn't.

"Okay." Wren turns to Aspen. "Thank you so much for inviting me. I had so much fun, and thank you all for keeping an eye on Madeline."

"That was all Marsh," Grant speaks up. "He's been hogging her since he got here." He doesn't mention that Madeline was having a meltdown when I got here, but that's okay. That would just make Wren worry and possibly turn down future invites. I definitely don't want that to happen. I can sense that my brothers feel the same, as they all stay tight-lipped about the incident.

It takes our group a good fifteen minutes to say goodbye before I'm loading Madeline and Wren up and heading toward their place.

"How was your night?" I ask once we're on the road.

"Good. It was a lot of fun."

"I'm glad you went."

"Me too."

We fall into easy conversation about girls' night at Sawyer and Royce's place, her work, and she even mentions that she's still thinking about the sunset at the lake. I want to ask her if it's because she watched it with me, but I decide to hold my tongue. It's a beautiful sunset, one we both commented on. However, in my mind, the company had something to do with it as well.

"Thanks for the ride," she says when I pull into her apartment complex.

"I'll walk you up."

"You don't have to."

"I'm walking you up," I tell her. Once I'm out of the car, I grab Madeline and her seat and motion for Wren to lead the way. This time she doesn't try to stop me. She just hikes the diaper bag upon her shoulder and we begin the long trek up the stairs to her place.

"Thanks again," she says when we finally reach her floor. She unlocks the door and pushes it open. She drops the diaper bag just inside and reaches for Madeline. I don't have an excuse to hold her any longer, so I relinquish her to her mother, seat and all.

"Lock up behind me."

"I always do."

Without thinking, my hand cradles her cheek in my palm. "Goodnight, Wren."

She visibly swallows. "Goodnight, Marshall."

There's a pause, and I want to kiss her. I think she wants me too as well. In fact, I know she does, but I drop my hand, killing the moment. Leaning over, I look into the seat and see Madeline watching us.

"Good night, baby girl." Lifting her tiny hand, I kiss her knuckles. "I'll wait until you're inside."

"Marshall, I'm a grown woman who has been living on her own just fine."

"I know that, Wren, but I'm not that man. I won't leave until I know you're locked safely inside. I know you're smart and you've been living on your own, but I'm here. I would never forgive myself if something happened to either of you and it was because I didn't make sure you were locked inside safe and sound."

"You're an enigma, Marshall Riggins."

A small laugh escapes my lips. Leaning in, I press my lips to her forehead. "You have no idea," I tell her. Stepping back, I wait for her to close the door, and I don't walk away until the lock clicks into place.

CHAPTER TWELVE

A FEW MINUTES after eight, my cell phone rings. Glancing at the screen, I see Carrie's name appear. I'm close on minutes so I wait for the phone to stop before firing off a text.

Me: Low on minutes

Carrie: On my way

Me: K

It's been a few weeks since I've seen her so I was expecting a drop-in at some point. My guess is that she just got off work and she'll be bringing breakfast. That's how my best friend rolls. Dropping my phone to the floor, I roll over, the ache in my back present from sleeping on the lumpy couch. From down the hall, I hear Madeline cooing in her bed, and I know I need to get up and change her and get her fed.

The issue is that I'm exhausted. I barely slept a wink last night after Marshall dropped us off. A mountain of emotions kept me tossing and turning. The first was acceptance. I'm attracted to him and I can't deny it any longer. Not even to myself.

Another was guilt. Travis hasn't even been gone two years, and I'm already letting myself admit that I'm attracted to another man. The guilt grows deeper when I admit to myself that Travis and I never should have married. We were best friends, and I know he loved me, but I didn't love him that way. We worked. I have no doubt that if he were still here, walking this earth, we would be happy together. However, since spending time with the Riggins family, I see the love and passion each couple shares, and we didn't have that.

I want that.

The problem other than the guilt?

Two words.

Marshall Riggins.

One minute I'm barely getting by. I have Carrie in my corner and am fighting every day to make ends meet. I'm still fighting each day and I still have Carrie, but my circle has widened. I have Sawyer, Layla, Aurora, Aspen, and Sam. By association with these incredible ladies, I get their husbands, their kids, and their in-laws. A chance encounter with the kindhearted Marshall Riggins led to these new friendships. Sure, Aspen didn't know who I was that day, but then again, maybe she did. I make a mental note to ask her. Regardless, it feels as though it's fate, and it all started with Marshall.

Madeline begins to fuss, and I know my time is up. With a groan, I roll off the couch, feeling years older than my twenty-four years. When I reach her bedroom and push open the door, her cries grow louder. "Hey, sweetie," I call out to her. She immediately stops crying and turns toward my voice. My heart swells. This tiny human is the light of my life.

"Let's get you changed," I tell her, lifting her from her crib. She begins to root around my chest and I chuckle. She's hungry. "Just a minute. We have to get this soaked diaper off you. Oh, and guess what?" I keep talking while I make quick work of changing her diaper. "Aunt Carrie is on her way to see us."

My daughter couldn't care less about our visitor. She's hungry and is making sure I know it. I guess that's a small price to pay for her sleeping all night long. Diaper changed, I head to the living room, taking a seat on the couch, and pull up my shirt. The seasoned pro that she is, she latches on and settles in my arms. Grabbing the small blanket of hers that I use for feedings, I drape it over both of us just in time for a knock to come at the door.

"Coming!" I call out. I manage to pull myself from the couch, and not disturb my daughter's breakfast, and open the door.

Carrie grins, holding up a popular drive-thru food chain bag. "Breakfast of champions," she says, stepping past me into my tiny apartment.

"You know you don't have to bring breakfast with you every time that you come to visit."

"La la la," she sings, pretending to not hear me. "You know that if you would let me add you to my phone plan, we could catch up more often," she smarts off.

"Fair enough." I nod. "Thank you for breakfast." I don't bother to try and pay her. We've traveled down this road many times, and I'm always the one who gets left in the dust.

"Now, tell me everything. What's been going on with you?"

"You first."

"Fine." She sighs dramatically. "I might have gone out on a date."

"What? And you didn't tell me?" I shriek, making Madeline jump in my arms. I rub her back to soothe her. "You didn't tell me?" I say, softer this time.

"Phone minutes." She raises her eyebrows.

"Fine. I get it. Now, please proceed."

"Dr. Danning, well, Elijah, that's his name, he's the one who's been asking me out for months. I finally gave in."

"Finally!" I smile at my best friend. She's a workaholic and still healing from a broken heart. Her high school boyfriend destroyed her when he left for college. He told her they would try long distance. She went to surprise him and found him in his dorm with another girl. They were together for over four years, and Carrie was devastated. It's been nothing but a casual hookup here and there for her since then. No dating, until now.

"How was it?"

"It was… nice."

"Nice? Come on, Carrie, you can do better than that. Where did you go? Did he kiss you? Are you seeing him again?" I blurt out a scroll of questions to my best friend.

"We went to dinner and then hung out on Broadway. He walked me to the door, and yes, he kissed me. We're going out again next weekend."

"Eep! I'm so excited for you. When do I get to meet him?"

"Slow your roll, Wren." She chuckles. "It was one date. We both had a good time. He hasn't reached the 'let's meet the best friend' level just yet."

"Well, when you get there, you'll tell me? Call me? Send me a text?"

"I don't want to use up all of your minutes."

"To hell with the minutes. I'll scrimp to buy more. This is important information."

"Okay. I'll be sure to tell you if we happen to get there. What about you? What's been going on in your life?"

"Well, working like always. This little one is thriving, coming up on her six-month birthday." I smile as I pull my shirt back in place and sit Madeline up on my lap. She grins at Carrie, and my best friend wastes no time snatching her from my arms.

"I've actually met some new people."

"Really? Wren, that's amazing. I'm so proud of you for busting out of your comfort zone. Wait, where did you meet these new people?" She eyes me suspiciously. She knows that I don't go out, and the likelihood of meeting new friends at the grocery store or pediatrician's office is slim to none.

She already knows about Marshall and him saving me, paying for Madeline's prescription. I catch her up on the day in front of the bakery and everything she's missed since then. "So, yeah, I've met some new people."

"The ladies sound awesome, and I want an invite to meet them soon. However, that's for another time. Let's talk about this Marshall character."

I can't help but roll my eyes at my protective best friend. "He's a good guy, Carrie."

"I didn't say he wasn't. I think there's more you're not telling me."

"What?" I protest a little too quickly.

"Spill it, Wren."

"Fine." I tell her about all the moments that felt... more than just two friends. I tell her how he almost kissed me then confessed to doing so, how he pulled me down on the chair with him, drove me home, walked me to the door, and kissed my forehead. She's quiet, but I can see it written all over her face... she's excited about this new information.

"He's hot, Wren."

"I know."

"So are his brothers."

"I know. They are and are blissfully in love with their wives." Technically, Conrad and Aspen are not married yet, but they might as well be.

"When are you seeing him again?" she asks.

"Uh, well, I'm not. I mean, not that I know of. I didn't know I was going to see him last night. I mean, I knew there was a possibility when we picked up Madeline, but I didn't expect him to drive me home."

"She really stops crying when he holds her?"

"She does," I confirm. "You should see her when she hears his voice. She turns to find him, and if one of his brothers or his dad is holding her, she cries until Marshall takes her."

"What about the women?"

"I'm not sure," I confess. "The Riggins men are kind of baby hogs. And once Marshall gets her, he doesn't let her go."

"Oh my God. I think my ovaries just exploded," she says, bouncing Madeline in her arms. "Do you like Marshall, Madeline?"

Carrie, even though she's sworn off men until recently, is a romantic at heart. She's all sunshine and roses when talking about love. She's addicted to reading romance novels, and the girl has a DVR full of Hallmark movies. I expected this reaction from her.

"It brought tears to my eyes," I admit. "She's so comfortable with him. If I hadn't seen her cry and then quiet down when he took her from his brothers, I wouldn't have believed it. She's never around men. Why him?"

"It's fate."

"That's the romantic in you."

She shrugs. "Regardless, I believe in fate."

"And is it fate between you and Elijah?"

"I'm not sure. I know that he's been asking me out for several months, and I've kept my ear to the ground. He's not some sleaze who hits on all of the nurses. He even had one of the nurses ask him out, and he told her he was waiting on me."

"What? You failed to mention that earlier when it was your turn to share," I scold.

"I know. I'm sorry. I'm just trying not to get too excited and let myself fall too hard or too fast."

"It's been years since Rick the dick. It's time for you to open your heart again."

"I will if you will," she counters.

"We're not talking about me."

"Sure we are. We're talking about both of us. Look, Wren, I know this is hard to hear, and we don't talk about it often, but you settled. Travis was a great guy, and he was good to you, but you didn't have that overwhelming passion for one another. I want you to have that."

"Do you have that?"

"I did once." She nods. "I hope to have it again someday. Yes,

Rick broke my heart and my trust. It's taken me time to get to a point where I feel as though I'm ready to let someone else in. However, I won't settle for mediocre, not when I know that I can have the fairy tale. I'm in no rush, and if I never find my prince charming, so be it. But, if I do, and I have faith that I will, he will be the one that sets my soul on fire. I was young when I started dating Rick, and I still felt it. I can only hope that the feeling is ten times stronger as an adult. I've changed as a person. I should have seen the signs, but I ignored them. I won't make that mistake again."

"Wow. That's… more than I've heard you say about you and dating in a long time."

"Yeah, well, I've been thinking a lot about life and what comes next. I want the fairy tale, Wren. If that man turns out to be Elijah, then great. If not, I'll keep looking."

"I'm not sure if I believe in fairy tales." It's true. My dad lost the love of his life and I lost Travis. Both were taken from us way too soon.

"I have a feeling Marshall Riggins can help change your mind."

"It's not like that between us."

"He was going to kiss you."

"Yeah, but he didn't. I'm a single mom. He's young and one of the most eligible bachelors in this city. Why would he settle for a woman with baggage who can't even afford a cell phone other than prepaid minutes?"

Carrie wags her eyebrows. "Fate."

"You're sleep-deprived," I say, making her laugh.

"I'm that too. But in all seriousness, don't let his 'most eligible bachelor' status or his bank account keep you from pursuing him if that's what you want."

"Whoa, hold up, sister. No one said anything about pursuing anyone."

"He's bringing you back to life. Remind me to thank him."

"What the hell are you going on about?"

"Shh, language around my niece." I give her a "really" look, and she just grins. "Your eyes are brighter, and you've talked more to me today than you have since losing Travis. I don't know if it's Marshall or his group of women who's doing this for you, but whatever the reason, I'm glad to have my Wren back."

"I've always been here."

"In body, but not in mind. You've been hiding away, thinking that you have to give everything to Madeline, and I get that, I do. However, what would it have hurt to keep your bed and share a room with her? You're making sacrifices you didn't have to make. Not with an infant."

"I only want what's best for her. Travis would have wanted what's best for her."

"Sharing a room with her mother as an infant when she will never remember would have been what was best for her. Travis would want you to take care of you as well. Besides, have you ever considered that maybe, just maybe, Travis has something to do with the handsome stranger who just happened to appear into your life?"

"Now you're just talking crazy."

"Hear me out. What are the odds, that a sweet, caring, hot-as-hell man like Marshall Riggins would have been behind you in line that day? When the pharmacy was getting ready to close and you needed this little one's medication."

"How do you know he's sweet and caring?" I challenge.

"My niece loves him already. She's a good judge of character, all babies are. There's something about him that soothes her. That's good enough for me."

"You know that sounds ridiculous?"

She shrugs. "I don't care how it sounds. It's the truth."

"I think you need to have Dr. Danning check you out," I tease. It's easier than to let myself consider her reasoning.

"Oh, he's going to check me out, all right." She wags her eyebrows.

"Really, Care?" I laugh. "I thought you were taking it slow?"

"We are. However, I feel as though I've learned a lot about me and about others during this time of healing, and I think Dr. Danning is one of the good ones too. Oh! We should double date!"

"I'm not dating Marshall."

"Not yet." She stands from the couch and kisses Madeline all over her face, making her laugh. "I need to go home and get some sleep. I'm back on tonight for another twelve-hour shift. Think about what I said and text me with any new developments. Hell, send a carrier pigeon, don't leave a girl hanging."

"I'll see what I can do. Thank you for breakfast," I say, even though neither of us touched a bite of it. We were too busy catching up. "Make sure you take yours with you."

"Nah, I'm all set. Put it in the fridge and warm it up later." She pulls me into a hug. "I love ya, girl, and I'm so proud of you."

"I love you too. Call me or stop by after your next date."

"You got it. Bye, Madeline." She waves, and my daughter just coos at her.

Once the door is closed behind her, I set Madeline up on her play mat for some tummy time while I dig into my breakfast sandwich. All the while I can't stop thinking about our conversation, and whether or not I believe in fate.

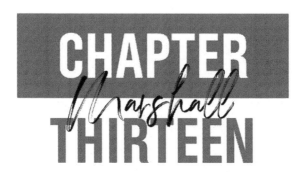

CHAPTER *Marshall* THIRTEEN

"**T**HANKS FOR DINNER, Mom." I snake my arm around her shoulders and press a kiss to her cheek.

"You're welcome. This is for you." She hands me a container filled to the brim with leftover meatloaf, mashed potatoes, and corn.

"You spoil me."

"I spoil all my sons."

"Yeah, but Marsh is the baby," Conrad says. "He needs more love than the rest of us."

I discreetly flip him off behind Mom's back, making him laugh. "Don't be jealous, Con. Just because I'm the favorite."

"You know she tells each of you that you're her favorite, right?" Dad asks, stepping into the kitchen.

"Stanley!" Mom scolds.

We all laugh. He's not wrong. She knows that we know it, but it doesn't bother us. Our mother loves us unconditionally. "We're heading out," Royce says, with a sleeping Roan in his arms.

"You tired, little man?" I ask my nephew. I lean in and kiss the top of his head. "Love you, buddy," I whisper. Seeing him makes me think of Madeline and Wren. I wonder what they're up to tonight.

I'd love to say it's a fleeting thought, but I'd be lying. I thought about them all night last night and they've been on my mind today as well. How could they not be? Madeline is cute as hell and all snuggly. Then there's her mom. Wren is… consuming me. Mostly because of how I can't stop thinking about her. She's gorgeous and so damn strong. She's been through so much, and all I want to do is wrap her in my arms—and be her rock. She takes such great care of her daughter. Who takes care of her?

"I'm out too," I tell my parents. Reaching for the container of leftovers that Mom fills for me every week, I smile at her. "Thanks, Momma."

"Kiss ass," Grant mutters under his breath.

"Hey, you all have wives to feed you. It's just me," I argue.

"Marshall Riggins!" Sawyer says, placing her hands on her hips. "Are you insinuating that's all your sisters and I are worth?"

"Nope. But you have to admit y'all have quiet nights in, and that includes eating." Her shoulders relax. "You know I love you, sis. I love all of y'all." I make eye contact with my other three sisters, who are now crowded into the kitchen, along with Owen. "But you know I'm right."

"If only you would open your eyes." Layla smiles sweetly.

"My eyes are wide open, sis." I place a kiss on her cheek. "I see you." I wink.

"Marsh," Owen growls, making the entire room erupt into laughter. He's so head over heels for his wife. They all are, and I admit that knowing they're going home together, each of them, and I'm going home alone, well, it causes a pang of loneliness to creep in. My brothers all have lives of their own, their own families, and I'm still me—fun-loving Marshall.

"Believe in the magic, brother," Owen says, Layla tightly wrapped in his arms.

"On that note, I'm out. Love you!" I call out to my family.

It's just after seven in the evening when I roll into the city limits. Again, Wren and her daughter pop into my mind, and I can't help but wonder what they're doing tonight. I let my mind drift, remembering how badly I wanted to kiss her last night. No matter how many times I tell myself that she's off-limits, I crave to taste her lips and feel their softness against my own.

It's not until I'm pulling into the parking lot that I realize that I'm at her apartment complex. Glancing over, I see the container of leftovers in the passenger seat. There's plenty for two, but then what about Madeline? I can't go in empty-handed. Putting my car into reverse, I pull out of the lot and head to the nearest twenty-four-hour pharmacy. Inside, I head to the baby aisle. I can't buy her food. I don't know what she's eating just yet, so I look at the toys. There's a book and a small set of keys that she can chew on. Perfect. Taking my picks to the register, I check out and head back to their apartment.

I have no idea what I'm doing. Hell, she might kick my ass to the curb and refuse to let me in. What I do know is that she's all I've been able to think about, and I need to see her. Life's about taking risks, right? I know she has a baby and that they're a package deal, and I'm good with that. I don't even know if I'm pursuing her. I just need to see her. I need to lay eyes on the beauty and her little girl. Friends can bring friends dinner and buy gifts for their kids, right?

Grabbing the pharmacy bag and the container of leftovers, I climb out of the car, hit the lock button, and make my way inside. With each flight of stairs, I begin to second-guess myself. This is crazy. I can't just show up randomly with food and toys. Despite this, I keep climbing the stairs and eventually reach her door. I don't let myself hesitate as I knock softly. I don't know what time Madeline goes to bed, but the last thing I want to do is wake her up.

When Wren opens the door, her mouth drops open, and so does mine. Hers is from shock, and I guess you could say that mine is from shock as well. She's got her short hair pulled up with tendrils of hair framing her face. She's in a skintight tank top that's see-through and a pair of tiny pajama shorts. Did I mention her tank is see-through?

"M-Marshall. Hey," she says, her eyes wide.

"Hey, Wren." I hold up the container. "I brought dinner." I'm not even remotely hungry, but I'll eat again if it means I get to share a meal with her.

"Oh, um, why?"

I shrug. "I missed you." Her eyes widen, as do mine. I didn't mean to say that. I didn't even realize that missing her was exactly what this nagging feeling has been all day. Not until she opened the door and I got to lay eyes on her.

"Y-You missed me?"

"You and Maddie. Where is she?"

"She's having some tummy time. She just had her bath."

"Good, that will give us some time to eat." I don't wait for her to invite me in. No, I step inside the door, squeezing past her. Her tits that are on full display brush against my chest when I pass, and I have to bite my cheek to keep from groaning.

"I hope you're hungry. Mom packed a lot."

"Your mom made dinner?"

"Yeah. Every Sunday, we all try to get together at her place for dinner, lunch, whatever fits everyone's schedules the best. She always sends me with more leftovers than I can eat on my own."

"And you thought it was a good idea to stop by and share them with me?"

"Yep." I flash her a grin. "Plates?"

She jumps into action, closing the door, and joining me in the small kitchen area, gathering plates from the cabinet, and hands me two forks. "Do we need to warm it up?" she asks.

"Nah, I just left, so it should still be warm."

"Okay. I, uh, don't really have anything to offer you to drink. Water and coffee," she says meekly.

"Water is perfect." I keep my tone light. Now that I'm here, in her space, I know this was the right choice. Sure, I caught her off guard, but seeing her makes me smile. "Here, this one is yours." I hand her one of the plates. "Should we eat on the couch so we can keep a close eye on Maddie?" This place is so small we can see her perfectly fine from where we are, but I'm hoping that sitting on the couch and having her daughter close will help ease some of the tension in her shoulders.

"Sure." She doesn't sound sure, but that's okay. I'm sure enough for both of us. She hands me a glass of water and together we make our way to the couch.

"Hey, Maddie," I greet the baby. She turns her little head, following my voice and rewards me with a toothy grin. "How was your day?" I ask Wren before taking a bite of meatloaf. As always, it's just as good the second time around.

"Okay. Yours?"

"Good. Anytime my family gets together, it's a good time. What did you do?"

"We stayed in today. I need to go to the store, but I didn't want to pack Madeline down the stairs knowing I need to do it again tomorrow."

"How do you manage that? Packing Maddie and the groceries up the stairs?"

"I have a grocery cart. I carry her in one arm and pull it up the steps with the other."

"You pull a cart and carry your daughter up three flights of stairs?"

She shrugs. "That's my only option."

"We need to get you out of here," I mutter under my breath.

"What's that?" she asks.

"Nothing. I can't believe this building doesn't have an elevator."

"It's full, so it doesn't seem to bother people."

"That's a lot for you to handle on your own, Wren."

"I'm a big girl, Marshall. I can handle it."

I know she's a big girl. Her tits that keep taunting me are a constant reminder. But I hate that she's dealing with this shit. I have plenty of space in my condo. It's on the tip of my tongue to tell her to pack her shit and move in with me. I open my mouth to say that exact thing when Madeline begins to fuss. "I'll get her." I set my plate on the floor and move to lie next to Madeline.

"Hey, baby girl, how was your day?" She grins and raises her hand to reach for me. "I brought you something." Jumping to my feet, I rush to the kitchen. Well, it's more of an area than an actual kitchen. Grabbing the pharmacy bag, I make quick work of opening the toys I bought her. A few steps and I'm back in the living room. I sit on the floor with my back against the couch and lift Madeline onto my lap.

"Look." I hand her the keys first and she immediately places them in her mouth. "I knew you'd do that," I tell her. "Now, let's read this book, shall we?" I open the book and Madeline rests her back against my chest, chewing on her keys while I read the small book to her. "The end."

"She likes it." I turn to look at Wren, and she once again has watery eyes. The corner of her sexy mouth is lifted with a smile. "You good, Momma?" I ask her.

"Yeah. I'm good." She nods.

We spend the next hour just chatting, getting to know one another. I'm the one doing most of the talking, but I learn a good bit about her, and she me. I don't dare ask a question. I'm not willing to answer myself. I've learned that she's the same age as me at twenty-four. I know that her favorite food is anything Italian and that her hair used to be long, but she cut it when she found out she was pregnant.

"It's just easier to take care of," she explains.

"I know what you mean. I keep mine short for that very reason," I say, making her laugh. It's a beautiful sound, and it does something to me knowing I'm the one responsible for her smile.

"Stop." She pushes on my arm, and I feign hurt. "Maddie, help me." I lift her from my lap and toss her just slightly in the air and catch her. Her laughter, much like her mother's, has me feeling some kind of way.

"Favorite color?"

"Hmm, I'd say teal."

I nod. "Good choice. Mine used to be black."

"Used to be?"

I settle Madeline against my chest and turn to look at Wren, who is now sitting next to us on the floor, her back also against the couch. "Now it's blue. The color of your eyes," I add. I don't know what it is about her, but I keep saying things that I should be keeping to myself. Her cheeks turn a light rose color, and now I'm glad that I said them. In fact, I'm wracking my brain for any other compliments I can give her just to see that blush stay on her cheeks.

"I need to feed her and put her to bed," she says, changing the subject.

"Can I help?"

"Oh, um, no, I've got it."

"Okay, Maddie, it's time for dinner, and then night night time." I kiss her cheek and hand her over to Wren.

"Thanks. Um, do you mind handing me that blanket?" She points behind me. Reaching back, I grab the small thin pink and white blanket and hand it to her. "Thank you."

Madeline knows what time it is, and she's rooting around, and that's when I know what's about to happen. If I were the gentleman that my momma raised me to be, I would stand and leave, or at least go to the bathroom to give her some privacy, but right now, I can't find that guy. No, all I have is the man in me that is fascinated with this woman, and she's about to pull her boobs out. Even if it is to nourish her daughter, I can't look away because it's Wren. There's a pull between us that I don't understand, but it's keeping me rooted into my spot and my eyes glued to her.

Lifting my gaze, we lock eyes. I see her hands moving, but I don't dare look away from her baby blues. I turn to the side so I'm facing her. Reaching out, I lace her fingers with mine. Something is happening. My heart is hammering in my chest, and I know she can feel the clamminess of my hands. "Wren." Her name is a whisper on my lips.

She swallows hard. "What are you doing?"

I move closer. I can't seem to get close enough to her. "I don't know. Whatever it is, it feels right."

"I'm a mom."

"You're a fantastic mother. Your beautiful little girl looks just like you." She looks down at Madeline, and my eyes follow hers. My heart trips over in my chest when I see Madeline's eyes on me as she eats. The moment is intimate and personal, and to think I could have missed it had I not knocked on her door earlier.

I'm still holding Wren's hand that's not holding her daughter, and the other, well, I slide it behind her neck and lean in close, resting my forehead against hers. "What are you doing to me?"

"Marshall."

"You feel it too, right? I wish I could describe this… the pull I have toward the two of you. Every time I see you, it grows stronger. I don't know what it means, but damn it, Wren, I want to find out." I pull back so I can look into her eyes.

"What does that mean?"

"Let me spend time with you. Both of you. I don't know what it means, baby. All I know is that something brought me to your doorstep tonight. All I've done is think about you today, and on my way home, this is where I ended up."

"You brought her a gift."

"She's a part of you, Wren. You're a package deal. What I don't know is what's happening between us. I don't know why you're all I can think about. I don't know why I can't be this close to you without touching you."

"I like spending time with you." Her confession is soft, almost as if she doesn't want me to hear her.

"Good. You're going to be seeing a lot more of me." Looking down at Madeline whose eyes are drooping, I gently run my index finger over her cheek. "Both of you." When my gaze meets Wren's, I can see the worry there. "Talk to me. Tell me what you're thinking."

"I'm scared."

"I've got you." There's conviction in my voice. "We'll go slow. I just want to spend more time with you and Maddie."

She nods. "Okay."

I don't bother to hide my smile. "Thank you." Leaning in, I kiss her cheek.

"I need to put her down."

"Need some help?"

"No. I'll be right back."

I watch as she somehow manages to stand gracefully with Madeline sleeping soundly in her arms. She disappears behind a door, and I assume the other door is the bathroom. They must share a room right now. Damn, I should have gone with her so I could see where she sleeps. That sounds creeperish even to me, but I'm just curious about her — everything about her.

"She's out," she says over a yawn a few minutes later.

"I should let you get some sleep."

"Thank you for dinner."

I stand and pull her into my arms, hugging her to my chest. "I'll call you tomorrow."

"That's not a good idea."

"I thought we agreed to spend time together."

"This is embarrassing," she mumbles. "We did, but my phone it's a prepaid, and I don't get a lot of minutes. Just enough to call for help if I need it with Madeline."

I nod, processing this new information. "Fine. What time do you get off work?"

"Five."

"The nursing home on 8th, right?" She nods. "I'll be there to pick you up. We'll get Maddie from day care and have dinner at my place."

"I don't—" she starts, but I place my finger over her lips.

"Let me take care of you, please." She nods. "Good night, Wren. Lock up after me."

"A-Always," she croaks.

Hand in hand, we walk to her door. I give her one final hug, and she fits perfectly in my arms. Reluctantly, I release my hold on her and slip out into the hallway. She waves and closes the door. I wait until I hear the lock engage before I start my trek down the three flights of stairs to my car. I don't know what I expected, but the night turned out better than I ever could have imagined.

CHAPTER
When
FOURTEEN

THERE'S NOTHING WORSE than watching the clock as it slowly ticks by. I barely slept last night, and when I did, it was Marshall who appeared in my dreams. Last night was… unexpected. Marshall's not alone. Whatever this is between us, I feel it too. It scares the hell out of me, but it also excites me.

Fifteen more minutes and my shift is over. I know without calling or texting him that he's going to be outside waiting for me. Marshall isn't the kind of man who says one thing and does another. Travis was the same way. He'd grown up being jostled and told one thing only to have another happen.

Guilt washes over me. I miss Travis every single day. But he's gone, and Carrie's right. I'm young, and I don't want to live the rest of my life alone. I don't know if that's what this is, this thing between Marshall and me. I'm in the dark where we're concerned. However, since meeting him that first day, the weight that was always holding me down seems to be lifted. The burdens of the world don't seem so heavy with my new acquaintances. Sure, he's more than just an acquaintance at this point, and so is his family, but you know that I mean.

At five, I make my way to the break room and gather my belongings. When I reach the front door, the florist is there delivering flowers. "Wren, wait up," the receptionist, Beth, calls.

I stop and wait for her to finish signing for the delivery. To be honest, the interruption is nice. It gives me a minute to wrap my head around the fact that Marshall is here to pick me up, and we're having dinner tonight at his place with Madeline. I know it's rude to keep him waiting, but an extra minute or two won't hurt to allow my heart time to settle into a steady beat.

"Hey," I say, walking up to her desk. She's smiling like she's got a secret.

"These have your name on them." Her grin grows wider.

"What?" I breathe.

"They're yours." She spins the flowers to face me, and I pluck the small card with my name written on it from the folder.

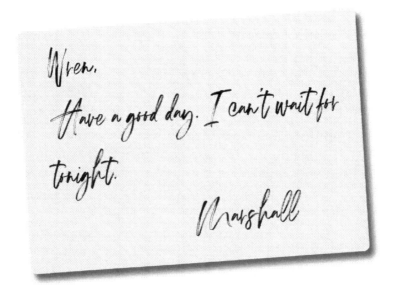

Wren,

Have a good day. I can't wait for tonight.

Marshall

"So, who're they from?"

"A friend." That's not a complete lie. Marshall is my friend. At least, I think he is. I don't know what else to call him. We're not really dating. He's not my boyfriend or my lover. Though the thought of him being my lover has a shiver racing down my spine. I've thought of *that* with him more than I should.

I take in the bouquet of lilies and think back to our conversation last night. I told him lilies were my favorite flower. He told me his was whatever made me smell so good. I blushed like crazy. Who knew there was a sweet talker underneath the power suits and all that sexiness he alludes to?

I can't believe he sent me flowers.

I've never received flowers before. Not outside of a birthday or holiday. Travis and I were always living on a budget while he was in school. This is… nice. Any chance I had of my heart slowing its rhythm is long gone. It feels as though it could beat right out of my chest.

"Thanks, Beth." I grab the flowers and rush out the front door. Suddenly my nerves are gone, and I can't wait to see him.

I spot him standing outside a black SUV, and I wonder how many vehicles he owns. He's leaning against the vehicle, with his arms crossed over his chest and his legs crossed at the ankles. "I see you got my flowers."

"Just now actually. Thank you. They're beautiful but not necessary."

"Just now? Hell, I could have delivered them myself faster than that," he grumbles.

"I got them. That's all that matters."

"How was your day?" he asks, opening the passenger side door for me. "I'll take those." He takes the flowers from my hands and presses a kiss on my cheek. Stepping back, he waits for me to relax into the seat before closing the door.

"It was long," I admit once he's settled beside me behind the wheel.

"So it wasn't just me?"

"Just you what?"

"Just me who couldn't stop thinking about tonight."

"No," I confess. "It wasn't just you."

"Good." He reaches over and places his hand on my thigh. "Now, point me in the direction of Maddie's day care."

I do just that, giving him directions to the small day care center just down the block from my work. "You walk to work every day?" he asks.

"Yeah." I shrug. "It's not too far, and it's good exercise." He opens his mouth to reply, but I open my door and climb out of the SUV. I make my way to the front door, and I'm surprised when Marshall reaches around me to open the door.

"I should see the process, you know, just in case I ever get to pick her up."

It's not lost on me that he says if he *gets* to pick her up, not if he *has* to pick her up. I'm not sure Marshall Riggins is a real man. Is it possible he's an alien in a man's body? Oh, maybe he's a robot in a man's body, and a woman programmed him to the sweetest caring man she's ever met. He certainly fits that description for me.

"Hi, Ms. Betty," I greet the manager of the day care. "How was Madeline today?"

"She's such a joy." Betty beams. "Let me go get her." She scurries off to the locked room that parents are not allowed to enter. At first, not being allowed in the center upset me, but Ms. Betty explained that it's for the children's safety. There are cameras everywhere, and the screen in the main room shows a view from every single angle of each age group of kids.

"Good security," Marshall comments.

"Yeah. It's expensive, taking half of my check each week, but it's worth it to know that she's safe and well taken care of. I'm fine with making sacrifices to ensure her safety."

His hand rests on the small of my back and he leans in close. "You're an amazing mother, Wren."

I feel his lips press to my temple, and it takes everything I have not to melt into his touch. He said he wants to see more of me. I agreed to that, but we didn't really discuss us *more* than that. I can't let myself depend on him. Not yet.

"There's Mommy," Betty says. She hands Madeline to me and I snuggle her to my chest.

"Mommy missed you," I whisper, placing a kiss on her soft cheek.

"Hey, baby girl," Marshall says softly. At the sound of his voice, my daughter turns to where he stands behind me and holds out her arms. *She's reaching for him.* "Come here, you." He plucks her from my arms and tosses her gently into the air.

"Here are her things." Betty hands me the diaper bag and infant car seat.

"Thank you, Betty."

"All right, baby girl. Let's get you strapped him. We've got dinner to make," Marshall tells Madeline. She babbles up at him as if he's the most magnificent thing she's ever seen.

I know the feeling.

Marshall gets her strapped in and lifts her in her seat with ease. "Ready?" he asks.

I nod, and just like that, we're leaving the day care. "I made sure I had the base this morning before I left the house."

"Thank you."

"Safety first, right, Maddie?" he asks, opening the back door of his shiny black SUV and placing her expertly in the back seat. He doesn't seem to mind that I double-check his work, and I wouldn't care if he did. This little girl is my life and it's my job to protect her. However, I didn't need to check. This isn't Marshall's first rodeo. I know he's very involved in his nephews' lives. His entire family is.

What would it be like to have that kind of support system?

Marshall is already behind the wheel when I take my seat. "What sounds good for dinner?"

"I'm not picky."

"I didn't ask you if you were picky, Wren, but that's good to know." Again, he reaches over and rests his hand on my thigh. "I asked you what sounds good to you."

"Honestly?"

"Always."

"Pizza."

"Pizza?"

"Yeah. It's not something I splurge on very often."

"That's your favorite?"

I nod. "It is."

"Okay. Pizza it is." He doesn't ask me why I barely indulge in my favorite food. Unless it's the frozen cardboard variety, I don't get it much. It's expensive to eat out. I do more Ramen noodles, spaghetti, soup, peanut butter and jelly, macaroni and cheese, things like that. Pizza, although my favorite, is a treat I can't afford.

"There are a few places that are close to my condo. They deliver. We'll get Madeline settled and you can choose."

"Anything, Marshall, really."

"Nope. It's the lady's choice tonight. If Maddie could tell me, I'd ask her."

"Thank you." My voice is soft as I'm overtaken with emotion. He's so good to Madeline and me. He's sweet and caring, and lethal to my heart if its rapid pace is any indication.

"For what?" He glances over at me, then quickly puts his eyes back on the road.

"For tonight."

"It's just starting."

"I know, but I don't want to forget to tell you." He doesn't comment, but the gentle squeeze on my thigh tells me that he heard me, and maybe he doesn't feel as though he needs to reply. I replay my words in my head, and it sounds stupid now that I play it back, but I get overwhelmed when he's close, and I truly didn't want to forget. Even if he was taking me straight home, just the little bit of time I've had with him today has been nice, and the flowers are beautiful, and they were unexpected.

"Wow, this is where you live?" I ask. We pull up to a two-story condo with a three-car attached garage. Three cars!

"Yeah, it was convenient in my younger days. My brothers and I used to hit the clubs a lot on the weekends, and we could walk everywhere we went. Conrad used to live just down the road, but he sold his condo and bought the house they live in now."

"You don't go to clubs anymore?"

"Nah. It was something I did with my brothers, and it's not much fun without them. Now we're usually at one of their houses, and I'm fighting with them to get time with my nephews. You might not know this, but my brothers are baby hogs."

"Soon you'll have two more babies to fight over."

"I know. It can't come soon enough. Owen needs to hurry up and have another one so we can even things out. We'll all have a baby to snuggle with."

"What about you? You don't want kids?"

"I do want kids. I just need to find their momma first." He winks, grabbing the keys from the ignition. "Come on, beautiful. I'll grab Maddie."

I do my best to school my features, and I hope he can't hear the rapid beat of my heart. I don't know if it's his sweet words or the wink that has my heart feeling as though it could beat right out of my chest.

I feel so far out of my element. His place compared to mine is just one more indicator that he's way out of my league. Surely, he can see that. Holding back my sigh and already invested for the night, I grab Madeline's diaper bag. "Can I leave my flowers in the car?"

"Sure. That will save us packing them when it's time to leave."

"That's what I was thinking too," I tell him.

With my purse and the diaper bag slung over my shoulder, I follow him through the service door in his garage that leads us into a mudroom. He keeps walking as we enter the kitchen. He sets Madeline's car seat on the island and makes quick work of removing her from her seat. "Let's find Mommy those menus," he tells my daughter. "Ah-hah." He pulls out a stack of menus and slides them across the island to me while bouncing Madeline in his arms.

"I can take her."

"Nope. You tell me what you want to eat, and I'll order."

"I'm not picky."

He steps around the island, moving into my personal space. He raises his palm to rest against my cheek. "Baby, this is your favorite. I want you to tell me what you want. We're going to order pizza and chill with the little angel, and then we're going to stuff ourselves with pizza."

"I'm boring. Just pepperoni."

A slow smile tilts his lips. "You're anything but boring. Wings? Breadsticks?"

"I like them both, so whatever is fine with me."

"Fine," he sighs. "You've left me no choice." I watch as he pulls out his phone and taps the screen before placing it to his ear. He rattles off that he wants to place an order for delivery and confirms his address. "I need a large pepperoni and cheese, a large breadstick, boneless wings, with all the sauce options on the side, and a brownie for dessert." He listens and nods before thanking the person on the other line and ending the call.

"We can't eat all of that," I say, my eyes wide.

"We can try." He winks. "Now, let's get Madeline set up in the living room." I follow along behind him, and there's a mat, similar to hers, only it's blue and green. He spreads it out on the floor and slides Madeline underneath it. Her eyes grow wide as she looks in the little mirror and all the brightly colored toys that hang from the bar.

"You keep baby toys just lying around?"

"I do now that I'm an uncle. I've watched Roan and Carter a few times when I can get my name thrown in the hat between my brothers, their wives, and my parents."

"I love how close all of you are to your family."

He nods. "I don't know what I would do without them." He furrows his brow, and I know he's thinking about me and how Madeline is my only family.

He surprises me when he settles on the floor, resting his weight on his elbow. He reaches over and bobs Madeline on the nose, making her laugh. "Come on, Mommy." He waves for me to join them, and the temptation is too hard to resist. I slide out of my shoes and take the opposite, mirroring his position.

"Tell me about your day."

"I thought we already had this conversation," I tease.

"You said it was long. Tell me about it. Any funny resident stories? Any coworkers that pissed you off?"

"You go first."

"Well, it was long. I kept watching the clock. I didn't want to be late to pick you up, and I was excited to see you. Both of you," he says, his eyes flashing to Madeline.

"My brothers and I had our weekly Monday morning meeting. We each give an update of what's going on in our departments, issues we might be having, and our schedules for the week."

"What's it like working side by side with your brothers?"

"Like working with my best friends. My parents started the company with just one truck, and now we're all over the United States."

"How were your positions decided?"

"It just kind of happened. Royce, as the oldest, it was always assumed he would take over as CEO. Owen is the numbers guy. Always has been. He's a whiz, so for him to be CFO made sense. Grant, he's a people person. He has this calm demeanor about him, so it was fitting for him to be CCO. Conrad was always into the latest technology growing up. He was fascinated by it. CIO was a no-brainer."

"What about you?"

"I'm like Grant. I'm a people person, but I had no desire to be their boss, if that makes sense. Yes, I have employees who report directly to me, but Grant, he has all the plant managers that report to him, and that's just never something that interested me. I didn't want to put out fires and have that weight on my shoulders. I was good at graphic design in college, and I minored in marketing." He shrugs. "CMO made sense.

"So, other than my weekly meeting with my brothers, I spent my day analyzing our latest marketing campaign results and thinking about you." As soon as the words are out of his mouth, the doorbell chimes. "That's dinner. Be right back." He hops to his feet, and I watch him walk away.

The beat of my heart feels as if there is a herd of wild horses tromping around in my chest. I told myself I wasn't going to fall for him. How is that possible when he says things like that?

CHAPTER
Marshall
FIFTEEN

"**O**NE MORE PIECE," I urge Wren. She groans and places her hand over her belly.

"I can't do it."

"Sure you can."

"I had two pieces, two breadsticks, and that pile of wings." She points to her plate. "I'm stuffed."

"You have to have a brownie still."

"Are you trying to kill me?"

"No." I laugh. I am trying to fill her belly, though. She loves pizza, yet she rarely gets it. I know it's not because she's watching her sexy-as-fuck figure, not with the way she just devoured her meal. Money is tight for her, and I've been sitting here all night thinking of ways that I might be able to help her. All I can think of is that she needs to have dinner with me every night—her and Madeline.

"I still have to go home and give Madeline a bath before bed. How am I supposed to do that if I'm too stuffed to move?"

"I'll stay and help," I offer. I know she's a mom and has responsibilities, but I'm not ready for them to go home just yet.

"You keep this up, I'm going to get spoiled," she says as I stand and collect our trash.

"What's wrong with you being spoiled?" I call out from the kitchen. She doesn't answer, so I finish tossing our trash, grab two more bottles of water, and make my way back to them. "Well?" I ask her.

"I don't want to get used to it."

"Why not?" I cock my head to the side to study her.

"If I allow myself to get used to this," she points at me and then herself, "it will hurt even more when it's gone. When you're gone."

Panic sets in. Why is she talking about this ending before it even begins? Hell, we don't even know what this is yet. "I'm not going anywhere."

"You can't make that promise, Marshall."

"You're right. I can't. I can promise you that if it's within my power, I won't be going anywhere."

She gives me a sad smile. "I should be getting home."

It's on the tip of my tongue to ask her to stay, but I know that's pushing my luck. "Let's get Maddie packed up, and I'll take you home." I don't like it, but it's out of my control. I hate that she lives there. I hate that her place is the size of a shoebox and that she has to carry Madeline everywhere. She can't use her stroller because of the steps. She can't carry the stroller and the baby down the steps at the same time. I hate that I have the means to help her, but I know that she won't accept the handout. Maybe if I could find a way to spin it by saying that Madeline needs it, I could get her into a better place? My wheels are already turning with possibilities and ideas.

She gets Madeline strapped in, and I pick up the carrier. "You ready to go home, baby girl?" She coos up at me, waving her arms and kicking her legs. She really is the cutest. "Ready?" I ask Wren.

"Yes." Together we head to the garage, and I work on getting Madeline's seat installed in the SUV.

"Thank you for dinner," she says once we're on the road.

"You're welcome." I reach over and place my hand on her thigh. I need that connection with her. I'm not sure how she feels about me always touching her. She doesn't stiffen or shy away from my touch, so I'm going with it. I've never been that guy. Sure, I like to show affection just as much as the next guy, but this constant need to have my hands on her? That's new for me.

"What's your schedule the rest of the week?" I ask. "Can we do dinner again?"

"You want to do dinner again?" she asks. I can hear the surprise in her voice.

"I told you that I wanted to spend more time with you."

"I know you did. I guess I just didn't think it would be so frequent."

"Are you tired of me already?" I hold my breath waiting for her answer. If she says yes, I don't know what I'll do. I crave time with her.

"No." She's quick to reply. "It's not that. I just... never mind."

"Tell me." I pull into her lot and put the SUV into Park. "It's nice that we live so close," I say when I turn to face her.

She gives me a soft smile that causes my heart to skip a beat. "You're out of my league, Marshall. I don't know if this is pity or what, but you don't have to take care of me. I'm doing okay on my own."

Her words light a fire inside me. Without further thought, I lean over the console, slide one hand behind her neck, and bring her lips to mine. I kiss her like I've been dying to do. She's still at first, but I won't let that deter me. *Kiss me back, baby.* I trace her lips with my tongue, and she moans, and just like that, Wren is kissing me back.

My body is telling me to devour her, but my head is urging me to take this slow. I don't want her to think I'm trying to get her into bed. Sure, I've imagined her riding my cock, but that's not what this is. I'm not sure exactly how to name it, but I know it's more than that. Gradually, I slow the kiss and rest my forehead against hers.

"Never again, Wren," I say, trying to catch my breath. "I don't ever want to hear you say that again. Money, name, status, none of that matters. What matters is what's in here." I grab her hand and place it over my heart.

"I like you too much already," she whispers.

"Good." I kiss her lips, just a quick, chaste kiss, before pulling away. "That means you're not immune to my charms." I wink, trying to lighten the mood a little. "Now, let's get Maddie upstairs and into the tub so we can tuck her in."

"We?"

"I told you I would stay and help."

"You offered," she counters.

"Well, now I'm following through." Not giving her a chance to argue, I grab the keys from the ignition and climb out of my SUV. Making my way around the back of the car, I pull open the back door and release Madeline's seat. I wait for Wren to grab the diaper bag. I know if I try to carry that too, she'll argue with me. Once she has everything she needs, I place my hand on the small of her back, and we make our way inside.

"Uh, come on in," she says once she unlocks the door.

I try my hardest not to let my eyes scan the room. Instead, I focus on Madeline. The last thing I want is for Wren to think I'm judging her. I'm not. It's just that this place is so small, and she really needs a ground floor space or something with an elevator. The thought of her hauling her groceries up, pulling a cart while carrying Madeline doesn't sit well with me.

"I'm just going to go get everything ready. The bathroom is kind of small, so you don't have to help."

"I want to. You get situated, and I'll come keep you company. How's that?"

She nods. "Okay."

"I'll watch Maddie while you get everything ready." She hesitates only for a fraction of a second before disappearing into the door that I assume is the bathroom. I hear her moving around and then see her buzz across the small hallway. I unbuckle

Madeline from her car seat and lift her in my arms. She stretches her little body, then rests her head against my shoulder.

"Ready," she says a few minutes later.

"Time for a bath," I tell the baby as I walk toward the bathroom. Wren holds her arms out, and I transfer Madeline to her.

"So, you never did answer me. What are your plans for the rest of the week?"

She glances at me from over her shoulder before turning her attention back to Madeline. "It's not like I have a booming social life. I go to work, then Madeline and I spend a quiet night at home before doing it all over again."

"I see a change in your future, Wren Wheeler." I flash her a grin even though she can't see me.

"What did you have in mind?" she asks.

"Dinner. Maybe we can take Maddie to the park? Or we can set up some playtime with Carter and Roan?" I suggest. I want to make sure that I include Madeline. She doesn't have many people in her life, and I want to reassure Wren that I know they're a package deal.

"We could do that," she agrees cautiously.

I don't push her any further. That's all the agreement I need. I'll take care of planning us getting together. Madeline having a routine is important. I've heard my brothers and their wives talk about that with their kids. We can hang out here. I'll bring dinner. Hell, I could watch Madeline while she runs errands or even takes a nap. I wonder how long it's been since she's been able to just stop and relax. Raising kids is hard work, and she's doing it all on her own.

"Shoot. I forgot a diaper," she says, pulling me out of my thoughts.

"Where are they? I'll grab one."

"Just across the hall underneath the changing table."

Stepping out of the bathroom, I turn and enter the bedroom. My mouth drops open. The room before me is vastly different from the rest of their apartment. The room is painted in a pale pink with white trim. The furniture is a light gray, and the bedding is a mix of pink and gray, and white. On the wall above the crib, gray letters with white lace spell out Madeline's name. There is a white rocking chair in the corner and a white bookcase filled with children's books. The room is beautiful, the perfect setting for a little girl. However, there is one thing missing.

A bed for Wren.

Grabbing a diaper from underneath the changing table, I turn and make my way back to the bathroom. "Here you go," I say, handing her the diaper.

"Thank you." She smiles up at me from her place on the floor. "You ready to get dressed and get your belly full?" she asks Madeline.

I watch as she stands from the floor, grabs the diaper, pajamas, and a bottle of lotion, and makes her way to the living room. Taking a seat on the couch, she makes quick work of getting a diaper on the baby and continues on with their nightly routine. Once Madeline is dressed, Wren reaches for the blanket on the back of the couch and covers her chest before lifting her shirt.

I take a seat next to her and turn so that I'm facing her. I need to see her expression when I ask her this question. "Can I ask you something?"

"Sure."

"Where do you sleep?"

She closes her eyes and sighs. "I told you that you were out of my league, Marshall."

"Stop. Tell me. Where do you sleep?" I hold her gaze, waiting for her to tell me. I know the answer. The only possible answer is the couch we're sitting on.

"I sleep here."

"The couch?" I ask for clarification.

"Yes."

I swallow hard. It's on the tip of my tongue to tell her to come home with me. I have enough space for both of them. Instead, all

I can manage to do is nod. I keep my mouth clamped shut. I don't want to offend her, and I'm not sure if I were to speak at this moment that I wouldn't.

"I had to give up our apartment. I couldn't afford it. I used the small life insurance to live on until Madeline was born and to buy what I would need for her." Her voice is soft.

Defeated.

"Wren." Reaching out, I take her hand that's not holding onto her daughter into mine. "If you ever need anything, anything at all, I want you to come to me." I feel sick knowing that the amazing, beautiful woman is struggling when I have the means to help her. I know she won't take my help, though. She's too proud and already has this misplaced concept that she's beneath me. That couldn't be further from the truth.

"We're doing okay." She smiles down at her daughter.

I nod instead of speaking. I know that if I were to speak right now, anything that I could or would say wouldn't sit right with her. Like, come home with me, hell, move in with me. The thought of her living in my space doesn't scare me at all. I'm more worried about the two of them living here. Even though Wren is taking excellent care of Madeline, she needs someone to take care of her. I can do that. If only she would let me.

"I'm going to put her to bed," she says, pulling me out of my thoughts.

I stand and follow her down the hall. She carefully places Madeline into her crib and kisses her fingertips, placing them on her forehead. I sneak up behind her, place one hand on her hip, and kiss the fingertips of the other, placing them in the same place as her mother. "Night, baby girl," I whisper.

Together, we walk back out to the living area, and Wren has to stifle her yawn.

"I should let you get to bed," I say, swallowing hard. The couch is her fucking bed.

"Thank you for tonight."

"I had fun spending time with you."

"We had fun too."

"I'll bring dinner by tomorrow night."

"You don't have to," she starts, but I stop her by pressing a soft kiss to her lips. "I'll be at your work at five, and we can pick something up and bring it back."

"Marshall—" she starts, but I kiss her again.

"See you tomorrow, Wren." I step away from her and walk to the door. "Lock up behind me."

"Always. Goodnight."

"Night."

I step outside and wait until I hear the click of the lock before descending the stairs and heading to my SUV. The entire drive home, my mind is racing with how I can help her. That same worry goes well into the night. By the time my alarm clock blares, I've had a few hours' sleep at best. However, I'm not irritated. I get to see her again tonight, and maybe, just maybe, an idea will come to me today.

"What's this special meeting for?" I ask, walking into the conference room.

"I have something I want to talk to you all about," Royce says cryptically.

My other three brothers file into the room, asking similar questions and getting similar answers. I pour myself a cup of coffee. I don't usually drink it, but I need something to keep my ass awake today. I also grab an apple strudel from the tray. It's not as good as anything that comes from Warm Delights, but it will do.

"I want to run something by you," Royce says, standing at the end of the table. He looks very much the CEO that he is.

"What's up?" Grant asks.

"Sawyer and I were talking last night. We love that Mom and Dad are watching Roan."

"And Carter," Owen chimes in.

"And Carter," Royce nods. "However, with two new babies coming soon, we're afraid it might be too much for them. On top of that, I know they have things they want to do. Travel, and whatnot. I feel guilty that they're tied down watching my son."

"You know they love it," I tell him.

He nods. "They do. And I appreciate knowing my son is safe, and I know that Owen does too. However, I think we need to look at an alternative solution. There are five of us. If we all have two kids each, hopefully, more..." He grins. "...that's going to be a hell of a lot to ask of our retired parents."

"What are you suggesting?" Conrad asks.

"Well, I have two suggestions, actually. We have the second floor that we're not currently using. I say we convert the entire floor to a day care. We would do intense backgrounds on all workers, and our kids would be here with us all day long. I'm thinking video cameras everywhere, extra security on the doors and windows," he rambles. "Mom and Dad can have unlimited access to come and see the kids, or even choose to keep one or more of them some days. But it won't be something they feel like they have to do. They can enjoy retirement and being grandparents."

"I like it," Owen says, sitting up in his chair.

"Would this just be for Riggins' children or anyone who works in this building?" I ask as my wheels are turning.

"I say we open it to all employees. Offer them a discounted rate on childcare," Royce says.

"We could do payroll deduction," Grant adds. "Make it even easier for them."

"Why don't we just offer free day care for all Riggins employees in this building?" Owen asks. "We don't need the money, and we can use the deduction as a tax write-off."

"You're the numbers guy, O. If you think that's feasible, then I'm good with it," Conrad tells him.

"Me too," Grant says.

"Me three," I agree.

"Let's do it." Royce grins.

"I have someone we can hire," I blurt as my wheels begin to spin. Wren is an incredible mother, and I have no doubt she would be the same with other children. She would be a Riggins employee and could bring Madeline and get free childcare. That would free her up financially. She said day care is a huge chunk of her pay. Hell, maybe she can run it?

"Who?" all four of my brothers ask at the same time.

"Wren." I go on to tell them her financial situation, swearing them to secrecy. I also tell them about her background in early childhood education. I don't know if her certifications are up to date, but that should be easy enough to do if not. At least I think it will be. I make a mental note to check into it.

"Sounds like she's qualified," Grant comments.

"I thought she was a nurse's aide?" Conrad asks.

"She is. She couldn't find work, so she took a twelve-week CNA program when she was pregnant with Maddie. She needed a job close to home since she sold her car."

"Damn," Owen mutters.

"Bring her on," Royce says. "She can help us set it up. Our wives can help too. Wren is a mom, and we could use her input. I know our wives would agree. They've grown quite fond of her."

"They're not the only ones." Grant smirks.

"She's cool." I nod. "And thanks. I'll run this by her and see what she says."

"No." Royce shakes his head. "Let Aspen do it." He looks at Conrad. "Can you get Aspen to handle it? I feel as though it will be better received coming from her than a handout from Marshall."

"I hate to admit it, but I think you're right," I agree.

"It's settled," Owen speaks up. "I like the idea of my boy being close. With Layla and me working here, I know she will as well." His smile is wide. Layla and Carter really have softened my big brother.

"What was the other thing?" Grant asks.

Royce smiles. "I think we should use the extra space on the bottom floor for Warm Delights." He looks at Grant and then Conrad. "We could have them close, and let's face it, all five of us stop there almost daily. We could have them in-house for meetings, etc. Plus, I know that Owen and I love working so close to our wives. I could only imagine that the two of you will as well."

"Hell yes." Conrad grins.

"I'm not going to say no to that."

"We currently have three elevators. I want one dedicated to the day care only. I want to install a code, so if you don't have the code, you're not going up. The other will take you to any floor except for ours and the second where the day care is."

"Can we do that?" Grant asks.

Royce laughs. "If we throw enough money at it, we can. The third elevator will go directly to our floor. The receptionist will have to enter a code to send up visitors, and all will be announced."

"Why the extra security all of a sudden?" I ask.

"Well, with having the kids here, I was thinking we could take that huge storage room at the end of the hall that we never use and make it a nursery of sorts. If we want time with our kids, we can have a place with just family. Also, as they grow older, we can let them run around and not worry about anyone grabbing them."

"Are we ever going to get any work done?" Owen laughs. "I can see my boy racing through these halls."

Royce laughs too. "That's the idea."

"Let's do it. Who's going to present that to Aurora and Aspen?" Owen asks.

"Sawyer," we all say at the same time.

"I'll get my plans for both down on paper, and we can meet again at the end of the week. I want to move fast on this."

We all nod and head back to our own offices. Just like that, I've found a way to help Wren. I just hope that Aspen can convince her to change jobs and come and work for us. It would be a huge help to her, and I'll make sure she's well compensated even if I have to pay her check out of my own pocket.

CHAPTER
Wren
SIXTEEN

I 'M NERVOUS. MARSHALL and I have been spending more time together. Actually, we spend a lot of time together. Every day over the last month, I've seen him. We make dinner at his place or mine throughout the week. On the weekends, we take Madeline to the park, and last weekend we took her to the aquarium. I tried to argue that she was too little to remember, but Marshall didn't seem to care. He insisted we take her.

I have to admit it was a great day.

Now, here we are at a restaurant, waiting on Carrie, and her new man, Elijah, to meet us for lunch. I'm nervous that my longest friend is meeting Marshall for the first time. I don't know what we are. We kiss, we hold hands, and we snuggle on his couch and mine, but that's it. He's made no comments about us being more, and neither have I. That last conversation was when he said he wanted to spend time with me.

Another reason I'm nervous, we left Madeline with Lena and Stanley. Marshall picked us up early, stating he had to help his dad move something in the garage. While they were working, Madeline and I sat with Lena. When Marshall came back in the house and asked if I was ready, of course, they asked where we were headed. Then Lena graciously offered to watch Madeline for me. I hesitated until Marshall placed his hand on the small of my back. "Thanks, Mom," he'd said. "We like taking her with us." Something about that statement pulled at me. This amazing man is spending time with my daughter and me, and even though I didn't need a break from her, maybe he does. I blurted that they could keep her and that I would pay them. That got me a stern look from Stanley. He then proceeded to tell me that I was family and to go and enjoy a few hours of adult time.

That brings us to now. We're sitting side by side in a small corner booth. Marshall has his hand on my thigh as we discuss the menu. "What sounds good, babe?" he asks me.

"I'll probably just get a burger or something."

"Hey." He leans in, locking his eyes with mine. "You okay?"

"Yes."

"Wren." His tone is a warning, and I sigh. "I'm nervous for you to meet her and her you. I'm nervous Madeline is with your parents."

"Let's call them." Before I can stop him, he's punching numbers on his phone, and his mom appears on the screen.

"Hello."

"Hey, Mom. Just checking in on Maddie."

"Oh, well, she has your dad wrapped around her little finger." She turns the phone to show Stanley in his recliner, sound asleep with a slumbering Madeline on his chest. "He's a baby hog," Lena grumbles.

"Thank you for watching her," I say, emotion welling in my throat.

"She's such a joy, Wren. Anytime you need us to look after her, you just call."

"Thank you." I nod, feeling the hot sting of tears.

"Thanks, Mom. Love you," Marshall tells her.

"Love you too. Have fun, and don't rush home. We're good here." She ends the call, and Marshall places his phone on the table between us.

"Anytime you want to call and check on her, my phone is right there. Mom and Dad won't care if you call a million times. They're used to Owen and Royce." He chuckles.

"I'm good," I assure him.

"Hey, hey." I hear Carrie say as she approaches the table. She slides into the booth to sit across from me, and Elijah sits across from Marshall.

"Marshall Riggins." Marshall offers his hand across the table to Elijah.

"Elijah Danning," he says, taking Marshall's hand.

"Carrie, this is Marshall."

"Nice to meet you." Marshall offers her his hand as well.

"You too. Elijah, this is my bestie, Wren. Where's Maddie?" she asks.

"Oh, um, Marshall's parents are watching her." Carrie's eyes go wide at my confession, and she knows that it's a huge deal. It took me months of searching while pregnant for a day care with a good reputation to leave Madeline with every day. The only other person who has ever watched her is Carrie.

"That's nice of them." Carrie smiles at us.

"They pretty much insisted," Marshall tells her. Just as he says it, a message pops up on his phone. I see it's from his mom, and panic wells up inside me. "Go ahead and look, babe," he tells me.

Normally, I'd never take his phone and open his messages, but they have my baby. Swiping the screen, I open the message and a picture pops up. It's of Stanley and Madeline. They're both still sleeping, but Madeline is now sticking her little bottom in the air with her hands curled under her face. Stanley had his hand on her back, and neither of them is remotely aware that Lena took a picture of them. I can feel the smile on my face.

"Everything good?" Marshall asks.

I nod. "Yes. Everything is perfect." I turn his phone so he can see the screen, and he laughs.

"Dad is such a sucker."

"Like you don't ever sleep with her on your chest," I counter.

He shrugs unapologetically. "She's cute as hell and she's a good snuggle buddy."

"Let me see," Carrie says. I turn the phone to show her. Elijah leans in to look as well. "Aw." She smiles. "Looks like Madeline is being well taken care of."

That line was for me, but I appreciate her attempt to show me her approval. "That she is." I smile at Marshall and hand him his phone.

"You keep it in case she calls or sends another picture."

His trust in me and the fact that he doesn't care a single fraction of a bit that I have his phone does something to me. He's not the player that I expected him to be. At least he's not anymore. I want to lean over and kiss him, but I know that's not appropriate. However, Marshall doesn't seem to care about being appropriate when he leans in close and presses his lips to mine. It's a soft peck, but it feels like so much more.

"You can't look at me like that and me not kiss you," he whispers.

"Hi, can I start you off with some drinks?" our waitress asks.

The next two hours fly by as we talk and laugh like the four of us have been hanging out for years. "This has been so much fun," Carrie says as we stand to leave.

"We should do it again sometime," Marshall speaks up.

"Definitely," Elijah agrees. "Good to meet you both." He nods at Marshall and me.

"Marshall, I think I owe my girl's smiles to you. Keep up the good work," Carrie says, embarrassing me.

Marshall slings his arm around my shoulder and pulls me into his chest. "That's the plan."

Out on the street, we say our goodbyes, and then it's just the two of us. "Are you in a hurry to get back?" Marshall asks.

"Not particularly. That last message your mom sent tells me Madeline is being spoiled rotten." It's true. She sent a picture about fifteen minutes ago of Madeline sitting on Stanley's lap, and he was reading her a story.

"I have a few things I need to do. I wanted you to go with me."

"Sure." I shrug.

"Great. Let's go." He laces his fingers through mine and leads me to his SUV.

"So, where are we going?" I ask once we're on the road and headed out of town.

"Well, there are a couple of houses that just came on the market that I want to do a drive-by on. My realtor sent them to me late last night."

"You're moving?" I turn to look at him.

He keeps his eyes on the road as he shrugs. "Maybe. I'm ready to get out of town. I'm jealous of my brothers being about to sit out on their back decks and have a cold beer at the end of the day."

"Yeah, but you love your condo. You love that it's close to the nightlife."

"I used to love it."

"You don't anymore?"

"I don't know if you've noticed, but I'm not exactly out partying every night."

"I know, but you could be. I mean, when you're bored, you could be."

"I know what you're trying to say, Wren, and you're wrong. I'm not going to get bored of you. I'm not going to get bored of Madeline."

"This is a big step."

"I've grown out of the condo phase. It's time to buy a big boy house." He chuckles.

"I think you should think about this before you do it."

"I have thought about it. Why do you think I'm looking at houses?"

"You've never said anything about it."

"I'm saying something now." He turns into a driveway of a house that takes my breath away. "I've been considering it for a while now. Conrad hooked me up with his realtor, and she's been on the lookout for something that fits my wish list. Last night she sent me three, and all three are close to what I want."

"What is it that you want?"

"Some land, an awesome backyard. I have a big family and want to be able to have them over. An open floor plan. Five bedrooms, a basement, and at least a three-car garage. I can build another garage for my toys, so that's not a deal breaker for me."

"Why do you, a single man, need a house that big?"

"I'm not going to be single forever." He winks at me.

My stomach flips and knots at the same time. The thought of him not being single causes the knots to form. We're hanging out, but we've never labeled us, and he never presses me for more than kisses. I'm so confused, but I don't dare ask what's going on. I already know he's just passing the time. Why else has he made no move for us to be more?

"Come on," he says, grabbing his keys and climbing out of the car.

"Are we allowed to be here?" I ask, trailing after him.

"Yes. The owners have already moved out."

"Okay," I say hesitatingly. He reaches back and takes my hand in his as we walk around peeking in windows. "You know, realtors can actually get you inside," I tease.

"I know, but I've looked at the pictures. I just want to get an idea of the lay of the land and see if the outside is what I want. The inside can be changed."

"Good point," I agree.

"This one's okay," he finally says, "but I think the other one is going to be better. At least from the pictures. It's hard to tell."

He leads me back to the car, and we drive to a house that's maybe two miles from Grant and Aurora. "Wow," I say when we pull into the driveway.

"Right?" he agrees. "This one ticks off all of my boxes. Twenty acres, five bedrooms, four-car garage, full finished basement, open concept, the inside is immaculate from the pictures, huge walk-in shower in the master bath."

"Sounds nice."

"It is. There's a huge patio in the back, with a sunken fire pit, a pool, and a hot tub. That's what I want to see," he says, rubbing his hands together.

Together, we walk around, peering in windows, and from what I can see, this one is so much nicer than the first. When we walk around to the backyard, or should I say back oasis, I know this is the one he's going to choose.

"This is it," he says as if reading my thoughts. He pulls his phone out of his pocket. "Marshall Riggins," he greets whoever he called. He rattles off the address. "Perfect. See you then." He ends the call and smiles at me. "That was the realtor. Her assistant is in the area just finishing with an open house and is coming over to show it to us." He grins like a kid who has just been taken to a candy store and told to go crazy with anything he wants. It's infectious and endearing.

"Well?" Marshall asks. We've just pulled out of the driveway of the house that I'm certain he's going to buy.

"I think it's a beautiful home."

"I love it."

"You're buying it, aren't you?"

"Hell yes, I am. I told her to offer full asking."

"You didn't even negotiate?"

"Nope." He reaches over and places his hand on my thigh. "You ready to go get your girl?" he asks.

"Yes."

On the short drive to his parents,' he talks about the house and how it's exactly what he's been hoping to find. He talks about it being close to his family, which is important to him. The Riggins are a tight-knit group, and I love that about them. I envy what they have. The entire drive, he never removes his hand from my thigh. It's a move he does all the time and one I've come to crave from him.

When we get to his parents,' Madeline squeals when she sees us, but Marshall makes it to her first. He gives her a hug and then holds his hand out for me. I take it, and he pulls me into his chest as well. "Thanks for watching her," he tells his parents.

"Thank you."

"Anytime. We enjoyed it," Stanley says.

"Next time you're going with them, you baby hog," Lena teases.

"Hey, it's the Riggins charm," he quips, making us laugh.

"Wren, you must come for Sunday dinner tomorrow," Lena says.

"Oh, I don't want to intrude."

"Mom, I've been trying to get her to come for weeks. Good luck," Marshall grumbles.

"Darlin.'" Stanley comes to stand in front of me. "You and that angel of yours are always welcome in our home. We'd love to have you," he tells me.

How do I say no to that? "Okay." I nod. "Thank you for the invitation. What can I bring?"

"Yourself and that baby of yours. Marshall, you'll make sure they get here?" Lena asks.

"I'm all over it. I don't even care that you gave into Dad and not me. I'm just really glad you're coming to Sunday dinner. Finally," he exaggerates.

"Stop." I smile up at him.

"We'll see you tomorrow," he says.

Just like that, I've agreed to have dinner with the entire Riggins family.

CHAPTER
Marshall
SEVENTEEN

"**H**EY, DON'T BE nervous," I say, pulling into the driveway of my parents' house.

"Easier said than done," Wren mutters.

"Wren." I say her name in *that* way. Do you know the look that you get when someone wants you to look at them? I know that she knows that's what I want, but she ignores me. She's freaking out. She has nothing to be nervous about. She's hung out with my family many times, hell they watched her daughter yesterday, but this, today, it feels different. This is a family gathering. Meant for family. I know what she's thinking, that she and Madeline aren't family, but they could be. I shake out of that line of thinking. Today is not the day to go there.

"Maddie, tell Mommy it's going to be fine," I say. I know Wren well because she turns to look at her daughter in the back seat, but I stop her, capturing her face with my hands. "We want you here. You know my sisters love you, and so does everyone else. My parents pretty much insisted that you be here."

"What about you?" she asks softly.

"I want you both here," I say, giving her a smile that I hope eases her fears.

"Okay." She nods, pushing back her shoulders.

"There's my girl." I lean over the console of my SUV and kiss the corner of her mouth. "I'll get Maddie." With that, I grab my keys and climb out of the SUV. Opening the back-passenger door, I lift Madeline, seat and all, before closing the door. Wren is standing beside me with the diaper bag in hand. "If at any time you feel as though you want to leave, you tell me, and we're gone. I don't want you feeling uncomfortable."

"You can't leave your family dinner."

"I can and I will. You say the word and we're gone," I say again.

"Thank you, Marshall." Rising on the balls of her feet, she presses a kiss on my cheek.

Taking advantage of the opportunity, I slide my arm around her waist, holding her close. "Anything for you, Wren. Anything." My voice is soft, but the seriousness of my tone isn't lost on her. I can see it in her eyes. Moving my hand to the small of her back, I lead her up the front steps of my parents' house. Inside, I set the car seat on the floor and expertly release Madeline from its confines. "Ready to be loved on, baby girl?" I ask her.

The adorable little girl coos at me, and I kiss the top of her head. "Come," I say, holding my hand out for Wren. Hand in hand, we make our way to the kitchen, and I stop. Something is wrong. Mom's not cooking. "What's going on?" I ask. "I thought we were having dinner? What's happened? Who's sick?" I fire off questions to my parents.

"Nothing is wrong," Mom says with a blinding smile. "No one is sick, and we are having dinner. We're switching things up today."

"As soon as Royce and Owen get here, we'll explain," Dad tells me.

"Everyone's okay?" I ask, needing to make sure.

"Everyone is fine," Dad assures me.

"Where are Con, Grant? I saw their trucks outside."

"They're… here," Mom says cryptically.

"These people are hiding something, Maddie," I tell the baby, snuggling her to my chest.

"Want me to take her?" Wren asks.

"Nah, babe. I've got her." She always asks, and I know she's just making sure I don't feel obligated. "We're best buds, right, Maddie?" I ask the baby, bouncing her a little in my arms, making her giggle. That sound always brings a smile to my face.

"Hey, where is everyone?" Royce asks. He has Roan in his arms and Sawyer clutched to his side.

"Why's it so quiet in here?" Owen asks, stepping beside Royce. Carter is in his arms and already reaching for my dad. Layla smiles as she watches Dad steal Carter from Owen. My brother grumbles about him stealing his son, but otherwise, he's too distracted, wanting to know what the hell's going on.

"Well, we have a surprise for you," Mom tells us.

"Wait, where are Con and Grant?" Owen asks.

"As I was saying"—Mom gives him a pointed look that we all know means, hush and let her finish. It's one we've seen a lot over the years—"today we have a special Sunday dinner."

"What?" Royce, Owen, and I ask at the same time.

"Go on out back and see." Mom smiles.

"Why are the blinds closed?" Royce asks before I get a chance to.

"Just go on outside, boys." Dad chuckles. Carter must think that's his cue to laugh because he begins to giggle for no reason.

"They're your sons," Mom tells Dad. I can hear the exasperation in her voice, and that, too, makes me grin.

"Boys," Dad says in his stern dad voice. "Just go outside, would ya?"

"Boys?" Owen scoffs and the entire room erupts in laughter.

"Just go," Mom says, holding her stomach from laughing.

"Come on." I reach for Wren's hand and we make our way to the door.

"Sure, let the baby of the family go first," Royce grumbles.

"You losers were dragging your feet. You snooze, you lose," I tell them, dropping Wren's hand to pull open the patio door.

"What?" I stop in my tracks.

"Let me see." This from Royce.

"Move, Marsh," Owen whines.

My parents' backyard has a huge white tent. Underneath the tent, there are white chairs with ribbon and some other decorations. "Mom? Are we having a bigger party than Sunday dinner?" I call out.

"Wait? When is their anniversary?" Owen whispers. "We didn't miss it, did we?" he asks.

Laughter from beside the house breaks out, and we all turn to look at Grant and Conrad. "We didn't think y'all would ever get here," Conrad complains.

"What's going on?" Royce asks.

"Well, boys, today is my wedding day." Conrad puffs out his chest, and I swear if he smiles any wider, his face is going to crack.

"No shit?" Royce, Owen, and I all murmur.

"Why are you the privileged one?" I ask Grant.

He shrugs. "I'm married to the sister of the bride."

"Can you all please go sit down so I can marry the love of my life? I'm afraid if I make Aspen wait any longer, she's going to change her mind."

"Not happening." I hear Aspen call out from somewhere in the house. Turning, I look up and see her and Aurora sticking their heads out of the upstairs window. They're in Conrad's old room.

"Love you, babe," Conrad calls up to her.

"Love you too. I'm coming down," she tells him.

"Finally." He winks up at her.

"This is really happening?" I ask Conrad.

"This is really happening," Conrad confirms.

I break away from our small group that's gathered on the back deck, Madeline still in my arms, and pull him into a hug. "I'm happy for you," I tell him, getting choked up. That's no surprise. As brother number four, who claims to have found his magic and grow our family, not only giving me another sister but another nephew, I'm used to the emotions that grab me. I've watched all four of them fall head over ass in love, and the women they've chosen only make our family better. Stronger.

"You okay?" I feel Wren's hand on my arm.

"I'm great." I smile at her. "Let's go grab a seat."

Hand in hand, we make our way to the tent and sit. Wren tries to take Madeline from me, but the sweet girl snuggles into my chest, hiding her arms. "She's fine, baby," I tell Wren.

There's a lot of commotion while my brothers and their families, along with my parents, choose seats. I'm getting ready to ask where the minister is when Dad steps up to the altar of flowers.

Placing my hand on Mom's shoulders, I whisper, "Is Dad marrying them?"

She turns to smile at me. "He is. He was ordained online."

"That's cool as hell," I reply.

"Marshall, watch your mouth around that baby," she scolds.

"Sorry, Maddie," I tell the baby in my arms, placing a soft kiss on her head. She doesn't seem to mind my language or my kisses.

Conrad takes his place standing before Dad, as Grant hits Play on his phone, and the "Wedding March" comes through the speakers that are placed throughout the tent. My eyes flash to Aurora and her parents, who are both waiting with bated breath for Aspen to appear. Then I turn back to my brother. With each of their weddings, aside from the first wedding for Royce, I've watched them. I know I'm supposed to watch the bride, but it's the expression on each of my brothers' faces that I will always remember about their weddings. The day they get to see the love of their life walk down the aisle to them.

Conrad smiles and bites down on his bottom lip. I can see the tears as they pool in his eyes. I watch as his throat bobs with his thick swallow, fighting back his emotions. He's unable to stand still as he shifts his weight from foot to foot. I watch as my dad, who keeps his eyes on Aspen, places his hand on Conrad's shoulder. My brother visibly relaxes, but it's not until Aspen reaches him and he has her hands wrapped in his does he still.

Reaching over, I place my hand on Wren's thigh, and she wraps her arms around mine, snuggling into me. This is the first of my brothers' weddings that I've brought a date to, and I did it right, bringing two. Glancing down, I see that Madeline has fallen asleep. The trust that this little girl has in me makes my heart beat faster inside my chest. Beat by beat. It's as if it's singing for her and for her mom. I don't understand it. I've never spent this much time with one woman, let alone a single mother.

In the back of my mind, I hear my dad telling me it's magic, and I'm not supposed to understand. I wish I knew. Is it the magic that my dad and brothers go on about all the time? Or is it the fact that Wren is amazing and her little girl is too? I like spending time with them, and when I'm not with them, I want to be.

"You may kiss the bride," my dad tells Conrad.

I watch as my brother lays one hand on Aspen's belly and the other cradles her cheek. He whispers something to her that has both Aspen and my dad smiling. Then, he kisses her. It's nothing over the top, but it's slow and intimate, and even though I know that I should look away, I can't. I'm frozen still as I realize that I want what he has, what they all have. Pulling out of my fog, I glance over at Wren as she wipes a tear from her eye.

I want what my brothers have, and I want it with Wren.

Everyone stands and claps, and I join them, even though my life in the last five seconds has changed. I go through the motions, but all I can think about is that my brothers, and my dad, they might not be crazy after all.

The magic might be real.

What other explanation is there for what I feel for Wren and Madeline?

"Are you okay?" Wren asks me.

"Yeah, baby." I pull her into my side and press my lips to her temple. "I'm good," I assure her. It might not be the complete truth, but I will be. Once I process this new development, I will be.

Today was a great day. I didn't expect to be attending my brother's wedding, but it was perfect for Conrad and Aspen. I'm happy for them. Hell, I'm happy for all of my brothers. I glance over to the passenger seat and my mouth tilts in a smile. I'm glad Wren and Madeline chose today to be here. It's on the tip of my tongue to ask her to stay at my place tonight. I have this urge to just... hold her. Fuck, I've imagined holding her in my arms all night long so many times.

I'm trying not to rush her. I know she's been through so much the past few years, and I kind of just pushed myself into her life. She's not casual. I've known that from the beginning. The more time we spend together, I don't want her to be casual. I want her to be more.

She is more.

"I'll walk you up," I tell her when I park my SUV in front of her building.

"Thank you." She doesn't argue with me. She's learned that on this, she will not win. I hate that she's living here, sleeping on the couch, and with no damn elevator. I need to figure out a way to get her out of here. It's not terrible, it's in a decent neighborhood, but she deserves better. They both do.

"I'm going to put her to bed," she says softly, lifting Madeline out of her car seat once we're inside her apartment.

I nod. "Need some help?"

"No. I'm good. Thank you." She smiles and disappears into Madeline's room.

I take a seat on the couch, which is also her bed. Anger bubbles inside me. Life isn't fair. This amazing woman and her daughter have been through so much, and this is what they have to deal with. I hate that I can fix this for her, but she won't let me. I hope that the plan that my brothers and I have in place works. I need it to work.

"What's wrong?" Wren asks, she's standing in front of where I'm sitting on the couch.

"Nothing."

"This…" she reaches out and runs her thumb over my forehead, "tells me that's not true."

"I was missing you," I tell her, pulling her onto my lap.

"I was gone a couple of minutes at best."

"Too long." I smile at her. My hand slides behind her neck so I can pull her lips to mine. We start slow, tentative at first. When I feel her body relax into mine, I take the kiss deeper. My tongue pushes past her lips, and she meets my efforts stroke for stroke. Turning, I lie back on the couch with her resting on top of me. "This okay?" I murmur against her lips.

"More than okay," she says, fusing her lips to mine once again.

I lose track of time as our hands are all over each other. I can't seem to get enough of her. For every new curve my hands caress, I need more. She seems to have the same problem as her hands roam. I kiss down her neck, and she moans, grinding against my cock.

Fuck me.

I want her. I'm hard as steel, and the way she's grinding against me, tells me she's wet. I can only imagine sliding inside her heat. I need to win her heart first. I freeze as the thought filters through my mind. Holy shit. Wren is magic.

"You okay?"

"I'm more than okay, baby," I assure her. "It's so okay that if I don't leave soon, we might be taking this further than you're ready for."

"I'm ready," she says, kissing my neck.

I believe her, but I've already made up my mind, I want her heart first. The magic is a once-in-a-lifetime deal. If Wren is mine, and I'm pretty sure she is, I'm not going to fuck this up. I might have the worst case of blue balls in the history of blue balls, but she deserves the best, and I'm going to give it to her.

"We both have to be up early for work tomorrow," I remind her.

She sighs, sits up, then stands from my lap. She offers me her hands and pulls me from the couch.

"Baby, when I do make love to you, I need time. Lots of time. It's going to be an all-night kind of experience. I don't want it to be quick."

She opens her mouth to reply, but no words come. She shuts her mouth and nods instead.

"Walk me out," I say, pressing a kiss to the top of her head. With my hand on the small of her back, we walk the small distance to her front door. "Lock up when I leave."

"Always do."

"Night, babe." I kiss her soft and slow.

"Night, Marshall."

CHAPTER
Wren
EIGHTEEN

"**H**EY, YOU," ASPEN says when I open the back door of her SUV. "Hi, Maddie," she calls out to my daughter.

"Hi." I smile and work to get Madeline's car seat strapped in. Sliding into the passenger seat, I pull on my seat belt as well. "So, Sawyer's?"

"Yep. Girls' lunch with the kiddos, of course." She grins.

"What's the occasion?"

She shrugs, keeping her eyes on the road. "We don't have one. We just like to get together and catch up as much as we can. Aurora and I are blessed to have Sawyer and Layla as our sisters-in-law. I've heard so many horror stories about terrible in-laws." She grimaces at just the thought of bad in-laws.

"I have to agree with you there. They're lucky to have you as well. How are you feeling?" I ask her.

"Good. I'm ready to meet him."

"Do you have a name picked out?"

"We've been tossing around a few ideas—nothing concrete. Aurora says she'll know when she sees the baby what his name should be. Grant's on board with that. Conrad and I are more of the 'let's make a decision' frame of mind. However, we can't seem to settle on anything." She chuckles.

"It will come to you. It took me months to decide on Madeline's name. I think I decided a week before I delivered her. I kept second-guessing myself. I'd pick a name and wonder if Travis would approve. In the end, I named her after my mother. Family was important to him, and I knew, at least I hope that he approves."

Aspen reaches over and places her hand on my arm. "He approves. You're an amazing mother, Wren."

"I hope so," I whisper. Clearing my throat, I change the subject. "Are you sure there's not something that I can bring? I feel bad that I'm always coming empty-handed. Maybe we can stop at the store, and I can grab some snacks or something?" I suggest.

"Positive. This is our thing."

"I know, but my place isn't big enough to have everyone over. I feel like I'm mooching off my new friends."

"Never!" she says adamantly. "We love this, and we love that you're joining us. Please don't think that."

"Next time give a girl some notice and I'll whip up something. I'm sure it won't be close to what you and your sister can create, but it will be edible." I laugh.

"Fine." She juts her hand over in front of me and we shake on it.

"Do you all really just spur of the moment have these get-togethers? You didn't know before this morning that you all were getting together?" I ask her.

"Nope. The guys are at the office, working on a new project, so we decided that the five of us should spend the day together."

"Thank you for including me. I know I'm not family, but I love hanging out with all of you."

"We love having you," she says, pulling into Sawyer's driveway.

Before I can open my door, it's being opened for me. Peering up, I see Grant's smiling face. "Hi." I wave awkwardly and climb out of the SUV.

"Hey, Wren. How are you?" he asks.

"Doing well. You?"

He grins. "I'm living the dream," he says, glancing over his shoulder where his wife is standing on the porch waving at us. "Let me carry Maddie in for you," he offers.

"I can manage."

"I know, but I'm here, and I want to."

"I thought you had a meeting?"

"I do. I was dropping Aurora off and was just leaving, but I have the time for Maddie Mae." He grins.

It appears that Madeline's nickname that Grant has given her is sticking with the entire family. And the Mae? I'm not sure where that came from. Her middle name is Elizabeth, but I admit Maddie Mae has a nice ring to it. "Thank you, Grant."

"Anytime."

"I call dibs on the baby!" Aurora calls out to us.

"I'm on my way, Rory," Grant calls back. Without another word, he releases the car seat and turns to head into the house, stopping only to slip his arm around his wife's waist, and they walk in together.

"Told you that you were welcome," Aspen says, sticking her tongue out at me.

Playfully, I roll my eyes, making her laugh. I follow her up the steps to the house and find Aurora already holding Madeline. I take a seat on the recliner, placing her diaper bag and my purse at my feet.

"We need some girls," Aurora tells Madeline. "Yes, we do, sweet girl. There are too many boys."

"Layla!" Sawyer calls out. "It's your turn." Sawyer points at her sister-in-law.

"What? Why is it my turn?" Layla laughs.

"Because Carter is the oldest. You're the closest to having another. We need a girl. M'kay?" Sawyer says, and Madeline giggles.

"Shh, don't let Owen hear you say that," she whispers.

"Oh, is he ready for another?" Aurora asks.

"Pft, if he's anything like Royce, he was ready before you were released from the hospital," Sawyer comments.

"Pretty much," Layla agrees. "I want them to be close, but not Irish twins. That's too close." She shakes her head.

"How are you feeling?" Sawyer asks Aurora and Aspen.

"Great." They smile at one another.

"We're close." Aspen rubs her swollen belly.

"So close," Aurora agrees.

"You plan on hogging her all day?" Layla asks Aurora. "You're not the only one who wants baby snuggles."

"Where's Carter?" I ask her.

"With his daddy." She rolls her eyes, but the smile gracing her lips tells me she's not as annoyed as she wants us to think that she is.

"Owen took him with him to the meeting?"

"Yep." She smiles, popping the p. "Those two are joined at the hip."

"See." Sawyer points at Layla. "We need some girls to even out all this testosterone."

"Do you really think that's going to make a difference?" Aspen asks her. "You know what's going to happen when one of us has a girl, right?"

"What?" Aurora asks, passing a smiling Madeline off to Layla.

"Come on. You have to know that they're going to be daddy's little girls. What's worse is that our husbands are going to convince the boys of the family to 'protect' her." She does air quotes with her hands.

"Shit," Aurora mumbles.

"That's fine," Sawyer speaks up. "They can take the girls and let them wrap them around their pinkies. Then maybe the boys will give their mommas some love." Aspen reaches over and gives her a high-five.

"Are you all hungry? I made some sandwiches and some dips. I figure the guys will all end up here after their meeting anyway."

"I'm starving," Aspen and Aurora reply at the same time.

"Come on, Mommas, let's get you fed."

"You want me to take her?" I ask Layla.

"No. She's too sweet."

"Well, you better get your fill. Once I eat, I'm taking my turn," Sawyer tells her.

"Where's Roan?" Aspen asks.

"He's napping. He should be asleep for a while. He woke us up at five this morning and thought it was time to party. Instead of Royce letting him lay in his crib and chatter himself back to sleep, he got up with him, and they had a little party together." She shakes her head. "And who can sleep when your hot-as-hell husband is playing with your son at 5:00 a.m.?" She shrugs.

"I know what you mean," Layla tells her. "Gets me every time."

"See what you have to look forward to?" Sawyer asks Aspen and Aurora.

"Doesn't seem so bad," Aspen comments.

I can't help but be envious of their relationships with their husbands. Being a single mom, I don't have these kinds of moments. At least I didn't. Marshall has given me a glimpse of what raising a child with a partner might look like.

We spend the next hour or so laughing and eating. All of the girls take a turn holding Madeline, and she's eating up the attention. I send up a silent thank-you to whoever brought these amazing women into my life. I don't feel so alone, and that gives me hope. I hope that Madeline and I will get out of this slump we're in.

"What about you, Wren? Do you want more?" Layla asks. We're back in the living room, bellies full and talking about anything and everything.

I sigh. "I wanted a house full, but I don't think that's in the cards for me. I'm thinking Maddie and I will be a duo for life," I tell them honestly.

"Seriously? Do you not see how Marshall looks at you?" Aspen asks.

"He might want to… you know?" I can feel my face heat. I've never talked openly about this kind of thing to anyone but Carrie. "But Madeline and I are a package deal." I shrug as if my comment makes the most sense in the world.

I startle when all four girls throw their heads back in laughter. Not just ha-ha laughter, I'm talking "hold your belly, my baby is shaking in Aurora's arms" laughing. I mock glare at each of them. At least I try to. Their laughter is infectious and I crack a smile. So much for the mom glare.

"Sweetie," Aspen says gently. "There is something you should know about the Riggins men when they find someone they want. They don't let anything stop them."

"It's not like that with us," I defend, even though my belly flips at the thought of being someone Marshall would want. Sure, he wants to spend time with me and he's kissed me a few times, and—

Holy shit.

"There it is." Sawyer points at my face. "Recognition."

"I'm a single mom," I mumble as I process what I've just finally let myself believe. Marshall Riggins wants to date me. The truth has been there, lingering in the back of my mind, but I never allowed myself to believe it. He's way out of my league, something he and I have discussed, even if he didn't like me saying it. But I have to admit his attention and the kisses don't scream casual to me.

We had dinner every night this week. Two nights at his place and three at mine. Every time he goes to leave, my heart sinks. I love spending time with him. It's not until just now that I've admitted that to myself, and well, now a room full of his sisters.

"So?" Aurora shrugs.

"I have baggage. A little girl who would eventually think of him as her daddy. That's more than he's going to want to sign up for." Is it, though? He's great with Madeline, and even at just a few days shy of seven months old, she already adores him. "And she's not baggage to me," I add. "I love her with everything inside me, and I need a man who is willing to love her like she's a part of him." I get choked up saying the words out loud. "That's a lot of pressure. I don't expect that from him."

Sawyer snuggles Madeline to her chest and smiles. My eyes scan the others and they're all wearing the same expression. "I'm serious," I tell them.

"Why don't you let me make that decision?" a deep voice rumbles from behind me.

My eyes go wide, and this time I pull the mom glare perfectly as I shoot it at my new friends.

At the sound of his voice, Madeline turns to look for him. When she lays eyes on him, she smiles.

"I see you, baby girl," he tells her. "Let me set Mommy straight and then I'll be right there." The next thing I know, Marshall is kneeling in front of me. I can't look anywhere but at him, and I know my face is crimson. I don't know why he's here or if his brothers are with him. What I do know is that he's about to say something that could change us, change me, and his family is going to hear every word of it.

His warm hands gently cradle my face. He stares at me, not saying a word. I wonder if he can hear the rapid beat of my heart. Surely, he can hear it. Right now, beat by beat, I wait for him to speak.

"I know she has a daddy," he says, his voice gruff. "I know that he loved both of you, and if he could be here—" He shakes his head. "It would be an honor for that little girl to think of me as her daddy," he says. His voice is strong, and there isn't a single person in this room who wouldn't believe that what he says is complete truth. "I'll love both of you for both of us," he says.

"What?" I whisper, hot tears pricking the back of my eyes.

"I never met Travis," he says, "but I don't need to for me to know that he was a good man. He earned your trust and your love, and that tells me all that I need to know about him. I'm sorry you and Maddie lost him. I hate that for both of you, but if you'll let me, I'll love you both, for both of us."

Beat.

Beat.

Beat.

Beat.

My heart thunders in my chest. My eyes burn and my palms sweat. This amazing man kneeling before me, he's mended my broken heart. Beat by beat, it's healing, and it's all because of this man.

"What... what are you saying?" I ask. It's a stupid question. I know the meaning of the words, but I'm going to need to hear them again. I'm having a hard time processing this. We've only known each other for a short amount of time, but here he is kneeling, telling me he wants to love my daughter and me. Not just that, but he's going to love her for Travis. A sob breaks free from my chest.

"Don't cry, baby," he says softly. He leans in and presses a kiss to the corner of my mouth.

"What does this mean?" I ask. I should be embarrassed his family is witnessing this conversation, but I need to know. This isn't something you can table to a later date. This needs to happen now, regardless of our audience.

"Fellas?" Marshall calls out. One by one, his brothers ask him what he needs. "You listening?" he asks them.

Eight replies, male and female, give us a resounding "Yes."

"Good." He nods, smiling. "Wren, baby." He swallows again. "You want to know what this is?"

"Please?"

"This is me telling you that I love you. I love your daughter. This is me telling you that I've found my magic."

I don't get a chance to ask him what he means by that. I remember a conversation we had about the magic of love and his family, but he claimed it was a story for another day. He's pulled to his feet, and one by one, his four older brothers hug him tight.

"Sawyer," Marshall calls out, while holding his hand for me. I place my hand in his and allow him to pull me to my feet. "Hand over my girl."

My heart gallops in my chest, and there are a million butterflies swarming in my belly. "Let's take a walk," he says to me.

I nod. I can't speak. I have no words and I don't know that he could hear me over the roar of my heart. Sawyer hands Madeline to him, and she gurgles up at him. "Hey, baby girl." He smiles down at her. "Let's take Momma for a walk." He doesn't say anything to his family, and I don't either. I let him lead me out of the house and out to the spacious backyard.

CHAPTER NINETEEN
Marshall

WITH WREN'S HAND laced with mine and Madeline resting against my chest, I lead us out to the backyard. Neither of us say a word as the emotions and the meaning of what just happened sink in.

I'm in love with her.

This isn't new information to me. I also know that blurting my feelings out to her while we're surrounded by my siblings probably wasn't the best idea. I know that, but I couldn't hold it in. Not when I heard her say that they were a lot to take on. She needed to know that beat by beat, she and Madeline have captured my heart, and I never want it back.

When we make it to the swing underneath a huge shade tree, I sit and pat the empty swing next to me. Wren follows suit and snuggles into my side. My lips press to the top of her head and again to Madeline's, just because I can.

"When we were little, Dad used to tell us a story about the

magic of love. He'd always been hugging and kissing on Mom, and we would give him a hard time for it. He sat us all down and told us that one day we would find our magic love." I pause, waiting to see if she has questions and taking the time to remember all the magic of love stories our dad used to tell us.

"Anyway, when Royce was married the first time, Dad tried to tell him that she wasn't his magic. Royce, like the rest of us, thought that Dad had lost his mind. We should have known with Mom supporting him that there was something to it. Anyway, fast-forward a few years, and Royce's marriage fell apart. He vowed a life of bachelorhood. He threw himself into his position at Riggins Enterprises, and nothing any of us could say could change his mind. Not that my brothers and I tried all that hard, but my parents, they kept telling him he would find his magic."

"Sawyer," she whispers.

"Yeah, baby. Sawyer. He fought it at first. He was convinced that all women were like his ex. Luckily, Sawyer didn't give up on him. He finally pulled his head out of his ass, and he said it hit him like a bolt of lightning. He just knew that she was the only one for him. She was his magic. Once he let himself fall, things fell into place for him."

"They seem happy."

"They are," I agree. "We went from the five Riggins bachelors to four. Which wasn't so bad until Owen, the grumpiest of all of us, fell ass over heels for Layla. He met her on a business trip and convinced her to come home with him and work at RE."

"Layla's told me a little of their story. All the girls have, but I like hearing your version too." She smiles up at me.

"There is a reason behind the history lesson." I chuckle. "Anyway, we all knew the minute Owen called home and asked if there was a spot for Layla in the company that he was a goner. He learned from Royce and didn't fight his feelings. Layla, however, it took her some time, but they're blissfully happy."

"They are," she agrees.

"Grant, on the other hand, the minute he laid eyes on Aurora, he was all in. He pursued her relentlessly. He was patient until she realized she loved him, and well, you know how that story ends too." I laugh.

"That brings us to Con and Aspen. They'd known each other for a year or so, and neither one claims to have any interest other than thinking the other was attractive."

"Aspen told me about them being snowed in and their whirlwind romance."

"Yeah." I nod. "Much like our three older brothers, Conrad claims it just hit him while he was at the cabin, and he knew she was it for him."

"You have a great family."

"Thank you." We swing for a few minutes while I collect my thoughts. "That day at the pharmacy, I could see you were beautiful. Tired as hell, but beautiful. I didn't think any more about it. I had the means to help a mother who needed it, so that's what I did." I shrug.

"You helped us too much. I'll never forget your generosity." She peers up at me under her lashes.

"The day you walked into my office to give me back the money I slipped into your bag, I was… amused to say the least. I was also intrigued. I knew you needed it, but you didn't care about who I was. You didn't care about my last name or the size of my bank account. You just didn't want a handout. You were so different from any woman I'd ever met. I'd love to say that that's the day that I knew you were more to me, but sadly, that's not the case."

"I was so nervous," she confesses. "You're the most handsome man I've ever seen, and you intimidated me."

"Well, you didn't show it," I assure her. "Anyway, the day you showed up with Aspen, and Maddie only wanted me, I felt this burning in my chest. It was a fire I'd never felt before. As time went on, the fire intensified. I didn't understand it, but I wanted to. Us spending more time together was my solution."

Wren sits up and turns her body to face me. She has one leg resting on the swing as the other dangles over the side. "You've been doing a lot of talking." She smiles.

"I just wanted to explain what the magic comment was about. I wanted you to know that when I told you that I'm in love with you, I meant it. I don't just love you. I love you and Maddie."

"Marshall." She raises her hand to my lips. "My turn," she whispers.

I nod, letting her have the chance to tell me how she feels. However, I'm already starting my defense in my head. I'm not letting her walk away. I don't know that I could survive losing them. I know I couldn't.

"I know you've been taking things slow for me, and I appreciate that. Over the past couple of months, you've been there for me around every corner. You help me with taking care of my daughter, and you take care of me." She reaches for my hand and links her fingers with mine. "I loved Travis. He was my best friend. What I feel for you—" She shakes her head and blinks hard a few times, getting her emotions under control. "It's so much more, Marshall. I feel guilty for even saying it, but it's the truth. You bring light to my darkest days. I was going through the motions of life, doing my best to raise Madeline and give her the best life I could. All of a sudden, you ride into our lives like a white knight, and nothing has been the same. Now it's not just my daughter who makes me get out of bed every morning. It's you too. It's knowing that I get to see you that evening, or the potential for a text message during the day."

"I'll always take care of both of you," I tell her with conviction in my voice.

She smiles. "I know you will. That's why I love you."

"Look, I—Wait. Did you just say...?" My voice trails off.

She nods with tears in her eyes. "I did."

"Say it again, baby."

"I love you too, Marshall Riggins."

She moves to rest her head on my chest, and I have my arms around both of them. "My girls," I manage to say. My heart is racing so hard I fear it could beat right out of my chest. I know "happy." I've lived a good life. I have four older brothers who would do anything for me and two loving parents who showed me what it means to love and respect your partner. But right here, in this moment, with Wren and Madeline in my arms, I'm bursting with it. I've never felt this level of contentment in my entire life. What's even better is that I know I'm never letting them go. I meant what I said. I want to spend my life with her, and I want to be Madeline's daddy.

I open my mouth to make sure she understands that this is it, she's it for me, when my cell phone rings. I see Owen's name; he wouldn't be calling unless something was up. "O?"

"Hey, I know this is a bad time, but I thought you might want to know that Aspen's water broke. We're on our way to the hospital."

"Shit. Okay, we're on our way."

"What is it? Is everything okay?" Worry filters through Wren's question.

"It's perfect. Aspen's water broke. We're about to welcome another Riggins baby boy into the family." I smile down at her.

"Looks like I'm going to have to hitch a ride with you."

"Speaking of that, why don't you take one of my cars—" I start, and she's already shaking her head no.

"I love you for who you are, Marshall. You're this kind, energetic, caring man who wears his heart on his sleeve. I won't be one of those women who gets your heart and then go after your wallet."

"You have my heart, and it's not my wallet. It's a car. I have three and can only drive one at a time. I hate that you and Maddie are without wheels when I have more than I need."

"Not happening, Riggins." She stands and tugs on my arm. "Come on. We have a baby to meet."

"Bring it in, brother." I pull Conrad into a hug before releasing him and going to stand next to the bed. Leaning over, I press a kiss to Aspen's cheek. "He's beautiful," I tell her. "Good job, Momma."

"He looks like his daddy." Aspen smiles at me with tears in her eyes.

"Do you have a name?" Wren asks. She's sitting in the chair at the foot of the bed with a sleeping Madeline in her arms.

"Bryson Conrad Riggins." Aspen smiles.

"He's precious." Wren smiles warmly, and I get a vision of this same situation, only it's Wren and me who just had a baby. I want that. I want a house full of kids with her.

"I'm going to be calling you, I'm sure," Aspen tells Wren.

"You know how to reach me," she tells her.

"Congratulations, guys. We need to get Maddie home. We wanted to wait to see you. We'll be back to visit tomorrow. Get some sleep."

"While you can," Wren adds.

"Thanks for sticking around."

"Can we bring anything tomorrow?" Wren asks.

"Not that I can think of," Aspen replies.

"We'll see you later." I wave to them. "You want me to take her?" I ask Wren, pointing to a sleeping Madeline.

"Sure. Let's get her strapped in first." Together we work to get Madeline in her seat.

"Hey, Marsh," Conrad calls as we're just about to walk out of the door.

"Yeah?" I turn to look at him over my shoulder.

"Welcome to the club, brother."

I smile. "You're never too old to believe in magic." I wink. Aspen and Conrad's laughter follows us out of the room.

When we're in my car, I pull out of the lot, reaching over and placing my hand on Wren's thigh. "Babe, what do we need for you and Maddie to stay with me tonight?"

"Um, I think we're good. I have some extra clothes and diapers, and since I'm breastfeeding, she'll be okay, but she needs somewhere to sleep."

"I have a Pack 'n Play we can set up in my room."

"Are you sure?"

"Am I sure that I want the woman I love and her daughter to sleep in my house with me? Yes, I'm sure."

"Okay," she says softly.

Tapping her thigh with my hand, letting her know that I approve, I keep my tired eyes on the road and take us home. Once we're in my place, I lock the door behind us and lead us to my room in the dark. "I'll grab the Pack 'n Play. There are shirts in my dresser for you to change into if you want."

"Thank you."

I stop and kiss the corner of her mouth. "Love you," I mumble as I go in search of the Pack 'n Play I keep for when my nephews visit. I make a mental note to have Wren pick out Madeline's room in my new place once I move in. I want them both to be comfortable. Hell, if I could convince them to move in with me, I would do it. I know if I can't get her to drive one of my cars, no way can I convince her to move in with me. I'm just going to have to get creative. Not tonight, we're both exhausted, and all I want to do is fall asleep with her in my arms and wake up the same way.

We've been moving at a snail's pace in that area of our relationship. I needed to know that she was ready. I still won't push her, but damn, knowing that I get to hold her in my arms tonight has me feeling some kind of way.

When I push open my bedroom door, carrying in the Pack 'n Play, I freeze when I see Wren standing in a Riggins Enterprises T-shirt. It's way too big on her and reaches just above her knees. She has Madeline in her arms, singing softly, and I don't give a fuck if my man card is revoked. It melts my damn heart to see them here like this.

"Hey, baby girl," I say, approaching them. Madeline looks at me with sleepy eyes. "I'm going to get your bed all set up, sweetie. You have to use blue blankets tonight, but I promise I'll get you some girly ones for next time."

"Next time?" Wren asks. Her smile gives her away.

"Next time. And the time after that, and the time after that, all the times until I can convince you to move in with me." She opens her mouth, I'm sure to argue, but I shut her down with a kiss. "Which side of the bed do you want, babe?"

She shrugs. "I sleep on the couch, so whatever is fine for me."

"Tell me which side you prefer?"

"Either, really."

"How about we put you on the right side? That way, I'm next to the door, and we can put the Pack 'n Play in that corner of the room as well. Sound good?"

"Why do you want to be by the door?"

"So I can protect my girls. If someone happens to get through my security system, they're going to have to go through me to get to either of you."

"You make my heart beat faster," she murmurs.

"Good. You do the same to me." I get busy setting up the bed for Madeline, and change my clothes while Wren gets her settled. "Do we need to keep a light on for her?" I ask Wren.

"No, she'll be just fine."

"Climb in, babe." I nod to what I now deem her side of the bed. Clicking off the lamp, I climb under the covers and pull her into my chest. "Fuck, Wren. It feels as though I've been waiting a lifetime to hold you like this."

"You never told me."

"I was trying to go slow. I didn't want to rush you."

"You're a good man, Marshall Riggins."

"I'm your man. Night, baby. I love you."

"Love you too."

CHAPTER
Wren
TWENTY

A DEEP TIMBRE wakes me. My eyes fly open, and it takes me a minute to get my bearings and figure out where I am. It's not until I see Marshall standing at the foot of his bed with Madeline in his arms, talking softly to her, that it all comes rushing back to me.

He told me he loves me.

I told him that I love him.

I'm sleeping in his bed.

"Everything okay?" I ask.

"We were trying to let you sleep," he says, his voice soft. "Well, I was. I think Maddie is ready to protest if she doesn't eat." He smiles at me, and it's endearing. He's shirtless, wearing nothing but a pair of low-hanging basketball shorts. His hair's a mess, and he has sleep lines on his face, and he's holding my daughter as if she's the most precious thing in the world to him.

He's never been sexier in my eyes.

"I can go feed her." I throw the covers off and start to stand.

"You can feed her right where you are." He brings her to me and gently places her in my arms. "Mommy will make it better," he assures her.

"Sorry she woke you up," I say, lifting his T-shirt and adjusting Madeline, and she latches on, settling in my arms.

"She was hungry," he says, his eyes meeting mine. Slowly, his hand reaches for me and raises his shirt. "You don't have to hide, baby," he says huskily.

"Habit."

"We need to work on breaking that habit. It's just me." He moves to walk around his gigantic bed and climbs on, sliding over close to me. Resting his back against the headboard, he carefully adjusts me so I'm in his arms. "Better," he mumbles, placing a kiss on the top of my head.

The quiet of the room surrounds us. The low glow from the bathroom light through the small gap of the door is the only light in the room. My mind is moving a million miles a minute as I process where I am.

Life has changed so much for me since meeting Marshall. I still struggle with the guilt, but Travis has been gone for over a year, and I'm lonely. I know I'm not doing anything wrong, but I have my moments where I feel as though I am.

"She's out," Marshall whispers.

"She is," I agree, glancing down at my daughter. "Let me put her down."

"I can do it."

"I need to change her."

"I already did."

I'm not surprised. Marshall is great with her. Having him here and his help and support brings tears to my eyes. "Thank you," I croak.

"Hey, why the tears?"

"You're so good to us."

"You're not alone anymore, baby. I'm here. You have Carrie and my family. You're going to have more help than you know what to do with it."

"I don't know if that sounds more wonderful or scary?" I laugh.

"Probably a little of both," he teases.

Sliding from the bed, I gently lay Madeline in the Pack 'n Play. I stand here a few minutes, watching her, making sure she stays asleep. It also gives me time to get my emotions under control.

"You okay?" Marshall asks. He wraps his hands around my waist. The warmth of him has me leaning into him, seeking his heat.

"Yes." I won't tell him about the guilt that sneaks in on me. I know Marshall well enough to know he will wear that burden on his shoulders.

"Come with me," he whispers in my ear, kissing my neck. Stepping back, he laces his fingers through mine and leads me out of his bedroom. "We'll leave the door open so we can hear her if she wakes up."

"Where are we going?"

"Just across the hall," he says, pushing open the door directly across from his bedroom.

As soon as we step into the room, he turns and pushes me up against the wall. I shriek out in surprise as he buries his face in my neck, nipping and sucking. "Quiet, baby, we don't want to wake Maddie."

"What are you doing?"

"Devouring you."

"D-Devouring me?"

"That's what I said." He lifts his head, his body still aligned with mine, his grip on my hips digging into my skin. "Unless this is too much. I can back off if you want." He says the words, but I can feel his hard length against my stomach. Any other man, I might feel pressured or even worried being at his mercy knowing how badly he wants me, but not with Marshall. I know he would never hurt me.

"Don't stop." My voice is barely audible, but he hears me because he smashes his lips with mine. This kiss is hungry and passionate. He nips at my bottom lip with his teeth, then swipes away the sting with his tongue.

"Legs around my waist, Wren." It's more of a demand than a request, but that's okay. I'm all too willing to obey. His hands slide over my ass, gripping the back of my thighs, and he lifts. Doing as I was told, I wrap my legs around his hips. He presses my back against the wall and grinds into me.

"I can't get close enough," he murmurs against my lips.

"Take me to bed, Marshall."

"My fucking pleasure." He turns on his heel and walks further into the room.

"Where are we going?"

"To the bed," he says, trailing kisses down my neck.

"Your bed."

"We can't. Not until we get Maddie set up in her own room here."

"What?" I pull back and look at him. The room is dark, but I can imagine the furrow of his brow.

"I don't know what the rules are, Wren. I want to do so many things to you, and I just… can't do that with Maddie in the room. There's some kind of law against things like that, right?"

Beat.

Beat.

Beat.

My heart thunders at his words, at this kind, generous, loving man. I slide my fingers through his hair, pulling his mouth to mine. "There are no rules against it. In fact, I'm sure parents do it all the time."

"What if she wakes up and sees us?"

"She's a baby, Marshall. She won't remember."

"Is there an age cutoff or something? What about a book I can read to keep up with all of this? I never want to do anything to traumatize that sweet girl."

"I love you." I force the words past my lips since my throat is clogged with emotion.

Marshall kisses me hard, his tongue invading my mouth. His hands grip my thighs to the point of pain, but I'll never tell him to stop.

Never.

"I need you naked, Wren. Is that okay with you?"

"Y-Yes," I say as he thrusts up, and then we're moving. He tosses me gently on the bed, and I can't stop the laugh that sputters out of my mouth.

"I'm going to go check on Maddie and grab a condom, or ten. I need you naked when I get back." He doesn't wait for me to answer before stalking out of the room and across the hall. I jump into action, pulling his T-shirt over my head and working my panties over my thighs and down my legs, letting them both fall haphazardly to the floor.

When I see the shadow of his body fill the doorway, a shiver races down my spine. It's been a long time since I've been with a man. Travis was my last. "I'm nervous," I blurt into the darkness.

"I'll always take care of you, Wren. Tell me you know that."

"I know that, but I'm still nervous."

His shadow disappears as he steps into the room. I can faintly make out his body moving. I hear a flop of something falling to the floor, and I assume that's his shorts. The bed dips and then he's there. His hand rests on my hip before sliding down my thigh and back up, this time going high enough to cup my breast. The pad of his thumb traces over my nipple, and I can't stop the moan that releases from deep in my throat even if I tried to.

"So sensitive," he murmurs.

"From feeding Madeline," I explain.

"Nah, baby, that's all you," he says, bending and capturing my nipple in his mouth. My eyes roll back in my head, and my hands dig into his back, holding him close. I never want him to stop.

His mouth is heaven as he gently licks and nips at my sensitive breasts. He moves back and forth from one to the other, and all I can manage to do is hold on for the ride. And yes, there might be grinding involved. No matter how many times I lift my hips to connect with his, he doesn't stop what he's doing.

"I feel you, baby," he whispers. "I'm taking my time."

"You don't have to. I'm ready now."

He chuckles softly. "I know you are." As if he needs proof anyway, his mouth stays attached to my breast as his hand travels down my body, until he finds my center. "So wet for me, Wren."

"Yes. You." I'm panting like a dog in heat, and I can't seem to find it in me to care. I've never wanted a man's touch this badly. His hard cock rests against my leg, so I reach out for him.

"Oh, no." He laughs. "You can't touch me."

"No fair." I'm very aware that I sound like a pouting toddler.

"I want you too much, Wren. This is going to be quick, so I need to get you there before I slide my cock inside you."

"No, it's okay, really."

"Patience, baby."

"I'm all out of patience," I tell him.

"I better get started then, huh?" I hear the playfulness in his voice.

"Get started?"

He doesn't answer me. Instead, he slides to the end of the bed and pulls my legs apart. *Finally,* I think to myself. He's going to take care of this ache that only he can quell. I'm ready for him to settle between my thighs, and when I feel his mouth on my pussy, my back arches off the bed.

"So good," he moans, going back for more, his mouth attacking my clit, while his fingers pump in and out of me. "Just feel for me, baby."

My hands bury themselves in his hair as I close my eyes and allow myself to just feel like he's asking. This is something that Travis really wasn't a fan of. We tried it once, but that was it, so I'm taken aback at the hunger in Marshall's voice and his eagerness.

"M-Marsh—" I try to warn him that I'm close, but the tidal waves of pleasure coursing through my body keep me from saying his full name.

"Ride it out, baby. Let me hear you," he murmurs. I can feel his hot breath against my thigh as he speaks, and I crash into the abyss. An orgasm to beat all orgasms wracks my entire body. Marshall doesn't let up until my body stills.

My chest is heaving with exertion while I try and figure out what the hell just happened. Being with Marshall Riggins is life changing.

"Ready, beautiful?" he asks. This time he's hovering over me, his body nestled between my thighs.

Even though my arms feel like jelly—hell, my entire body does—I manage to slide my hands behind his head and pull him close. "I'm ready," I whisper before placing a kiss on his lips. I taste myself. It feels naughty, but it's also a turn-on. Something I never thought I would say or think.

"My girl," he says huskily before pushing inside me, one slow, delicious inch at a time. "Oh, fuck," he breathes as he bends to rest his forehead against mine. "If I'd known this is what magic felt like, I would have searched for you sooner."

"It might not have been me," I say, feeling pain fill my chest at the thought of someone else having him like this.

"Nah, baby. It was always meant to be you. We both just needed to be ready."

"Are you planning on moving anytime?" I ask, trying to lighten the mood. My legs lock around his waist, trying to get him to slide in deeper.

"Not yet. I'm trying hard not to lose my control here, Wren."

"I want you to lose control. You love me, right?" I ask even though I know the answer.

"I more than love you, Wren."

"Then this isn't a one-time thing between us. Take what you need. Show me how bad you want me."

"You don't know what you're asking, Wren."

I lift my hips, and he moans. It's a deep sound from somewhere in the back of his throat. "I know I love you. I know that I want you to take me. I want you to take what you've been so patiently waiting for. What we've both been waiting for."

He growls and pulls out before slamming back in. Over and over and over again. He keeps a steady rhythm. "I love you and your magic pussy," he pants. I'm glad it's dark because I'm smiling. He is so lost in me, in us, that he's spouting crazy.

"I'm not going to last. Touch yourself, baby. Get there for me."

Doing as he asks, I slide my hand between us and begin to rub slow circles against my clit. "So sexy," he pants. "You there, baby?"

"Y-Yes," I moan.

"You're squeezing the hell out of my cock, baby. I can't—Oh, fuck!" he roars as his body stills above me. He slouches over me, holding his weight on his elbows. He's breathing hard, as am I.

"I don't know if we are going to call it magic, but that was... something. Something I've never felt before." The words rush out of me as I try to catch my breath. It was more than sex. It was deep, emotional, and life changing.

Magic.

"That's because it's our magic, baby." He kisses me softly. "Don't move. I'm going to get something to clean us up with." He slowly pulls out, and I miss his warmth and being connected to him. He walks out of the room, only to come right back with a warm wet cloth. He manages to clean between my thighs even in the darkness of the room.

"Come on, beautiful. Let's go sleep in my room in case Maddie needs us."

Beat.

Beat.

Beat.

The way he thinks of not only me but my daughter has my heart pattering hard against my chest. I allow him to pull me from the bed, and he turns on the bedside lamp. Together, we get dressed. He links his fingers with mine and we head back across the hall to his room. We climb into bed, and he pulls me back into his chest, wrapping his arms tightly around me.

"Sweet dreams, baby."

"Night." I whisper the words. My mind is racing just as fast as my heart. I'm happy and content. After over a year of sadness bearing down on me, life is looking up, and I have Marshall Riggins and his family to thank for that.

CHAPTER TWENTY ONE

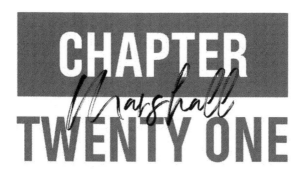

Marshall

I'VE BARELY SLEPT. I woke up sweating and irritated, until I realized why I was sweating. Wren has her tight little body wrapped around me, sleeping peacefully. I couldn't fall back asleep after that. I couldn't stop thinking about yesterday and my confession of love. Not just mine but hers as well. And then when we got back to my place, it's a day I'll never forget.

I was convinced my dad and brothers were talking shit. I should have known better. I saw my brothers fall. I was there when they found their magical love, and that should have been enough to make me a believer. The only reason I can come up with is that I didn't believe because Wren wasn't in my life. After meeting her, things changed. My outlook on life and everything I thought I wanted for my future.

I was certain that sleeping with only one woman for the rest of my life sounded like a life of boredom. I knew that I would get there eventually, but I assumed I had more wild oats to sow. I was so fucking wrong. I can say with absolute certainty that knowing

Wren is my only for the rest of my days is fine with me. It's better than fine. It's my future.

She and Madeline are my future.

They are all I want or need. Well, maybe give Madeline a brother or sister or two. Maybe more. I guess that's something we have to talk about.

She adjusts her position, and I know she's waking up. I'm watching her, so when she peers up at me, I get to see her sleepy smile. "Morning, baby."

"Are you watching me sleep?"

"Yep."

"Creeper."

"You call it creeping. I call it memorizing the moment."

She laughs softly. "Is she still sleeping?"

"She's been moving around a lot. My guess she'll be up soon." I kiss the top of her head and wrap my arms around her a little tighter. "So, I was thinking I could make my girls some breakfast, and then I'll get ready. We can go to your place to get you some clothes, stop by the hospital to see Conrad and Aspen, and then head to my parents' for Sunday dinner."

I hold my breath waiting for her answer. "Okay."

Madeline starts to jabber, making me smile. "I'll go start breakfast." I climb out of bed and slip into a pair of shorts, tossing Wren a T-shirt before going to the Pack 'n Play and lifting Madeline into my arms. "Look at you looking all cute with messy bed head," I say, kissing her cheek. She snuggles into my chest, burying her face in my neck. "Wren?"

"Yeah?" she answers, climbing out of bed and slipping on the T-shirt I just tossed her way.

"In case my confession of love and what we shared last night wasn't enough, I want to make myself clear in the light of day."

"O-kay," she says cautiously.

"I love this little girl." I kiss the top of Madeline's head. "I love you. You both are mine. From this point on, you're mine. You and Maddie."

I see her shoulders relax. Was she worried I would take it back? There are no take backs in love. At least not my love. "Go see Mommy," I tell Madeline. I hand her over to Wren and wrap my arms around both of them. "Love my girls," I whisper. Reluctantly I pull away and force myself to walk out of my bedroom to go make them some breakfast.

Once in the kitchen, I pull the high chair that I keep for Carter and Roan out from under the island. It's the kind that folds up and you strap it to a chair. I'll need to get a real one, full size for Madeline. I never have Carter or Roan for more than a night or a few hours, so this works, but I hope Madeline will be spending a lot more time here, and I want her to be comfortable and feel at home. It's important that babies have stability. I've learned that from my brothers and their kids.

I'm just pulling the scrambled eggs off the stove when Wren and Madeline appear in the kitchen. "Hey, I made scrambled, thinking Maddie might want some."

"That's perfect." Wren smiles at me.

"I have her seat all set up." I point to the high chair. "Go ahead and get her settled, and I'll make our plates. Coffee and orange juice okay?"

"Yes, please. Do you need any help?"

"No. You just take care of our girl and I've got the rest." I get busy making us both a plate of eggs and toast and fill the small rubber Blue's Clues plate that I keep for Carter with eggs. I use a fork to cut them up in tiny pieces so she won't choke, and like an experienced waiter, I carry all three to the table.

"Look at you. Were you a waiter in college?" Wren teases.

"No, but I could have rocked that sh-stuff," I say, catching myself.

"I'm sure you could have." She laughs. Her laughter follows me as I grab our coffee and orange juice before sitting opposite Madeline.

We dig into our food while we laugh at Madeline. She loves her eggs, but she's wearing more than she's eating. The entire morning is very domestic, and I don't hate it. In fact, I want this feeling. I want these two with me every morning. Hell, I want them every minute of every day.

"So, Wren," Sawyer says. We're all sitting in the living room at Mom and Dad's. The afternoon rain has us all holed up inside. The rain didn't stop Mom from making a huge pot of spaghetti and meatballs with salad and garlic bread. I assumed we would be having sandwiches since we're all tired from being at the hospital, but Mom pulled off a win. I ate way too much, but my mom is the best cook out there. Well, Aspen and Aurora have the dessert side covered, but Mom can give them a run for their money. "I have something to run by you."

I know what's coming, but I keep my face neutral. My brothers and I have been working on a plan that my sisters, their wives, and our parents were on board with. It worked out for me because I need her to make more money. I need her to find a better place if she's not willing to move in with me. I get the keys to my new place tomorrow, and I want them to move in with me, but I know she's going to argue.

"What's that?" Wren asks her. Madeline reaches for me, and I take her into my arms, tossing her gently into the air, making her giggle.

"Well, how happy are you with your job?" Sawyer asks.

"Um… I mean, it pays the bills," Wren says.

"I was hoping you'd say that. How would you feel about a change?"

"What kind of change?"

Sawyer looks over at Royce, and he nods. "Well, we're opening a day care at Riggins. The entire second floor is going to be a day care. We know Lena and Stanley have things they want to do, travel and whatnot. They can't do that if they spend their days watching our kids." She motions around the room. "Not only that, but we all love the idea of being able to drop in and see our kids anytime during the day."

Wren nods. "I can see the appeal. What does that have to do with me?"

"Well, we need someone we trust to run it."

"Okay?"

"That's you, Wren," Royce chimes in. I can already see he's got his CEO hat on, and he's ready to close the deal. "We know you. We trust you. We want the place to be for Riggins Enterprises employees. There is a state-of-the-art security system installed, and we need someone we know isn't there for any other reason than the safety, security, and well-being of our children and those of our employees."

"You want me to run it?"

"Yes." Royce's tone is serious. "I take the care of my son and nephews very seriously, and we need you. We need to know that someone is running the day care who is there for the kids." He's working hard to sell her on this.

"Did you know about this?" Wren turns to look at me.

"Yeah. We talked about it a few times."

"That's not the only change we're making," Royce tells her. "Aspen and Aurora will be reopening Warm Delights in the lobby."

"I... I don't know what to say."

"How about you and I go talk specifics?" Royce asks.

"Go on, babe. I've got Maddie."

She hesitates before nodding slowly. "Okay."

I watch as my brother hands Roan to Sawyer and stands. He motions Wren to follow him down the hall, and I know he's taking her to Dad's office. As soon as they are out of earshot, everyone starts talking at once.

"Do you think she'll take it?" Grant asks.

"She looked shocked," Layla comments.

"We need her to say yes," Conrad adds.

"We should have had you warn her," Owen speaks up.

"No, I think this was the best way. It's coming from Royce. She needs to know it's not just me who wants her to take this position. She'd think I'm trying to give her another handout."

"Another?"

"Yeah, I've tried to get her to drive one of my cars, but she refuses."

"So buy her one," Owen tells me.

"Right, she'd never drive it. She's stubborn."

"How are you going to get her to move in with you if you can't get her to drive your car?" Owen asks.

"Baby steps, right, Maddie?" I ask the baby who's sitting on my lap, chewing on my finger.

"Do you think he can convince her?" Dad asks.

"Yeah, I think so. If not, I'll do my best to try and talk her into it."

"Well, I hate to break up this party, but uh, we need to go," Aurora says.

"Now?" Grant asks, jumping to his feet. Aurora nods, and he scoops her up in his arms.

"Leave Carter with us," Sawyer tells Owen.

"I can keep him too," I volunteer.

"Well, I'm going to the hospital." Mom grins. "Stanley, grab your keys," she tells my dad. "We have a new grandson to meet."

Royce and Wren enter the room just in time to see Grant carrying Aurora out of the house. "Baby time?" Royce asks with a huge smile on his face.

"Baby time," Mom says, rushing out the door behind Grant.

"You go. I'll keep Roan and Carter."

"You sure?" Royce and Owen ask at the same time.

"Yes. We have Maddie. You all go and keep us updated. We'll bring the kids over if things go fast, if not tomorrow."

"Thanks, man."

"I'm going to need both of their car seats. I use my base for Maddie."

"Done," Owen says. "We'll do that before we head out."

"We're going too. We'll take them back to my place."

"We'll help you load them up," Royce says.

"I have to work tomorrow," Wren reminds me.

"That's fine. We'll swing by your place and get what you and Maddie need before going back to mine. Or you can stay at yours," I say when I see the uncertainty on her face. "I can take you to work tomorrow," I assure her. Or she can just drive one of my cars. This might be my chance to actually get her to do that.

"Okay." She nods, but she still looks unsure.

"Thanks, guys." Layla pulls Wren into a hug. "I always overpack wanting to be prepared for anything, so his bag should have everything he needs."

"Me too," Sawyer says. She also pulls Wren into a hug. "Thank you for watching him."

"It's no problem," Wren tells them, looking more certain with her choice to stay with me.

Making sure the house is locked, we all head to my SUV, where Royce and Owen transfer car seats while their wives toss their bags into the back. "You be good for Uncle Marshall and Aunt Wren," Layla tells Carter.

Wren whips her head toward me and I shrug.

"He's always good, right, little man?" I say to Carter.

"I good," he tells Layla.

"You too, bud," Sawyer tells Roan. "He's usually in bed by seven. Especially after a family gathering. All the attention wears him out."

"So, you love Sunday dinners?"

"Of course." She laughs.

There is a lot of hugs and kisses before my brothers load their sons into their seats. I load Madeline, and we hit the road. "I'll swing by your place and stay in the car with the kids while you grab what you need."

"Where are they all going to sleep?" she asks.

"We'll figure it out."

"I have another Pack 'n Play. I could bring that," she offers.

"Sure, we could do that for Roan, and Carter can sleep with us, or maybe I'll drag the mattresses to the living room, and we can camp out. That way, we don't have to worry about rolling over on him, and if he rolls off the mattress, it's not far to fall."

"That's a good idea, actually."

"Go grab what you need. Maybe get enough for a couple of days. Who knows how long she will be in labor and how long I'll have the kids."

"You have work tomorrow."

"I do, but we own the company. We can move anything we had scheduled, and our staff knows how to get a hold of us. All the more reason that we need a Riggins day care stat."

She nods. "I'll be quick."

"No rush. We're all good here." I point to the three car seats in the back, making her laugh.

I watch her as she grabs her keys out of her purse before opening the door and jogging into the building. "Maddie, looks like you get to stay with me again tonight," I tell the baby. I turn to look and find three faces staring back at me. "I spend night," Carter says, pointing at me.

"That's right. Who's your favorite uncle?" I ask him.

"Uncle Marsh!" he cheers. That makes Madeline and Roan giggle, and before long, all four of us are laughing at one another. These kids are a hoot. I need to get my girls moved in and a ring on her finger so we can add a few more to the clan.

CHAPTER
TWENTY TWO
Wren

"**H**OW WAS YOUR night with the boys?" Layla asks.

"It was fine. They were angels. Marshall dragged the mattress from his room and the spare room to the living room. Roan and Madeline slept in Pack 'n Plays, and we let Carter sleep on the other mattress. Marshall was worried about rolling over on him." This is the third sleepover we've had with the boys over the last few weeks. Next week, it's going to be Royce and Sawyer, and they're keeping Madeline. I'm nervous, not because I don't think she will be safe, but leaving her for that long and overnight is new for me, and for her. In fact, I'm not sure Marshall will make it all night. I smile to myself.

"He would have kicked you to death." Layla laughs. "That boy is all over the place when he sleeps. We don't let him sleep with us, but it's like there's a party in his crib every night."

"We took all the cushions off the couch and the extra bed pillows to build a barrier around him. We had the condo tore apart," I tell her with a laugh.

"Marshall is so good with them. Madeline too," she adds.

"He really is."

"So, this is it," Layla says as the elevator opens to the second floor. "So, there are three elevators. One only goes to this floor. One goes to all floors, and one goes to all but the second and very top where we all are. It took some work, but we eventually made it happen. The two that go to the second floor will have codes that the parents will have to enter, or they can swipe their employee badges. Only employees with children in the day care will have access to the second floor."

"Wow. This is incredible," I say as I take in the space.

"You know how the guys are. When they want something, they go after it. When it comes to their family, they'll move heaven and earth, or at least they'd try."

"Definitely," I agree with her. My mind immediately goes to Marshall and how he dotes on Madeline and me. Layla couldn't have described him any better. She's right—all of the Riggins men fit that same description.

"So, you'll have your own office. It's this way." She leads me down a long hall. At the end of the hall, she opens the door and motions me inside. "This is your office."

I take in the space. There is a large U-shaped desk in one corner and a rocking chair with soft fluffy cushions. There's a full-size refrigerator/freezer combo and a baby bed and changing table. "Layla?" I ask, confused.

"Do you like it? Sawyer and I picked it all out. We wanted you to have the option to have Madeline with you whenever you wanted. We don't expect you to work the floor. The plan is to be overstaffed, so each child gets proper care and attention. We just need you to hire them, to order in supplies, make the staff schedule, schedule fun activities for the kids, things like that."

"It's really your position to create," Royce says from behind us.

"I don't know what to say. This is… incredibly unexpected."

"Like I told you before. We want someone we can trust in this position. Someone we know is going to advocate for the kids and won't be afraid to kick an employee's ass to the curb if they are not doing their job. All of this"—he gestures around the room—"is to make your life easier. You're a single mom who's giving up your job and your security to come work for us. I told Sawyer and Layla to work their magic. If there's anything we've missed, let me know, and we'll make it happen."

"This is—" I feel tears burn my eyes. "So many amazing things have happened to me since meeting your family. This feels like too much, plus the salary is triple what I was making."

"Oh, and on top of that, as the director, Madeline comes for free." Royce grins.

"What? No. That's too much."

"It's done," Royce says. "I have to get back upstairs. Welcome to the Riggins team, Wren. Layla will walk you through the decisions we've made, and if there is anything you think we need to add or change, she will set you up with your company credit card. Between the two of you, I have full faith that you can make this happen. We have a soft opening in six weeks."

He turns to walk away, but I call out to him, "Royce." I can hear the wobble in my voice. He stops and turns to look at me. It takes me five steps and double that in racing heartbeats to reach him. Leaning up on my tiptoes, I hug him. "Thank you."

"You're welcome, sis," he says softly. I don't get time to ask him why he called me sis before he's releasing me and disappearing on the elevator.

"You ready to get started?" Layla asks.

I nod because that's all that I'm capable of. Meeting Marshall that day in the pharmacy has changed my life in so many ways. I've never really been a big believer in fate, but I don't know how else to explain that chance meeting and everything that's happened since then. Then again, maybe Stanley is onto something.

Maybe it's the magic?

My phone rings, vibrating across the desk where Layla and I are going over the different areas of the day care center and the age-appropriate activities for each area.

"If that's Marsh, you better get it. If he's anything like his brothers, and let's face it, we both know he is, he's going to keep calling." Layla chuckles. "I'm going to run upstairs and say hi to Owen. We've been at this for hours. We could both use a break. The fridge in your office is stocked with drinks, and there are snacks in the bottom-right desk drawer." She winks and walks out of the room.

"How's the move going?" I greet Marshall.

"Good. The movers just left. The condo is empty, and I have a lot of unpacking to do. The good thing is that they reassembled the furniture, so it's more just personal items that I need to unpack. How's the first day going? I wish I could be there with you."

"No, it's probably best you're not here. You're distracting."

"Is that so?" he asks, his voice suddenly husky.

"Anyway, I'm glad the move went well." I can't let him distract me with his sex voice while I'm at work.

"It did. Hey, can you and Maddie stay with me tonight? I'm going to work tomorrow, and you can take Maddie with you to the office, right?"

My heart swells knowing he wants us there with him for his first night in his new house. "Yeah. Have you seen my office?" I ask him.

"No, but I knew it was going to be nice. I know my sisters-in-law, and they love you, so I wasn't worried."

"Marsh, it's insane. It's an office and a nursery in one. I can't believe I get to work and bring Madeline with me every day."

"I'm glad you took the job, baby."

"Me too."

"How about I pick you up from the office and then take you home to grab what you need?"

"Sure. That would be great. I didn't bring Madeline with me today, but I did tell the day care today this would be her last week." I don't need to look in a mirror to know my face is light with excitement. This is my dream job and what I went to college for. However, I also still want to be a nurse. I feel that would only increase my qualifications for the job, and I know as a parent I would feel better with a nurse on staff at my day care. That's always been my dream, and now here it is coming true. Well, all but the nursing, but I'll get there.

"I wish you would drive one of my cars."

"After a few paychecks, I should be able to buy my own." Excitement courses through me. I want to save up to get a new place, where I can sleep in an actual bed every night, and then a car.

"Why spend your money? You know I can't drive all three of them at once."

"Marshall, we've talked about this. I can't take handouts like that from you. I love you for who you are, not what you can give me."

"Don't you think I know that? I wouldn't be offering if I didn't know you loved me for me, Wren. Come on, baby. Just think about it."

"Fine. I'll think about it," I say it to appease him. He's already given me so much and brought so much into my life. I can't keep taking from him. These past few weeks of us being together has been incredible. I love every minute that Madeline and I get to share with him. That's more than enough for me. I know that I'm being stubborn, but it's important to me that he knows that I love him for his heart, not his wallet.

"I have a few things to wrap up here. I'll be out front at five to pick you up."

"See you then."

"Love you, Wren," he says, and the line goes dead before I get the chance to tell him I love him too. Every time he says those three little words, I get butterflies in my stomach.

"Welcome home," Marshall says, spreading his arms wide as we walk into his new house.

"You mean to your home," I correct him. My heart skips a beat, and my mind races with thoughts of what it would be like to live here with him. To truly call this place my home. Our home.

"About that... Maddie and I have been talking," he says, setting the car seat on the kitchen island and unbuckling her.

"Oh, you have, have you? And what exactly have you and my almost eight-month-old daughter been talking about?" I ask, placing my hands on my hips.

"What do you think, Maddie? Should we tell Mommy what we talked about?" Madeline coos and places her hands on his cheeks, giving him a toothless grin. "I agree," he tells her, kissing the tip of her nose.

"I'm getting old over here," I tease.

"Mommy is impatient, Maddie." He grins at me. "Fine, I'll tell you. But I need to make sure you know that Maddie and I have discussed this at great length, and we feel as though this is the best idea we've ever had."

I'm smiling from ear to ear. This man, the way he loves my daughter and me, it's definitely magical. "Best idea ever. Got it." I nod.

"Here we go, baby girl." He walks over to where I'm standing and hands Madeline to me. He laces his fingers through mine and guides us to the kitchen, where he lifts us both to sit on the island, then proceeds to take Madeline back into his arms. "I need to make sure I have your full attention," he says, stepping between my legs. Madeline laughs, putting a hand on each of us.

"You have my full attention," I tell him. My heart once again flips over in my chest. That seems to happen a lot when Marshall is around.

"Okay." He clears his throat. "Maddie and I thought it would be the best decision ever if you and she would move in with me."

I watch his features, and all playfulness has left his face. Only serious Marshall remains. "I want you here, Wren. Both of you. I want you and Maddie to fill these empty halls with love and laughter. I want you to be my wife, and someday if you feel comfortable enough, I would like for Maddie to take my name too. I want to give her brothers and sisters, and I'd be incredibly honored to be her dad." He pauses and cups my face with his hand that's not protectively holding my daughter.

I have to bite down on my lip to keep the tears at bay. My palms are suddenly sweaty and I know for certain if I was standing, my knees would be weak. All because of this man and the way he loves me, and my daughter.

"I love you, Wren. All of you. I love Maddie, and I want us to be a family. I want to start that sooner rather than later." He places a kiss on Madeline's temple.

"Okay, baby girl, I need you to go to Mommy for a minute." He hands Madeline to me and lifts me from the island. My knees are shaking, and my heart is racing, and my breath hitches when he falls to his knees and reaches into his pocket.

"I know I'm supposed to pull out all the stops and give you all the romance for something like this, but I'm a firm believer in following my gut and doing what feels right. This, Wren, this feels right to me. Wren Wheeler, would you do me the incredible honor of being my wife? Wren, will you marry me?"

Tears flow down my cheeks, and I'm holding onto Madeline so hard that she squirms to get down. "I'm sorry," I murmur to her. My hand is shaking when Marshall holds the most beautiful ring I've ever seen up to me. I nod because I can't make the words come.

"I need to hear you say it."

"Y-Yes," I whisper. "Yes," I say again, louder this time.

Marshall stands, slides the ring onto my finger, and takes Madeline, who has been reaching for him. "Maddie, I know you're too young to understand, but I promise to love you and be the best father I can possibly be."

A sob breaks free from my chest. All I can manage to do is launch myself at him. The three of us stand here in an embrace until my tears subside. "So, does this mean you're moving in?" Marshall asks.

"If I pay some of the bills."

"I don't need your money, Wren."

"I don't need yours either. I have a new job, and the pay is pretty sweet." I smile up at him.

"Fine, we can work out the details, but this new living arrangement starts tonight."

"I have to pack up my place."

"Oh, honey, we're definitely going to be packing up your place. I've got my brothers on speed dial. The five of us, well three, Grant and Conrad get a pass since they're new dads, but trust me, we won't need them."

He proceeds to pull his phone out of his pocket and calls his brothers, asking for help moving Madeline and me into his place on Saturday. "That gives you all week to pack and tell me what we're keeping and what we're donating."

"Madeline's stuff is all that I need."

"Oh, that reminds me. I have to show you something." With Madeline perched on his hip and his hand on the small of my back, he leads us upstairs to the bedrooms. "Open that one." He points to the door that's located directly across from the master suite.

Pushing open the door, I gasp. "Marshall." I turn to look at him, and he offers me a sheepish smile. "It took me some time, but I found the same furniture that you have. I wasn't sure you would say yes to moving in, and I didn't plan to propose tonight. It just sort of happened. I was feeling it." He winks. "Anyway, I wanted you and Maddie to both feel comfortable when you stayed over."

"If I wasn't already wearing your ring, I'd be begging you to spend the rest of your days with me," I tell him. Going up on my toes, I kiss him softly. "Thank you for this. You have no idea what it means to me."

"I do, baby. And you have no idea what it means to me to know we're going to be a family. You've given me two of life's most precious gifts." I tilt my head to the side, waiting for him to explain. "Your heart and hers."

I'm a puddle of goo, and I can only imagine that this is what swooning feels like. I've read about it countless times but never personally experienced it. Not until Marshall Riggins walked into my life. I love this man with an intensity that is overwhelming, yet rewarding. I smile up at him as he makes faces at Madeline.

Marshall is our future.

CHAPTER
TWENTY THREE
Marshall

I T'S BEEN THREE weeks since Wren and Madeline moved in with me to my new place. I've never known this kind of contentment. Never in my wildest dreams did I imagine settling down would make me the happiest I've ever been.

"Wren, how's the new job going, dear?" Mom asks.

We're having Sunday dinner at my new place this week. I had it catered from a local restaurant in town. Not that I can't cook—Mom made sure that all of us could, and Wren can too, but that's not the point. Today is a housewarming/engagement party of sorts. All four of my brothers are here with their wives and kids. Jase and Sam are here with Aria, and Carrie and Elijah stopped by earlier but had to leave due to a prior commitment. Mom and Dad are sitting on the couch, both holding their new grandsons.

Mom's holding Bryson while Conrad looks over her shoulder, and Aspen smiles as she watches it go down. Dad's holding Everett Lee, with Grant sitting right next to him. In fact, if he was sitting any closer, he'd be sitting on Dad's lap too.

"It's going really well. The first week with the kiddos was a success." My fiancée beams with pride and excitement over her new job.

"That's wonderful news," Mom praises.

"We did a slow onboarding of kids, so this week it was just Carter, Roan, Madeline, and two other kids. Next week we have five more joining the roster," Wren explains.

"I plan to stop in and do story time here and there," Mom says, with Conrad hovering over her shoulder. "Aspen? Aurora?" Mom says, not looking away from Bryson. "Can you please pull your nagging husbands away so we can enjoy some time with our grandsons?"

Conrad scoffs and looks over at his wife. She gives him a cut-it-out look that our mother gave us growing up. I watch as his shoulders fall, and with one last look at his son, he steps away to stand behind his wife.

"You too," Dad tells Grant.

"Hey, I'm not hurting anything," Grant argues.

"You're cramping my style, son. Go spend some time with your wife or your brothers or your nieces or nephews. These two are taken." Dad makes a shooing motion with his hand. It's not lost on me that Dad referred to Madeline and Aria as our nieces. My family has accepted Wren and Madeline into the fold, and there's no going back.

"Baby hog," Grant mumbles, scooting over.

"How about a picture?" Layla suggests. "Lena and Stanley with all the grandkids?"

"Oh, I love that idea. Bring me more babies." Mom smiles.

Grant stands, moving out of the way, and Owen places Carter next to Dad. Carter immediately moves over closer to Gramps to look at Everett. Royce hands Roan to Mom, so she has a baby in each arm.

"Wren, what are you waiting on? I have an empty arm." Dad holds his arm in the air to prove his point.

"Oh, I just thought—" Wren starts, but Mom cuts her off.

"This is a picture with all of our grandkids," Mom says, leaving zero room for negotiation in her voice.

"Bring me my granddaughter, darlin'," Dad says gently.

Wren is unable to hold her tears as she covers her mouth with her hand. Madeline thinks it's a game and mimics her mom. I want to run to them and wrap them in my arms, but I hold strong, staying in my spot, leaning against the wall where I've been enjoying having my family in my new home. I don't move, letting my parents take the lead on this one.

Wren composes herself and takes small steps to the couch, where my parents are sitting. She places Madeline on Dad's lap, and she looks up at him and grins. "Hey, pumpkin." Dad greets Madeline with a kiss on her cheek.

"Say cheese," Layla calls out.

"Cheese," Mom, Dad, and Carter call out.

"Aria needs in here too," Mom tells Jase and Sam. Sam takes Aria and sits her next to Carter. Aria has every adult in the room laughing when she puts her arm around Carter's shoulders and pulls him into her, then says cheese, with the biggest brightest smile I've ever seen on a child.

Layla snaps a few more pictures before it's time for the babies to eat. Grant and Conrad jump at the chance to take their sons back from our parents. Carter and Aria have had enough and climb off the couch before darting down the hall to the playroom. Yeah, I'm the cool uncle. The area's not just for them. It's for Madeline as well. She's going to be too young to play upstairs while we're downstairs, so I made the downstairs bedroom a playroom and made sure to lock that bathroom door. I know Wren, hell, I know me, and no way am I sleeping downstairs, leaving her upstairs all on her own. As our kids get older, we can transition our room to the downstairs and move the playroom to the basement.

Wren is still watching my dad with Madeline, and her eyes are still swimming with emotion. I'm no longer able to stay away. Pushing off the wall, I make my way to where she's sitting in the recliner. I kneel beside her. "You doing okay?"

"More than okay." She nods. Leaning over the arm of the chair, I kiss her lips softly.

"Hey, Wren," Sawyer calls out. "We're thinking of running to Target. Aurora needs diapers. You want to come?"

Wren looks at me and I nod. "I've got Maddie."

"Sure. Uh, when are you going?"

"Now." Sawyer laughs.

"I need a few things too." Layla stands.

"Sam?" Aspen asks.

"We're actually heading home," Sam tells us. "Logan and Kacen are coming over later. There's this new band Kacen has been working with that he wants Jase to hear."

"Next time?" Aspen asks.

"Definitely."

Jase and Sam say their goodbyes before wrangling their daughter, who cries to stay and play with Carter. It's on the tip of my tongue to tell her she can stay and play, but Jase reminds her that her cousins are coming over, and that does the trick to get her to dry her tears.

"Take the SUV," I tell Wren. She opens her mouth to argue, but Aspen beats her to it.

"Thanks, Marsh. Lena, do you need anything? I'd suggest you go, but you look like you're in grandbaby heaven." Aspen chuckles.

Mom looks down at Roan. "I'm good, and yes, I am," she says, looking over at Madeline. "Swap?" she asks my dad.

"I don't know. She's actually letting me hold her while Marshall's in the room," Dad tells Mom.

"You boys go do… something," Mom tells us.

"Hey, I'm feeding my son," Conrad defends.

"Me too," Grant tells her.

"Fine," Mom grumbles.

"Keys are hanging in the laundry room." I kiss Wren quickly

and invite Royce and Owen down to the basement. I have a pool table set up and a projection screen TV.

The wives are off for a diaper run. My parents are doing what they do best, spoiling our kids. Conrad and Grant are new dads, and they refuse to let their boys out of their sight. Royce, Owen, and I head to the basement to play a game of pool or two, and it's a perfect day surrounded by family in my new home.

"We need to drive separately today. I have a lunch meeting and don't know how long it will run."

"That's fine. I don't need a car. If I do need something, I can walk," Wren tells me the next morning when we're getting ready for work.

"That ring on your finger, that means we're getting married, right?" I come up behind her and wrap my arms around her waist, resting my chin on her shoulder.

"That's what it means." She smiles at me in the mirror.

"That ring also means that what's mine is yours. Is it that you don't like my cars? We can sell them and get you whatever you want. In fact, I think we should get rid of the car and get another SUV. Soon we'll have two car seats, and an SUV would be easier. I'll keep the truck, though, in case we need to pull the boat or something."

"I'm not with you for what you can give me."

"Baby, I know you aren't. But you have to get used to the fact that I have money. A lot of money. I'm going to spoil my wife and kids. That's something you have to get used to." She nods. "Tell me what you want. We can get you whatever you want."

"The SUV is fine," she says hesitantly.

"It's yours. We'll go this weekend and see if there is one you like better. If not, you keep it, and I'll get another SUV. Hell, maybe we should look at vans," I muse.

"What? Why would we look at vans?"

"Babies, Wren. I want lots of babies." I kiss her shoulder and release my hold on her. "I'm going to start breakfast." I scoop Madeline up out of the Pack 'n Play, where she chills while we're getting ready for work. In the kitchen, I pour a few puffs onto the high chair after getting her settled and start some eggs and toast for my girls.

It's just before noon, and I need to leave soon for my lunch meeting. However, there's something I want to run past Royce before I go. "Knock, knock." I tap on the frame of his office door.

"Come on in," he says, scooting back from his desk. "What's up?"

"Well, you know that I'm paying for Maddie to attend our day care. I told Wren it was a perk for managers. And it is, but at a discounted rate. I'm paying the difference."

"You know that's going to bite you in the ass, right? She runs the day care, Marsh. She's going to see who pays what."

"I know," I sigh. "I'm going to have to tell her soon. Damn, I just got her to agree this morning to take one of the cars to drive as her own. She's stubborn."

"Nothing worth having is easy," he says.

"She's worth it. Listen, I know she wanted to go to school to be a nurse. I want her to achieve her dreams. That might be nursing, or maybe business to assist her with running the day care. Whatever it is, I want her to have it. Maybe she'll expand her early childhood education degree, I don't know, but I intend to make it happen for her."

"Understood." Royce nods. "So, what do you need me for?"

"I want to offer her tuition reimbursement from the company."

"If she chooses business, we can do that easily."

"I know, but I'm not sure that she will choose business. Regardless of what she chooses, I want her to think it's 100 percent paid by the company."

"You're playing with fire, brother," Royce warns.

"I know." I rub my hands over my face. "I know I am, but she won't let me help her. Hell, even if we were already married, I doubt that she would let me help her. I just… I want to give her the world."

"That's the magic." Royce smirks.

"Whatever the reason, I want to make it happen."

"And?"

"I've read the policy. It's very vague, so even if she looks it up, I think it's going to be fine. I know that the invoice for classes will come across your desk. I need you to give it to me so I can pay it."

"If it's Riggins related, we'll pay for it."

"Well, nursing might not be."

"If she's running the day care, I can see the benefits of having a nurse on staff," he muses.

"That's why she wants to be a nurse; she saw the benefit as well. However, a lot has changed in her life so that might not be her dream anymore."

"You don't know?" Royce raises his eyebrows at me.

"Last we discussed it, nursing was a pipe dream for her."

"Well, if she chooses nursing, the company will take care of it."

"But not 100 percent. The policy doesn't give specifics, but I checked with human resources. We pay 50 percent."

"We'll figure it out."

"Whatever happens, if it doesn't fall into the realm of Riggins reimbursement qualifications, then give the bill to me."

Royce nods. "I'll take care of it."

"Thanks, man." Rising to my feet, I walk to the door. "You were right," I tell him. "It just wasn't my time. I was waiting for Wren."

He nods. "I understand that. Glad you found her."

"Me too." I turn and walk out of his office. Glancing at my watch, I curse. I wanted to stop in and say hi to Madeline and Wren before leaving for my meeting, but if I do that, I'm going to be late. I hate to be late, especially for a business meeting. I guess I'll just have to get my fix when we're at home tonight.

CHAPTER
Wren
TWENTY FOUR

M Y EYES FLUTTER open at the feel of his hand on my bare belly. "Merry Christmas, baby," Marshall says huskily.

"Merry Christmas," I reply. I try to roll over to face him, but his hold is tight.

"Let me love you," he whispers. At first, I'm confused until he lifts my leg and slides inside me. "You're my present," he murmurs, trailing kisses down my neck and over my bare shoulder.

Goose bumps break out against my skin at the feel of his hot breath. "This is definitely not a present I'll be returning," I pant as he thrusts deeper. His movements are slow as he lazily pumps in and out of me. It's delicious torture that I would happily wake up to every single day.

"More." My words are a whisper into our quiet bedroom. We've gotten good at being quiet so we don't wake Madeline. He tightens his hold on me, and my back is aligned with his front.

The warmth of his skin seeps into me. His face is buried in my neck, and all I can do is feel, with my hand gripping his forearm that's holding me close to him.

"I'm so close, baby." Marshall's lips are right next to my ear. "Touch yourself. I'm not going without you."

Not needing to be told twice, I slide my hand between my legs, and that first touch sends a jolt of lightning through my veins. "Oh," I moan from deep in the back of my throat. Closing my eyes, I get lost in the moment. My breathing accelerates and another low, deep moan erupts from my chest. I'm close, so close to falling over the edge.

"Now. Come for me now," Marshall growls as his body grows stiff and stills behind me.

His grip on my thigh is so tight it's painful, but I wouldn't have it any other way. I love knowing I can make him lose control.

"That is the best way to wake up," he says, kissing my neck. He doesn't move as he peppers my neck and shoulder with kisses. "Now that I have my gift, it's time to get Maddie up to give her hers." He holds me for a few more seconds that feel like minutes, before pulling out and loosening his hold.

I smile, thinking about the mountain of presents downstairs underneath our tree. "You went overboard," I tell him, throwing off the covers and heading to the bathroom to clean up.

"It's her first Christmas," he defends, standing to follow after me.

"I'm using the restroom." I laugh.

"I have to take care of this." He motions toward the condom he's just slid off.

I wrinkle up my nose because… ew. I mean, I know they keep us safe and prevent pregnancy, but the aftermath is bleh. We don't even need them. "We don't even need them," I blurt.

He stops talking and tilts his head to the side. "What are you saying?"

"I'm saying we don't even need those." I point to the trash can. "I'm on the pill, remember?" I ask. "I never miss," I add just in case he needs the reassurance.

"Are you telling me I've had a barrier between us all this time, and we don't even need it?"

I shrug. "Oops."

"Oh, you're going to get it," he says, stalking toward me.

I take off running into the bedroom and dive on the bed, sliding under the covers. He bounces on top of me. He rips the cover out of my hold and begins to tickle me. I squirm and wiggle under him until I'm laughing so hard I have to pee. Again. "Mercy!" I shout, and he stops.

We're both breathing heavily as he hovers over me, his arms holding his weight. "I love you."

My hand rests against his cheek. "I love you too."

"When you're ready, you tell me, and we'll stop using them."

There's the sweet man I know and love. "I'm telling you now. We don't need them."

"If it weren't Christmas and if we didn't have a little girl to spoil, we'd stay in this bed all day long."

"We have lots of presents to open," I remind him.

"Nah, not too many."

"Have you seen our living room? It looks like five kids live here. Not one little girl who's not going to remember this day."

"Oh, but she's going to see pictures. What would she think if we only got her a few things? Besides, she needs all those things." He rolls off me, resting on his side.

"No. She doesn't need all those things. She's one little girl. How can she play with all of them?"

"She has lots of cousins that can come and play with her."

"You're impossible," I tell him, swinging my legs over the side of the bed.

"But you love me." He grins.

I nod because I do love him. I've never known the kind of connection that we have. It's scary and overwhelming and intense, but it's us, and I wouldn't change it for anything.

I stand and offer him my hand. "Come on, slowpoke. We have

to open ten million presents for a little girl who will be more interested in the wrapping paper, and then shower before going to your mom and dad's."

"Where are we going?" I ask a few hours later. "I thought we were going to your mom and dad's?"

"We are, but we don't have to be there until one."

"Then why did you rush me out of the house? I had at least another hour of lounging in my jammies." I'm not mad, but I am confused as to where else we would be going today.

"I made a promise and I intend to keep it," he says cryptically.

I don't bother to try and get it out of him. I know him well enough to know that if he doesn't want me to know until we get there, he's not going to give in and tell me early. It's not until we make the next turn that I realize where we are. "Are we going to the cemetery?" I ask, surprised.

"Yeah. I promised you that I would love you and Maddie for both of us. I thought we should come and tell him Merry Christmas. It's our first Christmas together, and I thought we could make it a tradition."

Beat.

Beat.

Beat.

This isn't the first time this man has made me feel as though my heart could tumble out of my chest. Beat by beat, he's healed parts of me I thought would forever be broken. I try to speak, but there is a lump in my throat the size of the state of Tennessee.

Marshall stops the car and turns to look at me. "If you don't want to get out, we don't have to. I just—" He pauses. "I sometimes feel guilty that he lost his life. I feel guilty that you and Maddie lost him, but at the same time, if that hadn't happened, I never would have found you. The thought of you and that precious little girl not being a part of my life tears me in two. Just the thought of losing either of you causes my heart to race and panic to set in."

"He would have liked you," I whisper. My heart squeezes in my chest, and I know with everything in me that I'm right. Travis would have loved Marshall. "In fact, I think he might have sent you to me. I don't know how else to explain our meeting that evening at the pharmacy. The same pharmacy he used to work for."

"Then I need to thank him." He smiles before leaning over the console and pressing his lips to mine.

"Okay."

Together we climb out of my SUV, and he grabs Madeline and an extra blanket. He holds her close, with the blanket thrown over her to ward off the cold. I lead us to his grave, something I think I could do in my sleep. It's been months since I've been here. I think the last time was when Madeline was three months old. The cab ride there and back was just too expensive.

I stop in front of his grave as I read the engraving on his headstone.

TRAVIS WHEELER
LOVING FATHER AND HUSBAND

"Hey, Travis," Marshall says before clearing his throat. "My name is Marshall Riggins. I want to thank you for sending me to our girls. I promise you they're in good hands," he says. "I'm sure you already know this, but I've asked Wren to marry me. She said yes. I know that her love is a gift, and it's one I will treasure for the rest of my life."

Hot tears race down my cheeks, but I don't bother to wipe them away. I know it's no use.

"I love them," Marshall adds. "I love them with everything that I am. I promise to take care of both of them. I'll love and protect them for both of us. I will be the father to Maddie that you wanted to be but missed the chance. I don't take this vow lightly."

"Hey, Maddie, Travis is your daddy. Can you say hi to Daddy?" he asks my daughter. She just smiles and laughs at him. Marshall is her favorite person, and she his.

"Merry Christmas," he says, his hold on me growing a little tighter.

I have so many emotions soaring through me. The biggest is that I feel so blessed to have loved both of these incredible men. I never thought I would be here with my fiancé and my daughter, but Marshall, he's one of the good ones. He's not someone who will shy away from the hard stuff, and at the same time, he's the one you want to have fun with, the one you long to hang out with.

"The wind is really picking up. Do you mind taking Madeline back to the car? I'll be there in a minute."

"Sure thing, baby. Take your time." He kisses my temple and releases me. He walks to the headstone and taps it twice with his hand. He then removes the extra blanket around Madeline and hands it to me. He snuggles her close and heads back to the car.

Wrapping the blanket around my shoulders, I stare at the headstone. "Hey, Trav," I croak. "Sorry, it's been so long. Times were tight for a while, and well, I just couldn't afford to get here.

"Madeline is getting so big," I tell him. "She's growing and thriving. Today is her first Christmas, which you know, but she loved the paper and the boxes more than the gifts." I chuckle softly.

"Marshall, he went overboard. The living room looked like a toy store by the time we were finished. We still have his family to go see. That's where we're headed. He has four brothers and his parents. They love Madeline like she's their own. So does he, but you already heard him. I went from having Carrie to having a huge support system. Madeline has cousins and aunts and uncles." I pause to catch my breath.

"You did well, Trav. You sent me a man who would love us both. His family, they love us too, and I know you're behind that. I wish you were here. I miss you every day. I wish you could have met your daughter. I know how important having a family was to you. Well, you might not be here to give that to her, but you made sure she got it. You made sure we both did.

"I love him, Travis. I feel guilty even telling you that, but I feel like you deserve to know. Hell, you're up there watching me, so you already know, but I feel like I needed to say those words to you. He's such a good man. I-I want him to adopt Madeline. I never want her to feel different from her brothers and sisters. No, I'm not pregnant, but we're getting married, and we both want to grow our family."

Taking the blanket, I wipe the tears from my cheeks. "I promise you she will forever know that you're her daddy. The one who helped me make her but had to go live with the angels. Marshall, he'll be her here-and-now daddy. I'll make sure she knows how much both of you love her."

A sob falls from my lips, causing me to suck in a deep breath to try and pull myself together. "I should get going. I don't want to be late. Thank you for the greatest gift of my life. Thank you for our daughter. I promise to come to visit more often, and I'll be sure to bring Madeline too." Walking to the headstone, I kiss the tips of my fingers and place them over his name. "Gone but never forgotten," I murmur.

I take my time, my steps small as I head back to the SUV. When I look up, I see Marshall leaning against the passenger door with his arms crossed across his chest and his legs crossed at the ankles. He doesn't say a single word when he opens his arms for me. I rush the last few steps and cling to him. I don't know that I will ever find the words to tell him what him bringing us here means to me.

When I finally feel as though I can speak without crying, I lift my head from his chest to look at him. "Today—" I start, but he shakes his head.

"I know, baby. Anytime you want to come back, you let me know. I know there's enough love in that heart of yours for both of us."

If I wasn't already irrevocably in love with him, I would be from that statement alone.

CHAPTER TWENTY FIVE

Marshall

"**S**O, A LITTLE birdie tells me that you're going back to college," Aspen says from where she sits on their couch, holding Bryson.

It's New Year's Eve, and the big party animals that we are, we're all sitting around Conrad and Aspen's house with the kids in tow. Mom and Dad are here, and so are Jase, Sam, Aria, Carrie, and Elijah. When I asked Conrad about having them over, he didn't hesitate. I knew he wouldn't, but still, it means a lot to me that he was willing to do that for Wren.

"I am," Wren says excitedly. "June from HR came to me the other day and reminded me that Riggins Enterprises offers tuition reimbursement. At first, I felt bad for accepting it, but Marshall reminded me I could still do my job and be a nurse and that it would be helpful to have a nurse at the day care."

"I agree with him," Owen chimes in. "That's definitely comforting knowing a nurse is on staff for the kids, hell to have a nurse in the family for the kids." He chuckles. "You see how rambunctious Carter is. I'm sure once the others reach his age, they're all going to be just like we were, getting into everything. We're going to need you."

"You should consider setting up a clinic room in your house." Dad laughs. "These boys had us running for bandages and stitches at every turn."

"Come on now," Royce defends. "We weren't that bad."

"Oh, I beg to differ," Mom adds. "I'm sure I could look up the receipts for the co-pays to prove it."

"That was years ago," Grant tells her. "You wouldn't still have all of that stuff."

"Probably not, but I do have your baby books that would showcase many trips just in the first five years of your lives." She laughs.

Wren looks at me and smiles. "Maybe we should consider it?" She's teasing; I can see it in the glint in her eyes.

"If that's what you want to do, we'll make it happen," I assure her. I love seeing her like this. With each passing day, she grows more comfortable with my family, and she's stopped fighting me on driving the SUV and even me spending money on the two of them. Sure she grumbles, but that's progress.

We live too far from work to walk. Sure, most days we ride together, but if she needs to go to the store or has plans with Carrie or one of my sisters, she takes it now without hesitation. Baby steps, but we're getting there.

"Well, since we have everyone here, there's something I need to say," Owen speaks up. He smiles down at Layla, who's holding Carter. "Lay and I are having another baby." He smiles.

The room erupts with cheers and hugs for the happy couple. I feel a tightening in my chest, and this time it's easy for me to name the feeling. Longing. I want Wren to be my wife. I want to make babies with her. I want to be the one standing in front of my family telling them that we're having a baby. I want to see Madeline as a big sister. I've been letting Wren take her time with setting a wedding date. I know that living together, the engagement, the new job, all of that has been a huge change for her. I wanted to give her time to settle into all of it before we move forward with the wedding. However, she's doing just fine.

I think it's time I push a little.

All the kids have crashed and most of the adults look dead on their feet. I smile. A couple of years ago, my brothers and I would have been at a club bringing in the new year. Now, here we are, all domesticated and shit and barely able to keep our eyes open to get our midnight kiss. Life has changed for the five of us so much, but for me, and hell, even for them, I know that none of us would have it any other way. I'll take quiet nights in with my girls over the noise of a club any day. I never thought I'd even think that, but it's the truth. I guess that's what magic does to you.

Grant passes out small plastic cups with sparkling cider as the room begins to countdown to the new year. "Ten, nine, eight, seven, six, five, four, three, two, one... Happy New Year!" everyone shouts, and then the room is quiet, all except for the music coming from the TV as they celebrate in New York for the ball dropping. None of us seem to care as we kiss our wives. Well, my fiancée in my case, but this year, she will be my wife. Hopefully, sooner rather than later.

"I got my kiss, and now we're leaving," Owen tells us.

"Yeah, we need to get home too." Grant stands.

We all murmur our agreement that we need to get going because, unlike the Riggins brothers from a few years ago, we all have little ones now who will be up early. We're parents, and our kids are our priority.

Carefully, I lift my daughter from her Pack 'n Play. Yes, I called her my daughter. In my heart, she's mine. I'll love her every single day as if it's my blood coursing through her veins. I couldn't love her anymore if that were the case. "I got you, baby girl," I whisper, snuggling her to my chest.

"I'll take her." Wren appears beside me. I nod and carefully hand her over to her mother while I pack up and gather the diaper bag. I hit the remote start button for the SUV and then pass out hugs and say our goodbyes before loading my girls up and taking them home.

"What kind of wedding do you want?" I ask Wren the next morning over breakfast. I'm sitting at the table next to Madeline, who is shoving eggs into her mouth from the tray of her high chair. I'm happy to say she now has a pink princess plate to eat off.

"I don't know. I haven't thought much about it."

"Did you have a big wedding the first time?"

"No." She shakes her head. "It was just Travis and me, and Carrie was there with a date. Some Todd guy, I think his name was."

"Did you want a big wedding?"

"No." She gives me another shake of her head. "Not without my parents," she whispers.

"Okay, so small wedding. Got it. Now, do you know what season? Winter perhaps?" I suggest helpfully.

She smiles, and I feel it deep in my soul. "Sure, November or December would be fine," she says casually.

"Think more, January or February."

"Hmm, that would give us more time. Are you sure you're willing to wait until next year?" She's biting on her cheek to keep from laughing.

"Hell no," I say, then grimace, looking over at Madeline. I usually catch myself with my potty mouth when she's around. "*This* year. This January or February," I correct her.

"Are you sure that's what you want?"

"Am I sure that I love you more than life itself? Am I sure that I want you to take my last name and be upgraded from fiancée to wife? Am I sure that I want to be this little girl's daddy?" I reach over and cover Madeline's ears with my hands. "Hell fucking yes, I'm sure," I say, releasing her ears and giving her a loud smacking kiss on the cheek. She giggles, and the sound warms my heart. She also offers me a bite of soggy egg, and I can't tell my little girl no, so I take it and quickly swallow, washing it down with some coffee.

"Okay, so… soon." She nods as if she's letting the idea sink in. "Nothing big, no wait. This is your first wedding. Do you want something big?"

"This is my only wedding," I say adamantly. "Honestly, I don't care. I want you to be happy. I want it to be the wedding you've always dreamed of. Big, small, Vegas, the beach, I don't care as long as at the end of the day you're Wren Riggins."

She's quiet for a few minutes while she processes what I've just said. "I really like the idea that Conrad and Aspen had. To just surprise everyone. Come as you are kind of thing."

"We can do that. Here? Mom and Dad's?"

A soft smile pulls at her lips. "Here. In our home. Seems fitting, I think."

"Come as you are, and here in our home," I repeat, the idea already cemented with me. "When?"

She shrugs, and I'm ready for her to blow me off. "I'm ready when you are. I love you, Marshall. When I agreed to be your wife, I was ready then."

"You should have told me. That was forever ago. We could have already been married and working on getting Maddie a sibling." Reaching over, I tap Madeline on the nose, and she giggles.

"You never asked."

"Woman! I was trying to give you time. I didn't want to overwhelm you with all the changes."

"There were a lot of changes going on," she agrees. "But none of them would have stopped me from marrying you."

"Next weekend. My dad can marry us like he did Conrad and Aspen. We can go this week to get our marriage license."

"Okay."

"Okay."

She smiles. "More eggs?"

"No. I don't want more eggs. I want your sexy ass to get over here and kiss me."

"Oh, is that all?" she asks with a smile. She places her plate in the sink and slowly makes her way to where I'm sitting. I scoot back from the table and pat my lap. She doesn't hesitate to take a seat.

I wrap my arms around her and hold her for just a minute. "I love you, future Mrs. Riggins."

Her hands cup my cheeks. "I love you too, Mr. Riggins." She smiles, a beautiful smile that lights up her face, and that's when it hits me. This beautiful, incredible woman is going to be my wife—next weekend. I glance over at Madeline. She's looking at us like we're crazy, but she's still shoving in eggs. She's wearing more than she's eating at this point. This is my life, my future, and it's never looked so bright.

CHAPTER
Wren
TWENTY SIX

T ODAY IS MY wedding day. This isn't my first wedding, but I can
say with absolute certainty that it's my last. No, I can't see into
the future. However, I do know that I will never love a man the
way that I love Marshall.

"Knock, knock," a deep voice says outside our bedroom door.
"Wren, it's Royce."

"Come in." I smooth down my simple white silk dress that
stops at the knees.

"You look beautiful," he says once he's entered the room. He
comes to my side and kisses my cheek.

"Thank you."

"I have something for you," he says, handing me a manila
envelope.

I take the envelope and carefully pull out its contents. I read over
the paperwork as tears blur my vision. "I know you said you were
in no rush for these, but I thought today, being your wedding day
and all, you might want to give this to him as a wedding gift."

"How did you manage to get these so fast?"

"We have an attorney on retainer. We call, and he does what we need." Royce shrugs.

"Thank you for this. Please let me know what I owe you or him or whoever."

"Wren." He reaches out, resting his hand on my arm. "You don't owe anything. You're a Riggins now. That means if you need the family attorney, you get his services just like the rest of us. Free of charge."

Tears burn my eyes. "You think he's going to be okay with this?"

"I know he is. He loves you and that little girl. He's already ecstatic to be making you his wife. When you give him this—" He shakes his head. "When you give him legal rights to his daughter, his entire world is going to be in alignment today."

"You called her his daughter."

"Isn't she? She might not have his name or have Riggins' blood in her veins, but she's still my niece." He leans down and kisses my cheek. "I'll see you out there."

Royce leaves, and I'm alone. I read through the papers one more time before placing them back in the envelope. I slide them under my pillow to give to him later. Needing something to calm my nerves, I grab my phone, yes, my new phone that Marshall bought the day after I agreed to marry him. I open up my email and find a message from the accounting department at Riggins Enterprises.

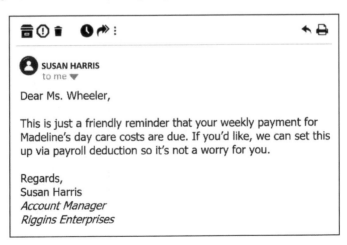

SUSAN HARRIS
to me

Dear Ms. Wheeler,

This is just a friendly reminder that your weekly payment for Madeline's day care costs are due. If you'd like, we can set this up via payroll deduction so it's not a worry for you.

Regards,
Susan Harris
Account Manager
Riggins Enterprises

I read the letter three times, and I can't seem to make sense of it. Instead, I dial Marshall. "Hey, beautiful," he greets me. "You ready to change your name today?"

"Yes," I tell him honestly. "Hey, I was checking my email and got one from Susan Harris in accounting."

"Okay?"

"She was reminding me that Madeline's day care hasn't been paid. I thought that was part of my position?" I ask him.

"Fuck." He curses.

"Marshall?"

"Look, at the time, I knew you'd argue with me. I knew you'd been struggling, and I wanted to help you. You do get a discount, but I've been paying the difference."

"What?" My mouth falls open in shock. The realization that he's been lying to me all this time takes root in my mind. "Are you kidding me? Why would you do that? She's my daughter. She's my responsibility."

"No," he says, his voice stern and his tone angry. "She's my daughter too. I have every right to do what I did."

"No, you did not. You lied to me."

"Because I knew you'd fight me on it."

"I don't even know you." I battle to keep my tears at bay. How is it possible for my heart to ache with love for him and with the pain of his betrayal?

"Baby, listen to me."

"No." I end the call and toss my phone on the bed. It immediately rings, but I don't look to see who it is. I know it's Marshall. How can I marry a man who lies to me? How will I ever know if he's being truthful? My heart cracks in two. I can't marry him. I can't go through with this.

The thought of losing him and his family tears me in two. Reaching behind my back to unzip my dress, I freeze when the bedroom door flies open. It's Marshall. He's breathing heavy, his tie is askew, and his hair looks as though he's run his fingers through it a thousand times.

"Wren." His voice cracks.

"No." I shake my head. "No. I don't want to see you. I don't want to talk to you. You lied to me."

"Please, let me explain."

"What? So you can tell me more lies?"

"No. I want to tell you why I made the decision that I did."

"Fine. Please, spew more of your bullshit lies. Get it over with, so I can get out of this dress."

"What?" His face pales. He's white as a sheet.

"I can't marry you. You lied to me." My voice cracks, as does my heart. It's thundering in my chest. And while I'm used to that feeling where Marshall is concerned, this is a different kind of beat. Instead of overflowing happiness, it's sadness and despair.

"No. No. No. You don't mean that. Let me explain it to you, please."

"Whatever you have to say won't change my mind, Marshall. I don't know if I can do this."

"No. You're my fucking wife. What? You think you can just go and take your love and my daughter away from me?"

"She's not your daughter!" I scream. I see the hurt flash in his eyes, and I feel the guilt weigh heavily on my chest, but the anger I have for him lying to me overpowers the guilt.

"You're wrong, Wren. She is my daughter. I love her. You're my wife. Right here." He taps his chest over his heart. "I don't need a fucking piece of paper to tell me either is true. Right here is where *you, my wife,* lives, and right next to you is *our* daughter."

"You lied to me. What else have you not been telling me? What else have you lied about?"

I see his face drop, and I know whatever it is he has to say, I'm not going to like it. "Tuition."

"What about it?"

"It's a 50 percent reimbursement."

"Are you kidding me? Why? Why lie to me about that?"

"Because!" he roars. "Do you have any idea what your smile

does to me? One tilt of those lips of yours and my entire day is made. When I met you, you were struggling. You were walking everywhere and sleeping on the fucking couch. I listened to you tell me how you gave up your dream for his, and you never got your turn. You never got the opportunity to follow those dreams, and I wanted to be the one to give you that. I want to see you soar, baby. I want to stand back with our daughter and watch you reach for those goals. I want to tell her that she can be just like Mommy and never give up."

The look in his eyes and the tone of his voice conveys what he's telling me. He's telling the truth. But he still lied to me. "Don't you see? I'm not doing it on my own. Not if you're paying for it."

"You're my wife, Wren. What's mine is yours. Why can't you see that? Why is it so hard for you to believe that nothing I have in life is worth shit to me if you're not by my side to share it?"

His breathing is so heavy his chest is heaving with exertion. I know because I've been staring at his chest this entire time. I can't look at him in the eye and not see the lies he's told. "How am I supposed to believe you won't lie to me again when it suits your needs?" I whisper. Even as the words pass my lips I know I'm being dramatic. Marshall has only ever done right by me and Madeline. I know I need to calm down, but the betrayal is still too fresh. Too raw.

He takes a step forward, and his index finger settles under my chin as he lifts my head. His eyes are swimming with tears as he looks me in the eye. "You believe me because it's the truth. My brothers tried to warn me it was a mistake, but I wanted to give you the world. I was going to tell you. I just—Fuck, you've been so happy. The stress that used to weigh you down is no longer there, and I didn't want to see it come back. I knew you would fight me every step of the way. I swear to you that's all I've ever lied to you about."

"The job?"

"The day care was Royce's idea. Sure, I suggested you for the job, but no way would they have given it to you if you were not the best fit. These are their kids we're talking about. My brothers are not just going to let anyone have that control. They needed someone that they trusted. And that was you."

"The salary?"

"Owen. He's the numbers guy. He chose what each position would make. It's all new for us, so we let Owen take the lead on that." He digs into his pocket and taps a few buttons on his phone.

"You good?" a voice I recognize as Royce's asks.

"No. Can you and the others come up to my bedroom?"

"Brothers?" Royce asks.

"Yes."

"On our way."

"What are you doing?" Why is he calling his brothers? This is between us.

"I want you to ask them anything you want to know. They were there with me when I made the decision to keep it from you. They warned me it was a bad idea, but I didn't listen. All I cared about was seeing you happy. I wanted to see that smile light up your face and the stress that life kept tossing at you to disappear."

"That wasn't your choice, Marshall. I'm an adult. I'd been doing just fine on my own."

"You were getting by," he says softly. "I agree that you were doing the best you could with what you had, but I could make it all better for you."

"I could afford day care on my new salary."

He nods. "I know. That was what my brothers tried to tell me as well, but I wanted to do it. I wanted to help take care of Maddie. Look, I know I lied to you, but I promise you it was all out of love. It crushed me to see you struggling. I was constantly thinking of ways to get you to move in with me so you could stop walking up three flights of stairs multiple times a day. I begged you for weeks to drive my car instead of walking. Can't you see? I just wanted to help you."

"You lied to me." I know I'm stuck on that, but it bears repeating. "How do I know you're not lying to me about everything else? How do I know you're not marrying me out of pity? You claim to love me but is it just this hero complex that you have? I mean, that's how we met, right? The almighty Marshall Riggins swoops in and saves the day." I see the pain in his eyes from my words, and if it was guilt I was feeling before, this feeling gripping my heart in my chest is shame, and regret, and remorse for my words.

I know he loves me, and I believe him, but this anger, it's speaking for me and ignoring my heart.

If I'm being honest with myself, part of my reaction is fear. I've never loved anyone the way that I love Marshall. Losing Travis killed me, but I survived. I put one foot in front of the other and moved on. I didn't have a choice. With Marshall, if I were to lose him, no matter what the reason, I don't know that I could do it. I don't know if I could pick up the pieces and keep on pushing forward in life.

"You know that's not true."

"Do I?" I ask automatically, as there's a knock at the door. They don't wait for permission to come in. No, instead, Royce, Owen, Grant, and Conrad all walk into the room wearing weary expressions. Great, just what I need. Five Riggins men are looking at me like a firing squad.

CHAPTER
TWENTY SEVEN

Marshall

MY BROTHERS WALK in and I plead with them with my eyes to help me. My chest feels tight and there's a fracture in my heart that only she can heal. I was wrong. I know that. I knew it when I lied to her, but it truly was coming from a good place. I just wanted to make her life easier. I had the means to do it, and I wanted to. Besides, Madeline is my daughter. I don't see an issue with me paying for her childcare. And as far as college goes, there's nothing I want to see more than to watch the woman I love to chase her dreams. I just need to prove that to her.

"What's going on?" Conrad asks.

"Wren knows I've been paying for Maddie's day care," I tell him. All four of my brothers nod in understanding. "I also told her about the tuition, that it's only a 50 percent reimbursement."

"We tried to tell you." Grant shakes his head.

"I know you did. Now can you please tell her what I told you when you tried to change my mind?" I wait as my brothers look between each other, then back to where I'm standing next to Wren. Her body is rigid, and I want to pull her into my arms and kiss the hell out of her. I want to kiss her until she forgets that I fucked up. I want to kiss her until she's ready to walk down those stairs and marry me.

"You said you wanted to change her life like she changed yours." It's Owen who speaks up.

Wren's shoulders begin to shake. I reach out to hold her, but she steps just out of my reach.

"Marsh, why don't you take a walk?" Royce suggests.

"What? Are you fucking crazy? The love of my life is ready to walk out on me, and you think I should take a walk?"

"Yes," all four of my brothers say at once.

"No. No way. I'm not leaving this room without her glued to my side."

"Marshall." Royce's tone is that of the demanding CEO. "Go down the hall to where the girls are getting ready. Spend some time with your daughter. I promise we won't let her leave here without you getting to talk to her again, if that's what she decides to do."

I turn my back to them to look at Wren. Tears streak her gorgeous face, and the fracture in my heart widens. "I love you, Wren. I love Maddie, and I want our family. I'm sorry for lying to you. I know it was wrong, but, baby, I just wanted to give you the world. You changed me. You make me a better man, and for that, I wanted to make life easier on you. I wanted to watch you achieve your dreams." She doesn't reply. I lean in and press a kiss to the corner of her mouth, tasting her tears. She still doesn't move.

"I'm trusting you with half of my heart," I tell my brothers. "I'm going to be down the hall with the other half when you're done." With one last longing look at my bride, I quietly make my way down the hall.

I knock on the door, and a chorus of come ins greet me. Inside, I find Carrie and Aspen with Maddie. They have her in the cutest little pink dress and white shoes. "Hey," I croak.

"What's wrong?"

"I fu-fudged up," I quickly correct myself.

"We were just coming to check on Wren," Aspen tells me.

"My brothers are with her. I just came to see my daughter." I take Maddie from her arms and snuggle her close. "I love you," I tell her. The tears are back, and I don't bother hiding them. My entire life is crashing around me all because my dumb ass thought I knew what was best for her.

"Aspen, do you mind if I talk with Marshall for a minute?" Carrie asks.

"Sure, you want me to take her?" She points at Madeline.

"No." I hold her a little tighter. "No. I need to be with my daughter right now."

Aspen gives me a small smile. "Okay. I'm just going to go downstairs and check on everything."

"Thank you." I manage to force the words out.

"So, what did you do?" Carrie asks.

I launch into the story, how I lied about the day care and the tuition. "I love her, Carrie. No, it's more than that. I don't even have the words to describe how I feel about her. I wanted to make it better, you know? I had the ability to do it, so I did. I knew she would fight me on it every step of the way, and she's done so much for me. She gave me her heart and this one." I kiss Madeline's cheek. "She gave me my family and I wanted to give her the world. Hell, I still do."

Carrie nods. "Anyone can see that you love her, Marshall. That's not what this is about."

"Help me," I plead with her. "Please tell me how I can make this better. How can I prove to her that I'm sorry, and I know I messed up? Lesson learned. I'll just argue with her the next time until I wear her down."

"Wren loved Travis." I nod because I know this. Of course she loved him. He was her husband. "But she loves you differently. Their love was safe and it was comfortable. What she has with you is not even close to what she had with him."

"And?"

"She's scared, Marshall. She loved him and lost him, and she survived. It was hell, but she survived. She knows she won't survive losing you. It would break her heart and break her spirit for a lifetime."

Realization sets in, and I know that what Carrie is telling me is part of our fight. I fucked up, and that's on me. I lied to her, and I never should have. However, I can also see the fear in her eyes now that it's been brought to my attention. I was mistaking it for anger. "She's not going to lose me. If I could just get her to believe that I haven't lied about anything else. This is our wedding day. I should be downstairs pledging my love to her in front of those closest to us. Instead, I made a mistake, and now I might lose my wife and my daughter."

"She's hurt. My guess is a lot of that is her pride. She struggled and worked her ass off to stay afloat. Suddenly you come into her life, and things are easy for her. She needs to know that she has a choice, Marshall. She doesn't want someone who is going to fix things for her. She needs a partner. Someone who will stand tall beside her, supporting her through the good times and the bad. She needs to know that you are that person."

"I am."

"I believe you."

"I need her to believe me."

"She loves you. And my guess is that once she calms down, she'll see that although stupid, you did what you did out of love."

"Today is our wedding day."

"I can go talk to her."

"My brothers are with her. They were with me when I made my decision, and they know why I chose to do it. They asked me to leave them alone with her. If that doesn't work, you're next in line," I tell her.

She smiles sadly. "Even if you don't go through with the wedding today, I have a good feeling about the two of you. Sure, you made a mistake, but it was one done out of love. I don't know what woman wouldn't forgive that."

"I hope you're right." I look down at Madeline. "I'm sorry, baby girl. I made Mommy upset. I was wrong. But I promise I'm going to fix it. I promise." I kiss the top of her head and close my eyes, breathing her in. I have to fix this. I can't lose them.

CHAPTER
Wren
TWENTY EIGHT

"**Y**OU LOOK BEAUTIFUL," Conrad speaks first.

I smile at him. "Thanks," I mumble.

Conrad gives me a sad smile. "I thought we should get that out of the way right off the bat." He shrugs.

"Wren, tell us what you're thinking." This comes from Owen.

"I'm thinking that my entire relationship is a lie. I'm thinking that I fell for a man who pulled blinders over my eyes."

"Now, that's what your head is telling you," Grant chimes in. "Now, tell us what your heart is telling you."

"My heart is telling me that he's a good man, and he had his reasons."

"I agree that he made a mistake. I tried to tell him both times, but he was convinced that he could give you more. He wanted you to be able to follow your dreams," Royce says.

"I know he lied, Wren, and there is no excuse for that, but when you think about his reasoning, it's all for the greater good, right?" Conrad asks.

"Put yourself in his shoes, Wren. What if you had a strong support system? What if you never had to worry about money or childcare, or cars?" Owen says. "What if you were in his shoes and he was in yours? What if he had big dreams, but life kept kicking him down? What would you do?"

"I'd do anything I could to help him achieve them," I tell him honestly. "But I would have been honest about it."

"Would you, though? From what I hear, Marshall, and in case you're wondering, that really means you, is rather stubborn."

"Ha ha," I deadpan. "I never want him to think I'm with him for his money. He told me once that the five of you never really knew who was nice to you for your name and money and who was nice to you for who you were."

"He's right. We did have that issue more often than not. However, we all found our magic. We all found that one person out there who's meant for us. That one person who will love us unconditionally regardless of the zeros in our bank account or the celebrity of our last name," Royce explains.

"Marshall has always been the happy-go-lucky guy. He's fun to be around, and if you need him, there's no doubt he's going to be there. No questions asked," Grant says.

"He's proven that to us over and over again," Conrad adds.

"Why do you think Marshall was the last to fall? Why do you think he was the last one to find his magic?" Royce asks.

"Because he's the youngest and was too busy partying to take the time to settle down?" I offer. I say the words but I don't mean them. I think he was hiding behind the magic their family is always talking about. I think that Marshall wanted the magic but was fearful he would never find it.

"Nah, sis," Owen says, making my heart squeeze. "He was waiting for you. You might not see it, but we do. We see the change in him. His happiness is off the charts, and that heart of his, which he wears on his sleeve, is bursting with love for you and your daughter."

My teeth connect with my inside cheek as I bite down to keep my sob from escaping my lips. The guilt of this entire situation sits heavy on my chest. I love Marshall with everything that I am, and I know he loves us the same. "I believe that he loves us. I just... I want him to include me in his life. In his choices."

"I'm sorry, but that's not always going to happen," Royce tells me. "You see, when we, and by we, I mean the Riggins family, when we love, we love hard. I can guarantee that he's going to mess up again."

"Definitely," Grant agrees.

"I can guarantee he's going to piss you off," Royce continues.

"Just ask my wife." Conrad shrugs.

"But I can also guarantee that no one will ever love you like he does." Royce holds my stare, willing me to trust in what he's saying.

"He's got a big heart, Wren, and he's given it to you," Owen explains softly.

Before I can reply, there's a knock on the door. Grant reaches out and opens it. Marshall is standing there with Madeline in his arms. She's hugging onto his neck, and there are tears in his eyes. He steps into the room and Grant closes the door. He walks to where I'm still standing beside our bed.

"Please don't take her away from me," Marshall says. His voice is thick with emotion, and the tears in his eyes make my knees weak. "I gave you both my heart, and I don't want it back. Ever. I'm sorry. I'll never keep something from you ever again." He turns to look at his brothers. "If you don't want her to know, don't tell me." He faces me again. "Never, Wren. I just wanted to give you the world. Hell, I still do. I never want Maddie to go a day not knowing a father's love. I never want either of you to have to sacrifice ever again. Not when I know there is something that I can do to make your life easier.

"I know—" he starts and then swallows hard. "I know you might not want to go through with the wedding today. I respect that but, please, baby, I beg you, let me make this up to you. I never meant to hurt you. I just... I just wanted to make your life easier. You make me feel so damn alive." He shakes his head, and it takes everything in me to keep from pulling him into a kiss. "It's unreal, Wren. I can't explain it, but when I have you and Maddie here with me, there's nothing else in this world that I want."

He takes a step closer, and I don't move. I can't. I'm powerless when it comes to the connection that we share. When it comes to him. "I know you have dreams, and I want to chase them with you. I can help you chase them, and I want to do that. I just want to love my girls," he says, pressing his lips to Madeline's head. There is nothing but honesty in his eyes, and suddenly all the anger evaporates and the fog in my head clears. This man is my future. He's our future, me and my daughter's.

"She loves you so much," I say, wiping at my eyes.

"That's because little girls are supposed to love their daddies," he murmurs. His voice is sad. Broken.

I know I'm at a crossroads, and I also know deep in my soul he didn't keep the truth from me to hurt me. Everything he kept from me was just as he said: to make my life better. If I'm being honest, even though I'm mad as hell, I've fallen just a little more in love with him, and I didn't think that was possible.

Glancing over his shoulder, I make eye contact with his brothers. "Can you tell everyone that we'll be right down? I just need a few minutes," I tell them. None of them make a move as they wait for me to tell them the outcome of today. "I can't get married with a blotchy face," I tell them.

I watch as all four of them have slow lazy grins that cross their faces. "You need us to take Maddie Mae?" Grant asks.

"No. But thank you for the offer." They nod, and each one takes the time to pat Marshall on the shoulder as they turn to walk out of the room.

"We're still getting married?" Marshall asks. There is so much hope in his voice and love in his eyes.

"Good times and bad, right?" I ask him. I hate that I questioned his love for me. I let a small piece of hidden truth, that I know came from a good place, almost allow me to lose the man who owns me heart and soul.

"All the times, baby. Every minute of every day. Every single beat of my heart is for you."

"No more secrets."

"None."

"Well, if I expect you to abide by that rule, then I need to be honest with you about something too." With each passing second, I realize that I overreacted, and the envelope that Royce gave me earlier is proof of that. I let my fear skyrocket something that shouldn't have even been this big of an issue. Especially not on our wedding day.

"It doesn't matter." He's shaking his head. "Whatever it is, it will work out."

"First, let me say I'm sorry. I overreacted. I let my fear of losing you, even though irrational, take hold of my emotions. I believe you were coming from a good place."

"I was. I promise." His eyes are still raw with emotion, and that same feeling of regret from earlier sits heavy on my chest.

"I did something. Something I wasn't really sure you were ready for. I mean, I thought so, but after today, well, I hope you like it." Turning, I grab the manila envelope from under my pillow and hand it to him.

"No way. I am not signing a prenup. Nope. Not happening." He tosses the envelope back on the bed.

"I didn't even consider that, but I should have. We should postpone the wedding until you can—" I start, but I don't get to finish when his lips crash with mine.

When he pulls away, he says, "No. No prenup. In fact, that's a bad word. Let's never say it again."

"Fine." I roll my eyes playfully, feeling relief wash over me that we are still us despite my overreaction. "That's not what this is anyway." I grab the envelope again and hand it to him. "Open it. Here, I can take her."

"No. I just… I need to hold her if that's okay."

I nod. "Yeah, that's okay," I agree softly. I always wondered if I would ever find a man to love us both, and I was lucky enough to do just that. Marshall loves Madeline and me with an intensity I've never witnessed before. He's all in. My earlier outburst and uncertainty seems even more foolish now that I'm seeing clearly.

"Okay, Maddie. Mommy has something for me to look at. You want to look at it with me?" She keeps her head tucked into his neck and her eyes glued to the envelope. It's almost as if she knows that those papers will change all three of our lives.

"This was going to be your wedding gift. Well, it still is. I just wasn't going to give it to you until later."

His eyes scan the document, and then he freezes. He lifts his head to look at me, and the tears racing down his cheeks tell me all I need to know. This man before me is a good man, a kind man with a loving heart. Sure, he might have kept a few things from me, but he did it with his big heart, thinking about me and what's best for my daughter and me.

Our daughter.

"She's mine?" he croaks. "Is this real?"

"Yes and yes. I had Royce help me with a lawyer to get the papers drawn up. It's not official. You have to sign them, and then we have to file the petition to the court. Since her biological father is deceased, the process should be a few months at best."

A noise comes from somewhere in the back of his throat. I'm not sure if it's a laugh or a cry. The smile on his face tells me it could be either. He tosses the papers on the bed and lifts Madeline into the air, making her laugh. "Guess what, baby girl?" he asks her, settling her on his hip. "I'm your daddy," he whispers. Then his eyes find mine. "Babe, I need a pen."

"You don't have to sign them today."

"I do have to sign them today. I need a pen." His eagerness has my heart bursting with love.

Turning, I open the nightstand and dig around until I find an ink pen and hand it to him. He takes it, and with one hand, sifts through to all of the Sign Here tabs and scrawls his name by each one. When he's done, he tosses the pen on the bed and pulls me into a searing kiss.

Pulling back for air, he whispers, "I love you, Mrs. Riggins."

"I'm not a Riggins yet," I remind him. Although the thought alone leaves me breathless.

"Then, we better get downstairs and make that happen." I nod, and together, hand in hand, with Madeline in his arms, we make our way downstairs. As we descend the stairs, I send up a silent prayer, thanking whoever might be listening that my fear didn't drive the man I love away. He fought for me. He fought for us and our family.

There's a loud round of applause when we reach the living room. Marshall doesn't stop until we reach the altar, which is in front of the fireplace. His father is already there waiting on us.

"Son, this isn't the way this is supposed to work."

"Well, that's how it works for us. I'm not letting go of either one of them," he tells his father.

"You heard the man," Owen calls out.

"Let's get you hitched." Stanley winks.

The ceremony is beautiful, and this is definitely a day we will never forget. Not just because of our blowout fight, but because we know without a shadow of a doubt that we can handle anything that's thrown our way. All we have to do is believe in the love that we share, and it will all work out in the end.

EPILOGUE
Marshall

TODAY MY YOUNGEST daughter turns one. It's mid-June, the sun is shining, the sky is blue, and we are surrounded by our family. To me, you couldn't ask for a better day to celebrate a birthday.

"Daddy, I think we're ready for cake," my mom tells me. She's currently sitting next to Marley, the birthday girl in her high chair.

"Yeah, Daddy, we want cake!" my middle daughter, Macey, cheers.

"Mommy said we had to wait for Uncle Grant to get here. The baby didn't sleep last night," my oldest daughter, Madeline, explains to her younger sister.

At five, I swear she's going on twenty-five. She's smart as a whip, and she mothers her younger sisters something awful. Madeline was two when Macey was born. And from the moment she laid eyes on her little sister, she was overprotective.

"My girls want cake. We're going to have cake," I say, knowing that Grant and Aurora just pulled up. They had a rough night last night with their two-week-old son, Cane. He apparently woke up at 1:00 a.m. and thought that it was time to party. I remember those days all too well. Mom and Dad stopped by their place and picked up their eldest two on the way over. Everett is four now, and Elaine, their daughter, turned two last month.

Making my way into the house, I laugh when I see Owen with his twin daughters, Paris and London, hanging off of each leg. At two, the girls are daddy's girls through and through. Owen wouldn't have it any other way. Carter, who's now six, and his second-oldest, Rebecca, who is four, are sitting at the table with their arms crossed over their chest.

"What are you in for?" I lean down and ask Carter.

"Dad's mad because we splashed the twins. It's a pool party." He rolls his eyes, and he, too, acts way older than his six years.

"Uncle Marsh, tell Daddy it's a pool party," my niece Rebecca pleads.

"Daddy, it's a pool party," I repeat, grinning at my older brother.

"Fine," Owen grumbles. "Apologize to your sisters and you can go back outside." His two oldest do their father's bidding and rush out the door.

"Hey, babe." I walk up behind my wife, who is standing at the sink, and kiss her neck. "The birthday girl is ready for cake." I reach around and rest my hands on her swollen belly—baby number four. We're not due for four more months, and I can't wait to meet him or her. We find out soon what we're having. Next week, in fact.

"It's ready. I was just taking some of these dishes, putting them into the dishwasher."

"I told you to leave all of that and I'll get it later."

"I'm pregnant, Marshall. Not injured," she grumbles.

"Wren, did you not learn from your previous pregnancies?" Owen raises his eyebrows at her in question. "Sit down, woman."

"I'm fine." She waves him off.

"I swear all the wives, all five of them are too damn stubborn," Owen rumbles.

"Damn!" the twins say loudly, repeating their father.

"Great. Do not repeat that word. It's a bad word, and don't tell Mommy," Owen lectures them.

"Girls, why don't you go out on the patio and find Mommy? It's time for cake," I tell my adorable twin nieces.

"Cake!" they cheer, release their hold on their father's legs, and take off running outside.

"How's Layla feeling?" I ask Owen.

He shakes his head. "Morning sickness is really hitting her with this one. I have her set up under the shade tree out back."

"Morning sickness is no joke." I nod. Wren was sick with Macey, and it killed me to watch her go through that and not be able to help her.

"Yeah," Owen agrees, running his hands behind his head. He looks exhausted.

"Hey, did we miss her eating cake?" Grant asks, walking into the house with two-week-old Cane already strapped to his chest.

"Nope. We were waiting for you. I heard you pull up," I say, motioning to the two cakes on the counter. One is for all of us, and the smaller one is for my baby girl, Marley, to go to town on all on her own.

Owen and I carry the cakes out to the back patio while a tired Grant helps to wrangle all the nieces and nephews.

"How's he doing?" Royce asks Grant.

"Oh, he's fine. He's sleeping like a log. I'm hoping that all the excitement will keep him awake or at least from a peaceful sleep, and he'll actually sleep tonight."

Royce looks down at our sleeping nephew and chuckles. "Good luck with that, brother."

"Yeah, wishful thinking on my part," Grant agrees.

"Why don't you let Everett and Elaine stay with us tonight? That way, you and Aurora can sleep when this little guy does." Royce reaches out and runs his hand softly over Cane's head.

"Yes." Grant laughs.

"Yes, what?" Aurora asks as she approaches us. She looks just as exhausted as Grant.

"Everett and Elaine are staying with us tonight."

"Oh, you don't have to do that," Aurora says.

"Babe, it's done," Grant tells her. "You know they love playing with their cousins."

Royce's oldest son Roan is five now. Next is his daughter Rachel, who is three, and their son Lincoln is two. Sawyer claims they are done, but I see the look in her eyes when Royce tells her he wants more. My guess is that we will be having another baby announcement soon.

"Who's taking who?" Conrad asks. He's holding his daughter Sage who is two, in his arms. She's resting her head on his shoulder, being shy—her older brother Bryson, who's four, doesn't have a shy bone in his little body.

"I'm taking the olders," Royce indicates to Grant, "so they can get some sleep."

"We're happy to help too," Conrad chimes in.

"Aspen is six months pregnant," Aurora states. "She doesn't need to be running after my kids and yours."

"What am I, chopped liver?" he asks, laughing.

"Sorry." Aurora is quick to apologize. "I'm exhausted."

Conrad puts his arm around her shoulders. "I know, sis, that's why you should let us help."

"All right, everyone!" I shout. "Time to gather around to sing to the birthday girl." My mom and dad are on either side of the high chair, and they clap, which causes Marley to smile and clap as well.

I stand back and wait for everyone to gather on the back patio. It doesn't take long for all my brothers, in-laws, nieces and nephews, my wife and kids, and our parents to get in position. Jase, Sam, and Aria are on vacation, so they're missing all the fun. However, as I look around at all the smiling faces, I understand the squeezing in my chest.

This is happiness.

This is love and family, and I know we are the lucky ones. Not everyone has what we have, and I thank God every day for giving us the magic of love.

Wren

"I CAN'T BELIEVE she's already a year old," Sawyer says.

She and the rest of my sisters-in-law are sitting underneath the shade tree that Owen has summoned Layla to. Not that we mind. We have a clear view of the entire backyard, and we've all been married for a few years now, but I know that I speak for all five of us when I say that watching our husbands with our kids is something that never gets old.

"I know. Soon, it will be the little guy," I say, rubbing my belly.

"Guy?" they all ask at the same time.

I laugh. "I don't know, but I have a feeling it might be a boy. I went to one of those mommy and me places and had a maternity massage. They talked me into the upsell of the ultrasound. They asked if I wanted to know the gender, but I felt guilty for finding out without him. I asked them to write it down and put it into a sealed envelope. I thought Marsh and I could do our own little private gender reveal."

"You know he's going to be jealous that you got to see the baby and he didn't." Aspen laughs.

"Oh, I know. That's why I scheduled another one for Monday morning. I took the next available appointment." I laugh. "I know my husband would be insistent for another look."

"We're blessed," Layla says softly. "I never imagined my life would turn out this way. I struggled for so long, and then Owen came along, growling about my shoes, and here I am." She smiles.

"Most definitely blessed," I agree with her. Aurora yawns as exhaustion settles in. "Girl, you look dead on your feet. Why don't you go grab that husband of yours and head home? Or you could leave Cane here with me for a while and you grab that husband of yours and go upstairs and nap," I offer Aurora.

"Nah. Royce and Sawyer are taking Everett and Elaine tonight. Wait, did you know?" Aurora asks Sawyer.

"Yes, Royce told me. I think Wren's right. You should go home and get some rest. Sleep when they do, remember?"

"It looks like all the kids are about to crash," Layla says. She points to where Marshall and Conrad are passing out popsicles to the group, and it's a very rare occasion that they're all sitting still.

The party has been going strong all afternoon. We played games, swam, let each of the kids try their luck with a piñata, then presents, and cake and ice cream. There was lots of running around the yard, and playing hard for all of them. The five of us are sitting under this tree for a little mommy quiet time, but the way the kiddos are slowing down, it's about to be over.

"I guess we should go help," Aspen says.

The five of us make our way to the back patio. Aspen and I are a little slower as we've both just started to waddle in our pregnancies. As soon as they have us in their sights, our husbands come to us. All five of them, as if we're beacons in the night.

"How you feeling, Momma?" Marshall asks.

"Good. I could probably use a nap." I chuckle.

"Done. Let's kick these jokers out and make that happen."

"They're our family," I remind him.

"And I love them all dearly, but it's my job to take care of you." He kisses me on the temple, and yep you guessed it. My heart rate kicks up. He still has that effect on me.

An hour later, the house is quiet. All three girls are napping, and Marshall and I are trying to as well. Except even though I'm exhausted, I can't hold in my secret any longer. "So," I say. I'm in bed with his back to my front, our joined hands resting on my baby belly.

"What's up, gorgeous?" he asks, kissing my shoulder.

"I had my massage yesterday."

"I know. You said it was relaxing. Do you need me to schedule you another one this week to recuperate from the party?"

"No." I shake my head. "They sold me on an upsell."

"Oh, what did you get, hot stone or something?"

"No. An ultrasound."

"What?" He climbs over me on the bed so we're looking eye to eye. "You had an ultrasound without me?" I can hear the hurt in his voice.

"I did. I'm sorry. It was too tempting. I have pictures, and before you get mad, I made an appointment for us to go together for another one first thing Monday morning."

His features relax. "Good. Where are the pictures? I want to see her." Marshall is convinced we're having another girl. He claims that he loves his girls, of which I'm included in, and he wouldn't have it any other way. However, I know he would be ecstatic to have a son.

"They were able to determine the gender."

"What do you think about Marissa?" he asks. Yes, we gave all of our girls M names.

"Well, I think if it's a boy he might get made fun of in school, but if that's the name that you're sold on." I shrug as best as I can lying down.

"Wait. What?" he asks, his eyes wide. "Did you say they told you the gender?" His voice rises an octave.

"No. They didn't tell me, but they did write it down and put it in here." I reach under my pillow and pull out the envelope I stashed earlier. I can't help but think about our wedding day and the envelope I stashed on this same bed, in the same location. The adoption papers that my husband was all too eager to sign.

"So, in this envelope is the gender of our baby?" he asks with awe in his voice.

I nod. "Yes."

"And you didn't look?"

"No." I cup his face with my hands. "I didn't look. I wanted us to find out together."

"Good things happen to me when you present me with envelopes that have been hidden under your pillow," he teases.

"Open it." I smile up at him.

"Come here." He moves to rest his back against the headboard and I do the same. He pulls me into his arms and kisses my temple. "You ready, Momma?"

"Yes."

He releases his arm from around my shoulders and slowly slides his finger under the flap of the envelope. I hear him pull in an audible breath as he reads the words written on the small white piece of paper.

"Tell me," I urge him. The suspense has been killing me.

"A boy," he says thickly.

"A boy?" I ask through the tears clogging my throat.

"A son." He smiles at me. "Happy tears?" he asks, even though he already knows that answer. That's Marshall; he's always putting me and the girls before himself.

I nod and tears coat my cheeks. "We're having a little boy."

"I love you so fucking much," he says, kissing me hard. "Thank you for this life you've given me. For our four children and the love—" He shakes his head. "So much love."

"It's the magic." I shrug, making him smile.

He grabs my hand and places it over his heart. "Beat by beat, baby."

"Beat by beat," I say, smiling through my tears.

Thank you for taking the time to read Beat by Beat.
While I'm sad to see the Riggins Brothers end, I'm excited for an all
new series, the Out of Reach Series, coming late 2021.
Book one of the Out of Reach Series is Available Now.
Beyond the Bases.

Never miss a new release:
http://bit.ly/2UW5Xzm

More about Kaylee's books:
http://bit.ly/2S6clWe

Facebook:
http://bit.ly/2C5DgdF

Instagram:
http://bit.ly/2reBkrV

Reader Group:
http://bit.ly/2o0yWDx

Goodreads:
http://bit.ly/2HodJvx

BookBub:
http://bit.ly/2KulVvH

Website:
www.kayleeryan.com

OTHER WORKS by KAYLEE RYAN

With You Series:
Anywhere With You | More With You | Everything With You

Soul Serenade Series:
Emphatic | Assured | Definite | Insistent

Southern Heart Series:
Southern Pleasure | Southern Desire | Southern Attraction |
Southern Devotion

Unexpected Arrivals Series:
Unexpected Reality | Unexpected Fight
Unexpected Fall | Unexpected Bond | Unexpected Odds

Standalone Titles:
Tempting Tatum | Unwrapping Tatum | Levitate
Just Say When | I Just Want You
Reminding Avery | Hey, Whiskey | When Sparks Collide
Pull You Through | Beyond the Bases
Remedy | The Difference
Trust the Push

OTHER WORKS *by* **KAYLEE RYAN**

Entangled Hearts Duet
Agony | Bliss

Cocky Hero Club:
Lucky Bastard

Riggins Brothers Series:
Play by Play | Layer by Layer | Piece by Piece
Kiss by Kiss | Touch by Touch | Beat by Beat

Co-written with Lacey Black:
Fair Lakes Series
It's Not Over | Just Getting Started | Can't Fight It

Standalones
Boy Trouble | Home to You | Beneath the Fallen Stars

ACKNOWLEDGEMENTS

To my family:
I could not do this without you. Your love and support mean more to me than you will ever know.

Wander Aguiar:
It's always a pleasure working with you. You and Andrey always go above and beyond to help me find the perfect image. Thank you for your talent behind the lens and bringing Marshall's story to life.

Roddy Handson:
Thank you for doing what you do. You brought Marshall to life. Best of luck to you in all of your future endeavors.

Tami Integrity Formatting:
Thank you for making the paperbacks beautiful. You're amazing and I cannot thank you enough for all that you do.

Lori Jackson:
You nailed it. You were patient with me, and worked your photoshop magic. Thank you for another amazing cover. It has been my pleasure working with you.

Lacey Black:
My dear friend. Thank you for always being there with life, and work. I value our friendship, and our working relationship more than you will ever know. I can't wait to see what our co-writing journey takes us.

My beta team:

Jamie, Stacy, Lauren, Erica, and Franci I would be lost without you. You read my words as much as I do, and I can't tell you what your input and all the time you give means to me. Countless messages and bouncing idea, you ladies keep me sane with the characters are being anything but. Thank you from the bottom of my heart for taking this wild ride with me.

Give Me Books:

With every release, your team works diligently to get my book in the hands of bloggers. I cannot tell you how thankful I am for your services.

Tempting Illustrations:

Thank you for everything. I would be lost without you.

Julie Deaton:

Thank you for giving this book a set of fresh final eyes.

Becky Johnson:

I could not do this without you. Thank you for pushing me, and making me work for it.

Marisa Corvisiero:

Thank you for all that you do. I know I'm not the easiest client. I'm blessed to have you on this journey with me.

Brittany Holland:

Thank you for your assistance with the blurb. You saved me!

Bloggers:

Thank you, doesn't seem like enough. You don't get paid to do what you do. It's from the kindness of your heart and your love of reading that fuels you. Without you, without your pages, your voice, your reviews, spreading the word it would be so much harder if not impossible to get my words in reader's hands. I can't tell you how much your never-ending support means to me. Thank you for being you, thank you for all that you do.

To my reader group, Kaylee's Crew:

You are my people! I'm honored to have you on this journey with me. Thank you for reading, sharing, commenting, suggesting, the teasers, the messages all of it. Thank you from the bottom of my heart for all that you do. Your support is everything!

With Love,

Kaylee Ryan
AUTHOR

Made in the USA
Coppell, TX
26 July 2023